Do Unto Evil

Do Unto Evil

William Kirt Parsons

Hardcover ISBN: 978-0-578-49959-8
Paperback ISBN: 978-0-578-49960-4

STRANGELAND

For my toughest critic and one true love, Mary Ellen.

PROLOGUE

On the day before Will's graduation from East Whittier junior high, he missed the bus home. He had been milling around with some friends, a nice light feeling in the air as they all looked forward to a long summer break from the classroom grind before starting at California High in September. Home was only maybe a two-mile walk—no big deal. He was about a half mile down Whittier Boulevard, the sun still high in the sky, when he walked into some serious shit. Suddenly, he was surrounded by four of the most notorious bullies in the history of East Whittier.

They were ninth and tenth graders—that is, if they were in school at all—and they were a bunch of low-functioning knuckle-draggers. Will wasn't sure of all of their names, but he knew that they had all been expelled from East Whittier Junior High and were rumored to have been inmates at Fred C. Nelles School for Boys, the state reformatory for incorrigible young criminals at the other end of Whittier Boulevard. These guys had stolen cars and broken into homes in swanky Friendly Hills. They had done some terrible things to kids smaller than Will. They had stolen lunch money right out of kids' pockets. Will had witnessed two of them make some fifth graders take off all their clothes in front of a group of girls. Then they laughed and laughed while the little boys cried and tried to cover up their wieners. If there is a hell, that's where these guys are headed, Will thought. He had managed to successfully outmaneuver them individually and in pairs several times in the past, avoiding confrontations in hallways, in the locker room, and on the playground. Now he could tell that, for some reason, they dearly wished to kick his ass.

He took off as fast as he could into a stand of trees next to Nixon's Drive-in, hoping to slip away. But they cut him off and boxed him in, the trees shielding them from sight of passersby—putting him at a severe tactical disadvantage. Some internal organ Will couldn't identify jumped high in his throat. Fight-or-flight juices were cascading. He needed to piss urgently. The ringleader, a guy named Hector, approached him, flicking a six-inch switchblade and wearing a twisted, sadistic sneer on his lips.

"You've been running like a little pussy from us for a long time, peckerhead. We can't stand yellow-bellied cowards like you. I smell the stink of your fear all the way over here. Or did you already shit your pants?" His laugh was shrill, a witch's cackle right out of *The Wizard of Oz*. He brandished his knife a few more times and smiled his wicked, ghoulish smile at Will. Hector looked at his knife and closed it. "Don't need this for a little cunt like you." He stuffed the knife in his back pocket. "I'm going to beat you ugly."

If he hadn't lost the power of speech Will would have liked to ask, Why are you so angry? What did I do to you to make you want to beat the shit out of me? There has to be an explanation. But maybe not. Maybe this is just the way evil people behave. Is there just some core of evil that compels the fiendish to hurt?

Hector feinted a punch, and Will flinched. Hector and his pals laughed loudly. "Better put them dukes up and fight, Willy lily liver."

Hector waded in on Will with a bolo punch. Will felt the rage spout out of the top of his head like an erupting volcano. The blow was closing on his chin when it came to a sudden stop. A billowing fury of purple clouds shut Will down. He didn't pass out. He just went away for a while. He dropped down a chute at the speed of light, seeing shapes, images, colors, sounds alien to his senses, all beyond recognition. Then he was back with a near-blinding blood-red burst of light, staring at Hector's bolo punch aimed at the middle of his chin but suspended in air as if frozen in time.

Will wasn't frozen, but he wasn't in control of himself, either. He could feel his rage erupt through his open palm as he struck Hector's solar plexus. He felt a surge so powerful that he thought his arm had been torn from its socket. Hector was sent into flight while time, for Will, seemed to move at a fraction of its normal speed. He watched the bully's slow-motion ascent into air end in a high branch of a tree. Hector's three partners in assault and battery were still inching toward Will with their fists raised. Their eyes were bugging out—Will wasn't sure whether that was because of the slow motion or their dawning surprise at Hector's launch. Before he could decide, another flash of energy exploded from Will's hands, sending each of the boys into the surrounding tree trunks. When the action ended, Hector and his companions were very unconscious.

When Will could finally bring himself to move, he fled, zigzagging through the trees, never looking back. He ran down Whittier Boulevard faster than he thought possible, not slowing until he had passed Hinshaw's department store. He turned down Painter and down the railroad tracks above his house. When he stopped, panting, he struggled to make sense of what had just happened.

ONE

On a wooden dock in the Port of Tacoma, Will Parish took in the mast of the troop ship USS *Darby* looming over him in the dense fog as dawn approached. The saltwater smell of the port was strong, and it carried the odor of rotting seaweed, fish, and creosote-soaked timbers. A foghorn sighed in the distance, and a long, looping olive-drab line serpentined before and behind him. Soldiers wearing fatigues each carried two duffel bags on their shoulders as they inched along like the feet of a giant centipede toward the gangplank. The color of the early October sky competed with the dingy, rusty battleship gray of the *Darby* to cast gloom over the dockside.

With each tiny, halting step he took toward the *Darby*, Will labored to subdue the panic attack butterflying in the pit of his belly. In a few hours he would be on a slow boat to China—more accurately, to the South China Sea, destination Vietnam. When he'd graduated from UCLA the previous year, he'd made a vow to himself that he would never go to Vietnam. He thought the war was indefensible and stupid. It had nothing to do with making America safe. Yet here he was, shipping out. Now he couldn't stop thinking that the only thing more stupid than the war was him.

The olive-drab line came to a dead stop. Will dropped his bags on the dock.

After graduation he had decided to go to graduate school for an MBA. He'd hated the idea of continuing the academic grind, but it was the only way he could maintain his student deferment. He'd gagged on the curriculum of accounting, finance, economics, and management. Not his cup of tea. He'd lasted only six weeks into the fall semester before he quit going to class. He'd figured he had five or six months to sort out a strategy for avoiding the draft before his selective service board discovered he had bailed out of grad school.

He was dead wrong. He had barely wrapped his head around a strategy for staying out of Vietnam when he received his notification of reclassification from student deferment to imminently draftable. Then he really had to hustle to find a reserve slot. Over two days he visited the recruiting offices of the National Guard, Army, Air Force, Navy, and Coast Guard. The last two were a stretch—he suffered violent motion sickness every time he was on a boat. Will was greeted by bad news from every branch of the service. They all had at least six-month waiting lists. He was screwed. No, make that fucked, really fucked.

Unless. Unless . . . he chose the low-integrity strategy. There were options, possibilities. He could file for conscientious-objector status. No, that one was fraught. He needed a history, a body of evidence pointing to his pacifistic nature, his Christian credo. Not a chance. Puncturing an eardrum was a reasonably attractive option relative to being smoked in Vietnam, but he was a bit of a pussy when it came to physical pain. Then there was the genuinely freaky pathway: pretend to be gay. But that path was really dicey. A friend of a friend had tried it, and it had ended very badly. The examining physician had grown sick and tired of the gay ruse and grabbed the guy's pecker to test the veracity of his claim. The guy had gone wild and nearly killed the doctor. He *did* succeed in avoiding Vietnam; the problem was he was doing it in prison.

The most alluring strategy of all for staying out of Vietnam was merely to become a draft dodger and skip out of the country to Canada or Sweden. The beautiful women of Sweden were a powerful attraction, but Will couldn't afford the airfare. So Sweden was out. British Columbia was looking pretty damn good, though. He had read about a small but growing cluster of expatriate draft resisters on Vancouver Island in the suburbs of Victoria.

Will spent several days researching and visualizing this scenario. It was gut wrenching. He thought of how his parents would react: It would be ugly. They would disown him. He thought about his younger brother Dana, who was a cop with the Los Angeles Police Department in the Hollenbeck

Division. His brother would consider him a coward, lower than a worm. He thought of his dozens of friends who had stayed in ROTC at UCLA and were on their way to Vietnam. He thought of his ex-girlfriend, who had gone off to New York City to follow her dreams. He found himself standing in front of his bathroom mirror, lathering up to shave. When he looked into his green eyes, he saw something looking back at him, something he hadn't ever seen before. Will became immobilized. Then he saw the path before him clearly. In that moment, he knew that if he were to flee to Canada, he would spend the rest of his life in pursuit of his self-respect.

Will had made up his mind, but his situation grew more desperate. A notice from the draft board for his preinduction physical had arrived in the mail. When it seemed that all hope was gone, he ran into his old roommate Rob Landau at Ell's restaurant in Westwood Village. Rob had dropped out of law school around the same time Will quit grad school. He had received his own notice earlier that day. Rob's quest to avoid Vietnam had run parallel to Will's. He had received the same bad news at every reserve recruiting office. But he was able to hold out a ray of hope for both of them. One of his fraternity brothers had told him to check out a recruiter for army intelligence whose office was in the federal building in downtown LA. The frat brother claimed that if they enlisted in army counterintelligence, they would be assured of staying in the states and out of Vietnam.

The day after meeting at Ell's restaurant, Will and Rob had gotten into Will's mechanically challenged '55 VW Bug and driven from Westwood east down Wilshire Boulevard to the US Courthouse on Spring Street, hoping to make an appointment with the US Army Intelligence Service recruiter. They knew this was their last chance at avoiding both the draft and getting their asses shot off in Vietnam. They were lucky. The recruiter had a break in his schedule, and he would grant interview time to both of them. After thirty minutes of filling in forms and questionnaires, they were sitting in a small reception room waiting for their appointments with US Army Intelligence recruiter Major Victor Pangloss. Rob's interview was first.

Will squirmed anxiously for another twenty-five minutes. He sat in a rickety chair and had a staring contest with the picture of the commander in chief on the wall across from him—President Lyndon Baines Johnson, good ol' Texas redneck, warmonger, and the architect of Will's present plight. Just when it seemed that LBJ was going to win the stare down, a smiling Rob Landau emerged from the major's office, giving Will an enthusiastic thumbs-up.

Major Pangloss motioned Will into his office. He shook Will's hand and prompted him toward a chair. Pangloss was fortyish and rather stately looking. Not much of the military bearing. He had a kind and open face. His prematurely silvering hair was swept straight back, close to his head. He had the Ivy League look: three-piece Southwick suit, Gant button-down in blue with a wide, striped Savile Row tie. His sole nod to his military standing was the high gloss on his Florsheim wingtips. Will was getting nervous, armpits starting to wet his oxford cloth. Not quite a panic attack. But close.

Major Pangloss smiled beatifically at Will, immediately putting him at ease. He said, "Well, Mr. Parish, it is indeed an extraordinary day when I have two UCLA graduates applying for enlistment in the United States Army Intelligence Service. I glanced over your paperwork, and it's clear that you are more than fully qualified for our counterintelligence work." Will wanted to jump and dance and shout for joy and leap into the arms of Major Pangloss. Just seconds earlier he'd felt the weight of the world on his shoulders; now he was as light as a feather, joyously buoyant.

"Congratulations and welcome aboard, Special Agent Recruit Parish," said the major as he rose from his chair and extended his hand to Will. "Welcome to the world of American intelligence." He told Will that he would get orders in a few days to report to the Los Angeles induction center for processing and transportation to a US Army post for nine weeks of basic training. "The next stop," Pangloss explained, "will be Fort Holabird, Maryland, the US Army Intelligence School outside Baltimore. You will be enrolled in the four-month counterintelligence course and graduate as a special agent. During that course, you will be trained in interrogation and counterespionage methods and techniques. It is likely that you will be assigned to a US Army installation near a major population center. For example San Diego, San Francisco, Portland, New York, even Miami.

"Your assignment will likely be conducting basic background checks on army personnel in sensitive assignments that require security clearances. Your uniform will be a coat and tie. You will be addressed as Mr. Parish. At entry level, your job is popularly referred to as 'a doorbell ringer,' the guy in the coat and tie who rings the doorbell of the neighbor of the person who needs the security clearance. Quite a desirable alternative to going to Vietnam. I think you will have to agree that this is the best of all possible outcomes," Pangloss added with an expansive smile.

Before he answered, Will paused to absorb the ecstatic beauty of what Major Pangloss had just said. A fleeting image came to him, of himself in Miami Beach attired in a lightweight blue Dacron polyester suit or maybe a stylish seersucker sports coat with a pastel paisley tie. He liked how he looked. An enormous smile that could only be described in the vernacular of fraternity row as "shit-eating" broke out across Will's face as he said, "It sounds beyond perfect, sir."

Perfection never arrived.

TWO

"Hey, soldier, I'm talking to you! Move your ass! Close ranks—you're holding up the line!" A staff sergeant in charge of the troop-loading operation was bellowing at Will, pulling his consciousness from where it had been hanging out, about a thousand miles south. What was no doubt a bright, warm dawn emerging in sunny Southern California was oppressively dank and gloomy dockside in Tacoma. Will grabbed his duffel bags and scurried forward twenty feet, closing ranks as the sergeant had ordered. The duffel bag carrier in front of him stopped, and Will stumbled into him. His heart sank when he saw the members of his detachment start ascending the gangplank of the *Darby*. The fauna of his gut—still butterflies, mainly—were taking flight, the not-so-subtle beginnings of an anxiety attack. His right foot hung suspended in air at the edge of the gangplank. Panic was near at hand. His foot fell in slow motion. He was numb. He stepped from the dock. Then it was over, and next came the calm that accompanies acceptance of fate . . . at least for a while.

Will continued to flow with the snaillike movement of the long drab line. He high-stepped over bulkhead after bulkhead, finally descending into the cattle hold of the *Darby*. He was shocked to see how deep the troop quarters plummeted into the bowels of the ship. With each level down, his claustrophobic disturbance rose. Finally, at the very bottom of the metal staircase, he and his group found a series of tiny compartments, their billets for this voyage to war. Each chamber was roughly nine-feet square with two-foot openings on either end connecting to the next. Each of the two walls perpendicular to the open ends held three sets of canvas bunk racks and an angle-iron post bolted to the ceiling and the floor. The canvas racks had two-inch-thick GI mattresses rolled up at their wall end.

Will dropped his duffel bags on the floor. He grabbed the mattress on the upper bunk harness closest to him and unrolled it. He lifted himself onto the bunk, trying but failing to avoid hitting his head on the pipes that ran into the ceiling. "Ouch," he said, rubbing the top of his head. He tried stretching out to his full six-foot one-inch length and failed at that as well. "I feel like a fucking sardine in a can."

His buddies Rob Landau and Bobby McQueen claimed the slots below his. Three other classmates, Jack De George, Jimmy Bacigalupi, and Dennis Wolfe, grabbed the three bunks across from them.

Will jammed his duffels into a corner. "This sucks worse than basic training, guys," he said.

"I'm going to avoid this place like the plague. This is like something out of Dante's *Inferno*," Rob said. The others grunted and groaned their agreement.

"Fuck, we're all going to have to sleep in the fetal position, especially you at six-four, Rob," said Will, shaking his head. "It's a goddamned torture chamber. Let's get the hell out of here, now!"

Will rushed to the stairs and leaned into them, taking two at a time fast, up the flights to the opening at the top deck. When he broke into the light, dank and gray though the view was, the claustrophobia departed. His buddies were right behind him. They gave a collective sigh of relief.

Will pointed up to the bridge deck. He could see what looked like a terrace eight feet above them with a dozen or more tables set with white tablecloths and linen napkins shaped into inverted fans. A group of officers and NCOs were milling around. Most of them were sipping from cups of coffee or glasses of orange juice. White-jacketed and white-gloved servers were refilling their drinks from carafes. The enticing aroma of coffee, bacon, eggs, and toast hung in the thick morning air. Hunger panged hard in the pit of Will's gut.

"Why the hell did I drop out of Air Force ROTC," he lamented. "Talk about being a second-class citizen . . ."

"We aren't even *that* high in the pecking order," Rob said. "I'd say we are more like the untouchables in this caste system."

Just then Major Charles, their detachment's commanding officer, came to the edge of the deck rail and looked down at them. He gave them a slight nod and turned away.

The detachment consisted of Will and his nineteen classmates who had recently graduated from the US Army Intelligence School. They had spent four of the last five months grinding their way through the Department of Area Studies Case Officer / Agent Handler course at Fort Holabird. In the early weeks of their studies, he and his classmates were excited and intrigued by the prospects of the cloak-and-dagger mystique, the secret-agent aspect of the training. They all thought they'd hit the big time. They were all so full of themselves, so cool. But they weren't. In fact, it was a bit of a joke. This "spymaster" course was reputed to be a condensed version of the CIA's case-officer training. But it was case-officer training light—very light. In Will's view, it was what gave rise to the saying "Army Intelligence, the ultimate oxymoron."

After they graduated from area studies, the whole class got orders to train at the army's anti–guerilla-warfare school at Fort Bragg, North Carolina, for three weeks before shipping out to Vietnam. Will and his classmates' collective delusion and wishful thinking had kept them from seeing the obvious: they were always going to be sent to Vietnam. The instruction at Fort Bragg wasn't any more impressive than at Holabird. At least, Will thought, the training and field exercises in reading USGS topographic maps might prove useful in Vietnam.

The rest of the detachment on board the *Darby* consisted of their commanding officer, Major Thomas Charles; Captain Dick Royce and First Lieutenant Tim Frasier, who had been their training officers at Fort Bragg; and Staff Sergeant Mick Perry, their so-called NCO in charge. The three officers had just graduated from the officers' version of the case-officer training at the same time as Will's class. SSGT Perry had been a not-so-happy member of Will's enlisted men's class. Not so happy because he was the only NCO in their class of all private E2s.

The detachment, all twenty-four of them, had orders to report to the 525th Military Intelligence Group in Saigon. The 525th was the headquarters and clearinghouse for all conventional intelligence assignments in Vietnam.

Will and his mates were told that once they arrived in Saigon, they could be sent almost anywhere in Vietnam and operate out of conventional units to recruit agents for intelligence gathering or be assigned to headquarters. Maybe the officers had an inkling of what they were going to be doing, but none of the enlisted guys in his class had the slightest notion of what lay ahead. It's definitely not going to be Miami Beach, Will thought.

The *Darby* had just started to pull away from the dock. That first gentle motion triggered a jolt like an electrical shock racing through Will's body. He quickly reached into his pocket in search of his vial of Dramamine. His motion sickness was legendary. Car, plane, boat—made no difference. His barfing was almost hair-triggered. He always had to fall or roll out of a car because his legs wouldn't work after the explosive vomiting. His older brother, Randall, who was not prone to motion sickness, never failed to point out how much he resembled a frog with his green face. Will always wondered why his father couldn't take the curves a little slower.

With Rob leading the way, the six would-be "secret agent" men circumnavigated the USS *Darby* several times. They wanted to get their bearings on this 306-foot-long, 37-foot-wide, 1,400-ton mass of gray steel. Back when it was launched from the Philadelphia Naval Shipyard in May 1943 it was one of the new Buckley class destroyer escorts. In its heyday during World War II, the *Darby* had been a formidable and lethal hunter of enemy submarines in the Atlantic and the Pacific. After the war it was decommissioned and placed in reserve. A few years later it returned to service as a troop transport ship in the Korean War. After Korea, it ferried troops and their dependents from various American ports on the Atlantic and Pacific most often to Bremerhaven, Germany.

And on the first day of October 1966, the *Darby* embarked on its first Tacoma-to-Vietnam voyage, a cruise scheduled for seventeen days to deliver some 160 enlisted men and officers to the port of In Harm's Way. Will's detachment was joined by Alpha Company of the Fourteenth Combat Engineer Battalion, a contingent of 136 enlisted men, NCOs, and officers. They were heading for Qui Nhon, the first port of call. Will's unit was getting off the ship at the second stop, Cam Ranh Bay.

As they scouted the *Darby,* Will and his friends found it was easy to get twisted around, lose their sense of direction, and become disoriented with all the narrow passages and the monotone grayness of the ship. They were looking for out-of-the-way places to hide from authority and escape from their sardine-can sleeping quarters. Will noted a couple of canvas-covered whaleboats that might serve as private reading rooms. Looking over the top of one, he became aware that the ceiling of low fog had lifted enough for him to see land.

The *Darby* had sailed out into Commencement Bay, passing north of Bainbridge Island. It was well past 9 a.m. There was still no sign of the sun, though it must have been well above the horizon. The pea-soup gloom seemed to thicken and darken like Will's mood. The Li'l Abner comic strip character with the thundercloud hovering overhead came to mind. Will smiled ruefully as he pictured that scruffy character, Joe Btfsplk—the jinx, bad luck personified. A chill ran up Will's spine and stood the hair up on the back of his neck. He shuddered with a vague premonition, a subconscious tendril from a recurring dream that his mind couldn't quite grip in a waking state.

"Will! Will, what's wrong, man?" asked Rob. Will looked at him without answering. "You look like a guy who just saw a ghost. You all right?"

He reflected a moment. A huge ship, lots of bombs—a waking dream?

No. No, my friend, I'm not all right, he thought. In fact, I think I'm going stark raving mad.

But he managed to say, "Yeah, I'm cool. How about you, Rob? Are you all right?" Rob avoided giving voice to it. He just shook his head gently from side to side with a sad expression.

McQueen, who was watching them, shouted, "Goddamn it! Come on. You guys are depressing me with your fucking mood disorders. Let's go find the mess hall and get some breakfast before it closes." So the six cruise mates marched to the starboard edge of the ship, went fore, then aft, and finally found the mess hall minutes before it closed. As they entered, Will saw a tray piled with thousands of little white tablets like the one he had just swallowed, a Dramamine label taped to the wall above them. He shoved a small handful into his pocket. He calculated that it could take as long as two weeks on the ship to get his sea legs.

Will pulled a stainless-steel tray from a tall pile and got in line behind his pals. He watched as they all held their trays out for SOS—"shit on a shingle," the armed forces' breakfast staple. Will had developed a gag reflex just at the sight of the stuff. Some guys loved it, couldn't get enough. It was creamed chipped beef on toast. The beef was rehydrated and had an odor and a flavor that Will was not able to abide. He went around his friends and got some cold scrambled eggs, bacon, toast, and hot coffee then joined them at a twenty-foot-long table. They were the only ones in the dining hall. He sat at a slight angle to the rest of the group to avoid watching them scarfing down their SOS.

After dining, they all went to take a second look at their desultory sleeping quarters. That tiny compartment hadn't grown any. If anything, Will thought, it had shrunk a little.

Will had started reading a fat paperback copy of *War and Peace* that he had found in the day lounge at Fort Bragg. He dug it out of his duffel now. He had struggled through the first fifty or so pages of Tolstoy's masterpiece with all of the unpronounceable, polysyllabic Russian names, but the hook was in him. He was committed. "Going upstairs to find a reading room," he told his bunkmates. "See you later." No one said a word. They watched him slip away.

Will felt trapped like never before in his life. He could see no escape. He was standing midship at the starboard railing. He gripped the rail with his right hand and held Tolstoy in his left. He felt the *Darby* gently rise and fall. His gut was fine. No motion sickness. He silently praised the creator of Dramamine. He looked out at what appeared to be another island. This one had to be Whidbey. He guessed they were in the Puget Sound by now. Clouds thinning. Ceiling rising. Visibility increasing. Rain-forest greens intensifying. The Pacific Northwest. Home of his fathers.

Will needed a powerful distraction. He needed to be transported. *War and Peace*. Pierre. He found a cubby at the edge of a firewall under a lifeboat. He disappeared into a fiction. Escape. It was Will's way.

THREE

During his fifteenth year, the summer of 1957, Will's mother, Katy, told him the story of the day of his birth.

Katy Parish had been told that she was cute. Some called her pretty. Some said beautiful. She wasn't sure about any of that, but she knew that even being cute wasn't all that easy when you were almost nine months pregnant. Before this, her second pregnancy, she had carried a hundred pounds on her five-foot-two frame. If you had met her before then, you might have thought she'd inspired the zany 1920s flapper tune that asks "five-foot-two, eyes of blue . . . has anybody seen my gal?" She was vivacious and energetic. And, boy, could she cut a rug. Now she tipped the scales at 140 pounds. She was sure she was going to give birth to twins, but the doctor said no, there's just one baby in there kicking the hell out of your rib cage. She remained skeptical.

Katy and her husband, Captain Bill Parish, had been living in married officers' quarters at Schofield Barracks on the enchanted Island of Oahu for nine months. Bill was commanding officer of Bravo Company of the Second Battalion of the Twenty-Fourth Infantry Division, the old Hawaiian Division. He had taken a commission as a second lieutenant in the US Army Reserve after graduation from UCLA in 1936. He had never seriously considered a military career after college until the Great Depression prompted him to hedge his bets a little and keep open the option of gainful employment with the US Army. His decision to stay in army ROTC turned out to be a wise one. He knew the winds of war were roiling in Europe. By the time he was called to active duty in the fall of 1939, he had been promoted to captain. Just a few weeks before his call to active duty, he was introduced to and immediately fell in love with the enchanting Katy. After a whirlwind courtship, they married in a small civil ceremony in Long Beach, California.

As soon as they returned from their all-too-short honeymoon in Santa Barbara, Bill received orders to report to the Eleventh Cavalry Regiment (Blackhorse), headquartered at the Presidio of Monterey. He and Katy found the perfect little rental in Carmel-by-the-Sea. Katy called the tiny place their Hansel and Gretel fairy-tale cottage. The newlyweds spent many idyllic hours on the pristine white sands of Carmel beach. They would remember these months as the happiest of their lives.

Nine months to the day of her marriage to Bill, Katy gave birth to Randall Noel Parish. It was a trouble-free labor and delivery. Mother and child were doing fine. Proud daddy Bill drove Katy and baby Randall home in their 1936 Dodge coupe. When they walked through the door of their tiny cottage near the corner of Monte Verde and Eleventh, Katy was surprised at how small the place seemed now with her newborn in her arms.

During the Parishes' magical year on the Monterey Peninsula, Bill participated in dozens of maneuvers on horseback with the fabled Eleventh at the Presidio's training facilities near Gigling Road at Camp Ord. He had grown very fond of the concept of mounted warfare and had become a skilled equestrian during his first seven months at the Presidio. But his dreams of mounted glory in the Blackhorse became a fading memory when the army's high command decided to abandon the concept of horse cavalry in favor of armored cavalry. Bill was forced to play a role in initiating the beginning of the end of the last great horse cavalry as the armored M3 Scout Cars replaced his beloved Trigger, Topper, Champion, and Duke as engines of war.

At the end of 1940, with the "deequinezation" (as Bill called it) of the storied Eleventh Cavalry coming to a close, Bill Parish received his orders to report to Schofield Barracks on Oahu. To Katy, it was just one more la-la land moment for the Kansas-born farm girl. In less than a year of her life, she had met and married the man of her dreams, lived in an enchanted cottage in Carmel-by-the-Sea, and given birth to a beautiful boy—and now here she was on a fancy cruise ship, setting sail for Honolulu.

It was just so much more glamorous than anything she had ever imagined growing up. The Parishes shared a delightful first-class berth on the Matson Lines cruise ship SS *Lurline* out of San Francisco. Because of Bill's rank as captain and because they were traveling as a family, they qualified for a generously sized suite. Katy happily strolled the promenade decks for hours with baby Randall in his pram. Bill spent a lot of hours in the bar with his fellow officers—maybe a few more hours than he really needed to, thought Katy. But she didn't let that thought get in the way of the absolute joy she took from this perfect cruise to Honolulu.

She particularly enjoyed dressing up in formal dinner attire for the evening meals. She loved seeing Bill in his dress blues—so dashing. She was madly in love with her husband. In fact, she was madly in love with life. A bright-eyed optimist, she saw only the best in people. Just being around her made people cheerful. She was a child of the Depression, but she never internalized the despair and want that surrounded her growing up. She watched her parents lose their Kansas farm to drought and the resulting dust bowl of the thirties, yet Katy never wavered in her belief that all was for the best. When things were at their most dire, she and her family left Kansas for Long Beach, California. They moved in with her aunt's family until they could get back on their feet again. Katy remained steadfast in her faith that something magical was just around the corner for her and her family.

With some modest financial assistance from Uncle Victor, her parents bought a small, dilapidated grocery in Hollydale. No strangers to long hours and hard work, Charlie, Millicent, and Katy Seavey turned that little dump of a grocery store into something to be proud of. In less than two years they were back on their feet and thriving, just as Katy had predicted.

Bill Parish's youth stood in marked contrast to Katy's. His parents were born and raised in Tacoma to relatively affluent families. Logan Parish and Luisa Bosworth grew up in very close proximity to the lap of luxury. Luisa had been in love with Logan's older brother Nelson. When Nelson broke off their relationship, Logan was in position to catch Luisa on the rebound. They married before they became aware of their toxic incompatibility. They fought incessantly and divorced shortly after Bill's birth.

When Bill met Katy, his gloom disappeared. Family and friends were stunned by his dispositional metamorphosis. In Katy's presence he suddenly had a lot to say. The sun was shining brighter. It was an astounding transformation.

Schofield was ensconced in a tropical paradise, and the Parishes had experienced a bliss-filled interlude there after disembarking from the *Lurline* some nine months earlier. They had bodysurfed together in the gentle rollers of Waikiki Beach until Katy got too big and didn't want to be seen in public wearing a bathing suit. They had explored the island several times seeking points of obscure historical interest. Bill was a natural historian—he'd taken his degree in US History at UCLA. They had dined at luau after luau until they were luaued out. Bill had introduced Katy to the joys of horseback riding on the Honolulu equestrian trail. The army maintained stables at the edge of Schofield for the recreational use of officers and their dependents. Katy was just starting to feel confident on a horse when her advancing pregnancy turned her confidence into concern. The idea of falling and possibly losing her baby led her to give up riding after little more than four months.

When Katy was nearing the end of her second trimester, she noticed that her baby started going through periods of intense hyperactivity. She marveled at the unborn child's extreme physical movements. It seemed at times that the baby was somersaulting in her womb, kicking and stretching. At times Katy's ribs were sore for days after an eruption of extreme motion by the baby. These outbursts were sandwiched between periods of total inactivity that could last a day or two. Katy puzzled at the difference between her firstborn, Randy, and the current resident of her womb. How could they be so different? And what was she in for when this crazy critter popped out? Katy and Bill had been hoping for a sweet little girl. No way, she thought, this has got to be another boy.

For Katy, the third trimester went on and on and on. He was way too big and physical to be a girl. By the start of her ninth month of pregnancy, Katy was beside herself, frantic to get a decent night's sleep. Even when the baby wasn't in a manic cycle, she was on edge, waiting in anticipation of his next fit. She sensed that the kid just wanted out. Maybe he was claustrophobic. Poor little guy—I mean, poor big guy, she said to herself.

During the late stage of his wife's ninth-month struggles, Bill could not sleep in the same bed with her. To preserve his sanity and get enough sleep to fulfill his duties as a company commander, he moved to the sofa. His heart went out to Katy: she looked so out of balance, so much bigger than she did with baby Randy. From behind, she still looked petite, but from the side, she looked as if she should tip over.

November was giving way to December. For months Bill had been hearing growing chatter about the coming war with Japan. In fact, the Twenty-Fourth had been girding for an outbreak of hostilities for his entire nine months at Schofield. The War Department considered Pearl Harbor the likeliest target of a Japanese attack, but Bill wasn't buying it or didn't *want* to buy it. His best guess was an attack on the Philippines. He admitted to himself that there was a lot of wishful thinking in his belief that an attack on Oahu was unlikely. He was terrified by the thought of a Japanese invasion because his very pregnant wife and toddler were right in the middle of harm's way. And the Japanese were notoriously vicious toward their conquered adversaries. The Japanese Imperial Army's Rape of Nanking in 1937 weighed heavily on his mind.

During September, October, and November, the Twenty-Fourth had been preoccupied with building up the defensive positions around Schofield. A ring of observation posts was built in the highlands above the barracks. During the previous three weeks, Bill's battalion had been deployed on defensive maneuvers that anticipated probable Japanese points of attack.

On the afternoon of December 5, the company received orders to participate in a two-night bivouac starting that evening and to deploy to the northeast periphery of Schofield near Wheeler Air Force Base. Bill was upset at the timing. Katy's due date of December 2 had come and gone. She had been experiencing Braxton Hicks contractions for the last three days. He took some comfort from the presence of Katy's best friend Valita, who had moved to Honolulu six months earlier. Whenever Bill was in the field on extended maneuvers, Valita either stayed with Katy at Schofield or Katy and Randy went to her place above Diamond Head.

"Gee whillikers, Captain Parish, you could scare a girl into labor moving that fast," Katy said when Bill suddenly burst through the screen door and startled her and Randy.

He stopped and shook his head. "You're right, sweetie. I'm sorry I scared you. It's just I'm in a devil of a hurry. I need to throw some gear together." He placed his hand on her belly. "Anything happening?" he asked. "Just the false contractions," she answered. Bill gave her a quizzical look then went into the bedroom.

The moment Bill went into the bedroom, Katy grabbed the phone and called Valita to tell her she and baby Randy were going to be available for a two-night visit. Valita was elated. Katy was happy to get to hang out with her best friend and even happier to get out of Schofield for a few days because it seemed to calm down the overactive guy in her womb. Katy would actually be able to get some sleep at Valita's place. And God could she use some sleep.

Bill came out of the bedroom and embraced Katy. His kiss was much more passionate than any other in a long time. Randy was on the floor with his favorite toy trucks and cars, making engine-revving sounds. Bill reached down, lifted his toddler, and gave him an uncharacteristically long hug. Then he set the lad down and turned to Katy. "Honey, I'm so sorry I have to go. I'll do everything I can to get back before the baby comes," Bill said as he planted another passionate goodbye kiss on her lips. Then he was gone.

Katy did some packing and called to arrange for a cab to Diamond Head. She grabbed a small wicker basket from the broom closet and started tossing in Randy's favorite toys, which were mostly cars, trucks, and tractors, and a teddy bear.

Then the doorbell rang. It was Katy's favorite taxi driver, Lenny. He gave her a crisp salute through the screen door. "And how are you this beautiful day in paradise, Mrs. Parish?"

"Oh, Lenny, I'm doing fine, but I'll be a lot better when I finally deliver this baby. It's way too big to be carrying around any longer. I swear I'm going to split open if it doesn't arrive soon," Katy answered as she opened the door and motioned him in.

"Well, now look at the little guy. He's growing like a weed. How're you doing Randy?" he said. Randy looked up at him and held his truck out. Lenny reached for the truck, saying, "That's a really nice truck." And Randy pulled it away just as Lenny's hand got close to it.

Randy smiled a sly grin at him. Then he resumed his revving. "*Rrrruuuhhmnnn, rrrruuhhhnnnn, rrruuuhhhhnnnnn.*"

"Wow, he's even got the sound effects down," said Lenny.

Katy pulled Randy up from the floor by his free hand and grabbed the toy basket with her other hand. Lenny lifted the suitcases and held the screen open while Katy locked the door. They proceeded to the street where Lenny's bright-yellow long-wheelbase 1938 De Soto awaited and loaded up. Lenny eased out from the curb and drove over to Trimble past the post theater and then to McCormack past the parade grounds, pausing at the main gate. He glanced left, then right, taking in the old Kemoo Pub near the Wahiawa Reservoir. He pulled out right onto Wilikina Drive, old Highway 99, accelerating his big barge into the flow of traffic. Soon, he turned right onto Kamehameha Highway heading toward Honolulu.

Traffic was light. They made good time to Honolulu and were cruising into Waikiki. The cab turned right off Kamehameha onto Kapiolani, then onto 17th via Waialae and a final right on Kaimuki. Lenny eased up in front of a stylish bungalow where Valita was standing on the front porch, waving her arms joyfully. She bounced down the sidewalk and opened the backdoor of the cab and said, "Welcome, welcome, welcome, you two."

Valita lifted and hugged Randy then threw her free arm around Katy, giving her a sideways hug. "I'm so happy to have you come and stay with me. This is going to be fun," she said.

Katy paid Lenny and asked him if he could return and pick them up at seven thirty on Sunday morning. He agreed, then removed the bags from the taxi's trunk and placed them on the sidewalk. He waved goodbye to the three of them as he pulled away.

The women immediately started talking at about ninety miles a minute, excitedly interrupting and finishing the other's sentences. Valita said, "I have big plans for every hour you're here, Katy. We are going to do some gourmet cooking first, and since 'tis the season almost, some major cookie baking too. When we have finished that, I have crafts and sewing projects. And do I ever have some gossip to catch up on with our old friends from Southgate High days."

"Well, I do have a big pile of Christmas cards in my suitcase to address, stamp, and write notes in. Looks like we are going to be two very busy girls," Katy said.

"Then let the merriment begin," said Valita.

For the next day and a half the two gals yacked and giggled nonstop. They cooked, baked, crafted, and entertained Randy. They oohed and ahhed over the spectacular night views of Honolulu from Valita's back deck. And though they stayed up until the wee small hours both Friday and Saturday nights, Katy still managed to get some of the best sleep she had had in months. The baby was strangely quiet.

The two gals matched each other's gregariousness to a tee. But that was where the similarity ended. When not pregnant, Katy was a petite, blue-eyed blonde. Valita was a willowy, brown-eyed brunette who could be mistaken for a runway model or a Hollywood actress. Their high school friends used to call them Mutt and Jeff because of the difference in their stature.

Sunday morning arrived in a flash. The time had arrived for Katy and Randy to return to Schofield, and Katy planned to make a delicious brunch to welcome her husband back from the field.

By seven thirty, Katy with Randy and Valita were huddled at the curb with suitcases and a basket of toys awaiting Lenny's arrival. The girls' high-speed dialogue continued unabated. At 7:40, Katy grew concerned. "I hope Lenny hasn't forgotten us," she said. Before the words were out of her mouth, a bright-yellow taxi came roaring up the street. "Oh, there he is," she shouted with relief.

Lenny got out of the cab and quickly circled to the curb. "Sorry I'm late. I had to drop a couple of GIs off at Waikiki. They tried to stiff me on the fare, but I got lucky: a couple of MPs drove up in a jeep just when they tried to walk on the fare. They paid the fare and a much bigger tip than they had in mind," he said, laughing.

"Well, better late than never, and I'm glad you didn't get stiffed," Katy said.

Lenny opened the cab door then placed the suitcases in the trunk. Valita gave one last big hug to Katy and Randy and said, "We have to do this more often."

"Every chance we get," Katy agreed as she and Randy got into the cab. Valita closed the door. Lenny pulled out from the curb and turned toward Kamehameha.

"So did you and your friend solve all the problems of the world during your visit?" Lenny asked.

"Not a one," Katy answered. "Not a single serious word was spoken between the two of us during the entire time. We talked and laughed and ate and laughed. Then we talked and laughed some more. It was a wonderful, relaxing tonic for me to be away from Schofield for a few hours. We reverted to a state of childlike enchantment. All of the problems of the world disappeared for a while. No talk of invasion by the Japanese."

"Sounds beautiful," Lenny said as he turned onto Kamehameha.

A few minutes later they were approaching Pearl City and the Makalapa Crater at the edge of the east loch of Salt Lake. Lenny turned his attention to Ford Island and said, "Look at those two monster battleships. I think they're the *Colorado* and the *Arizona*." Just as the words came out of his mouth, a violent explosion erupted from the closest battleship. The shock wave was so powerful that it lifted the cab off the ground a few feet and Lenny almost lost control. The sound was deafening.

Katy shrieked, and Randy started wailing. They saw what appeared to be a squadron of Japanese Zero fighter planes. This was what everyone had been predicting for months: the start of the Japanese invasion of the Hawaiian Islands. Lenny floored the accelerator of the big DeSoto and shot down the straightaway of Kamehameha Highway. He had a full jolt of adrenaline and was struggling to think clearly. Katy continued to whimper, and Randy cried hysterically. Explosions continued, but at a greater distance.

"Katy, Katy, Katy," Lenny shouted louder and louder. "Calm down. Calm down now. It's going to be OK. I'll have you back to Schofield in minutes. Please stop crying. Randy and your baby need you to calm down; get control. Take some long deep breaths. There. That's it. Deep breaths. Keep it up. That's better. We're going to be OK. We're going to be safe."

"Oh, God, oh, God, oh, God, no, no, no!" Katy's voice thundered into a crescendo of agony, higher and higher. "I'm having a massive contraction," she screamed. "Lenny, Lenny, oh, God, the pain, Lenny. Get me to the hospital. Please hurry, hurry!" She couldn't calm down. She was gasping for breath.

"Breathe, Katy, breathe. You're gasping. Try to control your breathing. Longer, slower breaths. That's it. Good. Take control." Randy continued to cry in convulsive rhythms. Lenny reached over the seat with his right arm and began gently stroking the toddler's head. "There's a good boy, Randy. Calm down. Mommy's OK," he said in a soothing voice. Just when she appeared to be calming down, Katy let out a bloodcurdling scream that launched Randy back into paroxysms of hysteria and nearly drove Lenny's head through the roof of the cab.

"Breathe, Katy, breathe," he commanded. He reached back and pulled Randy into the front seat next to him. "Lie down, Katy, on your back, door to door. Get your heels on the seat and take control of your breathing."

Groaning fiercely, she did as Lenny directed. As soon as she got her heels on the seat, her water burst. Lenny knew he had to get her to the hospital very quickly or he'd have to perform another back-seat delivery. He had done it once. He had been a medic in the Great War, with twenty years in the medical corps. He'd had some practice. He could do it again. But it was dangerous. And he had Randy to worry about. The kid was already so traumatized. He pushed the big sedan to the edge of what he thought was safe. He had never before exceeded fifty miles per hour, yet in the last five minutes, he had been driving at over eighty. Just ten minutes to the hospital now. Katy kept moaning.

"Hold on, Katy, hold on. We're almost there. Just a few more minutes. You can make it. You can make it," he urged her.

Then hell broke loose from the sky above. A Jap Zero came out of nowhere, firing a steady staccato, destroying the macadam paving several hundred feet in front of the cab. Lenny steered radically right, catching air as the cab lifted off the highway. He felt a strange energy flow through him and a sense of everything slowing down, barely moving. They collided gently with a thicket of shrubs that kept the DeSoto from rolling over. They came to a screeching halt against the trunk of an ancient banyan tree. The cab had been slowed by a slide through the hanging aerial prop-root system. The DeSoto had major damage, but the three of them, miraculously, were uninjured.

Katy was crying softly. Randy was sobbing and gasping in hysterics. Lenny felt his sanity ebbing away. The Zero made a second pass, strafing the banyan tree and striking one last chord of terror into the three of them. And then it exploded violently and disappeared mysteriously into a swirling violet cloud.

"Don't let my babies die, Lenny. Please save them. Don't worry about me. Just save my children," Katy begged.

Lenny rallied. "No one's dying here, Katy, least of all you. You and I are going to deliver that big guy right now." He grabbed Randy by the shoulders and hugged him. He said, "Randy, your mother needs you to be strong. We need you to sit here in this seat and play with your trucks." He grabbed two of the trucks that were loose in the front of the cab and handed them to Randy. "Remember how you go '*rrrruuuhhhnnnuuuuuhhhhnnn.*' Now go '*vvvrrrrooooooomm-mmmm, vvvvvvvrrrrooooommmmmmm.*'"

He got out of the cab and opened the backdoor on the side where Katy's legs were extended. He pulled a canteen of water from under the seat and washed his hands the best he could. He grabbed Katy's hands and asked her to look him in the eyes. She did. "We are going to do this, Katy, you and me. We are going to deliver your baby right now. And he's going to be healthy and strong. Are you with me?" he asked.

She whimpered and nodded through her pain and whispered, "Yes, I'm with you, Lenny."

"OK, here goes." He gathered her dress above her belly and saw that the baby was fully crowned and she was fully dilated. The next wave of contractions struck. She started moaning and panting, and her moans rose to a shatteringly high note. "Push, Katy, push, push, push." The baby's head was showing more. She heaved and pushed and howled like a wild animal again and again and again. Then her pain subsided enough for her to start breathing deeply.

"OK, Katy, the head is showing. When I yell push, you have to push with everything you've got."

The next wave hit, and Katy started shrieking. "Push, push, push, harder, harder, harder," Lenny shouted. And a baby boy with an uncommonly massive head popped out of her. He lifted the boy and cleaned out his palate. He had positioned the baby to give him a hearty slap on the backside when the lad let out a primal scream that caused Lenny to drop him on his mother's legs. The scream made every hair on Lenny's body stand erect. It was an uncanny sound that penetrated to the bone. It was like nothing he had ever heard. He picked the boy up tentatively and handed him to Katy, whose cries had become relieved, even joyful. Lenny took his Swiss Army knife out of his pocket and severed the umbilical cord. Randy was whimpering but still holding onto his truck.

After she finished telling her story to Will, with a haunted look in her eyes, his mother said, "A child was born in a cauldron of evil and violence on a day that shall live forever in the annals of infamy. And I named the child William Banyan Parish."

FOUR

Will had disappeared deep into the world of Tolstoy, losing himself in the kindred spirit of *War and Peace*'s Pierre. He'd mastered this technique for escaping reality as a deeply depressed high school freshman. Now he was being torn out of the pages by his concerned friend.

"Time to fall in, Will. Captain Dickwad's looking for you. He called formation three minutes ago. Let's go!" Rob urged.

Will shot out of his cubby a little disoriented and jabbed a marker in the book. "What formation? Where?" he asked.

"Come on," Rob said. "Now!" Will followed him up the steps and around a double bulkhead. Their classmates were lined up in two rows. Will and Rob joined the second line and came to attention. Captain Royce stared hard at Rob and Will—harder and longer at Will.

"All right, men, listen up. I know you've all been bellyaching about sailing to Vietnam when everyone else is flying there in style. But it's time to count your blessings. Every day aboard this tub is one less day in a combat zone where you might be ducking bullets and dodging mortar rounds. And here's another lucky break. I just met with the company commander of the combat engineers. He has volunteered to have his men pull all of the crap duty details on the ship. He needs to keep his men busy. He's under the impression that you men are all part of some exalted top-secret intelligence unit. So, I want to see some happy faces out there. Staff Sergeant Perry will pull daily inspection at 7 a.m. Personal hygiene will be maintained. That means shaving and showering daily. To maintain some semblance of fitness, we'll have PT right here every morning at zero seven fifteen. Any questions?"

Hearing none, he ordered, "Detachment dismissed—except for you, Parish." Everyone but Will moved on. "I thought I told you to get a haircut before we left Fort Bragg," the captain said. "You are starting to look like one of those mop-headed Beatles. You bear no resemblance to a soldier; in fact, you look more like a beach bum or a surfer."

Will didn't answer. What Captain Dickwad said was true. His hair was way too long. He had no military bearing. He was a joke when it came to esprit de corps. "I'm waiting for an answer, Parish," the captain snapped.

"I'm sorry, sir. I did try to get a haircut, but the post barber shop had closed an hour early our last day at Bragg," he lied.

"I don't believe you, Parish," the captain said, narrowing his eyes into tiny slits. "I'm going to make it my highest priority to find a barber among the engineers or the crew to give you a buzz cut. That's it, private, dismissed." The captain did a sharp about-face and walked away. Another anal West Point lifer, Will said to himself as he watched Captain Dickwad stalk off.

Will wondered what his chances were of making it back home alive and with all of his body parts intact. The scary thing was that his survival probably depended a lot on his ability to get along with officers and NCOs. So far he had been an abysmal failure in that department.

When he was honest with himself, Will knew at heart that he was the problem. He had a serious hang-up with authority. It had all started with his father, who had been a verbally abusive authoritarian and an alcoholic. He and Will had shared some profound moments with a wooden paddle. At school, Will had struggled with teachers and coaches from his earliest days. He found himself constantly challenging authority, and it always cost him: time-outs, detention, knuckles smashed with rulers, trips to the principal's office, and getting kicked off of sports teams. And with each altercation, every reprimand, there was his mother, saying "Will, you're just way too smart for your own good." He remembered her using those words over and over from the very first time he started getting into trouble at school.

He had never had a problem with lessons or homework assignments or tests. He was always at the top of the class in every subject as far back as he could remember. One night, late in his sixth-grade year, Will's father had been very late coming home from work. Will and his brothers were already in bed when their dad got home. His two brothers fell asleep quickly, but Will was wide awake, listening to his parents arguing loudly. He was worried about his mother because he knew how angry his dad got when he had been drinking. So he snuck out of his bedroom to eavesdrop.

It soon became obvious that his parents were arguing over him.

"They must have made a mistake. That's almost fifty points higher than mine. He's not that smart." They were talking about a test that Will and his classmates had taken. Will had a score of one hundred eighty-eight. His father said he didn't believe it.

"Yes, he is," she said. His mother told his father that she had met with Will's sixth-grade teacher, who'd told her about Will's unprecedented high score. The teacher recommended that Will skip junior high school and go directly to the ninth grade. He said that holding Will back would be a crime because he wasn't really learning anything at this level.

"Will's teacher said that he thinks his high IQ is why he gets in so much trouble and is such a discipline problem," said his mother. His parents argued on opposite sides. His father wanted to follow the teacher's advice and send Will right to high school. "Maybe that will give him the discipline he needs—either that or military school," his father said.

Hearing this scared the crap out of Will. He didn't want to be in high school. He was too little. He wouldn't know anyone. He would have no friends. His mother, with unusual firmness, took charge of the debate. She said in the most assertive voice he'd ever heard her use, "Bill, our son is not going to go to high school next year. I won't stand by and let that happen to him. He is not emotionally mature or stable enough to cope with that. This discussion is over."

Will remembered his mother's forceful words clearly as he headed back to the whaleboat. Not far in the distance, he saw the vague outline of a cityscape. It had to be Victoria, on Vancouver Island. He was struck by the notion of how close to freedom he was standing. Just a few miles away, he knew, there was a growing colony of draft-card-burning expatriates. Two guys he'd been friendly with at UCLA were the nucleus of the small group. They refused to fight in a war they believed to be immoral. Will asked himself, Is this war immoral? Yes. What does that make me? A moral coward? Probably yes. He wondered how his life would have turned out had he taken that path to Victoria. He lifted the whaleboat cover, pulled himself up by the davits, slid under the canvas, and disappeared.

FIVE

Will's stomach was growling up a storm. It must be dinnertime, he thought. He climbed out of the whaleboat and made his way to the crowded mess hall. He grabbed a tray and got in the chow line. Dinner was what looked like a highly edible meal: cheeseburgers and french fries. Will filled a tall glass with milk and joined his buddies, who squeezed him onto their bench.

In a highly social setting like this, Will would flip on his extrovert switch. Or was it flipped on by the setting? He wasn't sure, but he probably had no control over it. He became garrulous. "What's happening with you spooks and secret agent men? I'm really rather hating the accommodations here. I do so terribly miss my dry martini, shaken, not stirred," he said in his best Sean Connery brogue.

"Well, look who's suddenly all sunshine and light. What happened to the gloomy, depressed guy?" Rob asked.

"Ah, my beloved fellow spymasters, it was just a period of adjustment. I needed some time to get better used to the idea of going off to war and maybe getting my brains blown out," Will said. "The amazing thing is that every one of us enlisted for three years to avoid going to Vietnam. And look where we're going. We could have got drafted and accomplished the same thing. Then we could have looked forward to one less year in captivity."

"You're full of shit, Will," Rob shot back. "If we had been drafted, we would have been in a frontline infantry unit. At least being in an intelligence unit we have a good chance of avoiding the heat of the battle."

"Yes, hope does spring eternal. Your version of the future is much more attractive than mine," Will said.

The classmates continued in their feeble attempts to prognosticate the future. It mostly boiled down to wishful thinking. Not one of them had an intelligent clue of what was yet to come, Will included. Against his better judgment, he was sucked into a round of bridge. He struggled through the first rubber. Arguments over the official parameters of the conventions of Stamen, Blackwood, and Gerber finally drove him out of the game.

Outside, he started pacing the *Darby*, searching for his sea legs. He walked the lower decks—the upper ones were roped off for officers and senior NCOs only. As he navigated the deck with its ubiquitous armored steel plate, Will became aware of the dazzling chromatic light show ignited by the setting sun and clouds. That fiery amber orb was on the edge of the Pacific horizon, and the entire sky was dominated by a broad field of cirrocumulus stratiformis with globs of mammatus patched in floccus. For one breathtaking moment, the sky, from top to bottom, was ablaze. Will had never seen a sunset like this. He feasted on its majestic structure and infinite power. Had he slipped into a parallel universe? The scene was so overpowering that it made the hair all over his body stand up. Was he the only one on the *Darby* aware of this ecstatic moment? His impulse was to shout out at the top of his lungs for everyone to come running. Should he rush below and muster the troops? No, he refused to miss any part of it.

He continued to stand there with his mouth wide open, taking in every photon he could absorb. He experienced it with every sense, not just visually. He literally smelled it, tasted it, heard it, and felt it all over his body, every cell in his body tingling in full synesthesia. All quadrants of the sky were on fire. Behind him and above him were roiling magentas, structures of fuchsia and lilac fusing into royal purples. He knew these colors—he had experienced this recurring curious waking dream through the years. He turned back to the horizon for the green flash and the afterglow the color of burnt blood orange. Soon only half of the sky held magenta, then one quarter, then it showed the pink and the purple, and finally the intense purple. Then it was over. He stood there for several moments mesmerized, incapable of movement, a solitary figure rising and falling with the swell. The chill of the twenty-knot wind finally broke the spell and brought him back to reality. Then he shouted,

"Red sky in the morning, sailors take warning. Red sky at night, sailors' delight!" And Will was delighted.

Later that night, his first night at sea, the swell increased dramatically. The rise and fall of the hull of the *Darby* was considerable, and the rolling motion grew more noticeable. Will whispered his thanks to the maker of Dramamine as he swallowed two more tablets. A few of his bunkmates appeared to be sleeping. Others were reading. Will lifted himself gingerly into the sardine can that was his bunk, careful, this time, to avoid smashing his head on the pipes above. He lay on his back, studying those pipes and pondering their function. He knew that sleep was unlikely. He could read or hope to slip away into a self-induced reverie of pleasant youthful remembrance.

Will tried to force his thoughts to wander off to some vivid, pleasant memory of childhood. Sadly, there weren't a lot of them. One of his earliest memories was playing in the front yard on a warm summer day with his big brother, Randy, and a bunch of other kids from the neighborhood in Hollydale. A couple of the kids were seven or eight. One was a girl, Wendy, from next door. They were playing tag. Almost four, Will was too little to play with the big kids, but he kept trying. The bigger kids were getting annoyed with Will. Randy turned to him and said, "Here, little brother. I got you a candy bar. It's yummy white chocolate." Will took it from his brother and was about to take a bite when Wendy came screaming and flying out of nowhere and knocked the turd from his hand. Out of Will's sight, Randy had grabbed an empty candy bar wrapper from the ground and pushed a bleached, bone-dry dog turd inside it.

She said, "Don't touch that, Will! It's a dog poop!" His brother and the other kids were laughing their asses off.

Will looked at Randy. He wanted to beat him up. Then a wondrous thing happened. A flock of pigeons flew over the yard, and one of them dropped a big wet gob right in the middle of Will's big brother's face. You could hear him scream for blocks around. That beautiful memory was indelibly written in Will's mind, and he recycled it many times over the years. When he did, he thought, Somebody up there really likes me.

The *Darby* was still undulating steadily, gently rocking Will into REM sleep. He dreamed a not-unfamiliar dream. He was a child in an older car from the 1940s, sitting in the front between his father, driving, and his mother's father, in the passenger seat. They were heading down a mountain road lined with pines and cedars. He was watching his father's hands on the steering wheel, then he turned and looked at his grandfather, with his massive belly.

"Bompi, why are you so fat?" Will said.

His grandfather turned toward him and struck him in the middle of his face with an open palm. Will started screaming. Blood erupted from his nostrils and his mouth.

His father yelled, "Goddamn you! I told you never to lay a hand on my kids!" The tires screeched as the car veered to the side of the road. Will's father pulled the handbrake, turned off the ignition, and popped the clutch in a single motion. The car lurched as he jumped out in a rage, rushing around to the passenger side and flinging the door open. He reached in and grabbed his father-in-law by the collar of his jacket with both hands, pulling him to his feet. With a vicious right hook to the chin, Will's father laid him out cold in the grass and weeds on the shoulder of the road.

Will lurched awake from this dream with a gasp, bumping his head on those damn overhead pipes again. This dream was not new. He couldn't remember the first time he'd had it. How old was he? He wondered how much of it came from repressed memory and how much was planted there by his father. Did it really happen? Was it true?

His memory wandered to the telephone call he got from his dad when he was a junior at UCLA. His father told him that his grandfather Bompi had just died during surgery. There was a brief silence. Will felt no sense of loss, no sadness. He asked his father if his mom was doing OK. He felt sad for her because he knew she, an only daughter, worshipped her father. His dad replied that she was taking it pretty hard. Will still felt nothing. He thought about that, why he felt no compassion for the man. How could he not care?

Two days later he went home for the funeral. At the beginning of the memorial service at Rose Hills, there was an open casket visitation. He and his brother Randy each took one of their mother's arms and walked her up to the half-open coffin. The sight of his grandfather lying there dead. At peace? His mother sobbing gently. Randy all teary and sniveling. Will stood there while his mother lingered, almost inaudibly whimpering. He waited for some tiny fragment of emotion, and still nothing came.

Later that night at his parents' place, after his mother had gone to bed, Will sat with his father drinking whiskey. His father was on his sixth or seventh. Will was on his second or third, feeling few inhibitions. Will said, "You know, Dad, now that Mom's gone to bed, I gotta tell you I didn't feel anything over Bompi's passing. I never really cared for him. I know he didn't really give much of a shit about me. I had the feeling he didn't even know my name. He usually left the room whenever I walked in. He sure loved Randy, though. He always had something special for him when he and Nana came visiting. A new pocket knife, a bag of marbles, jawbreakers, magic tricks, a silver dollar, always something for his beloved Randy. Sometimes he would glance over to make sure I was watching before he handed it to him. But there were never any goodies for Will."

"There's a history that explains it all," his dad said through slurred speech. "Now that he's gone, I guess it can't do any harm to tell you. You were probably too young when it happened to have any memory of it. You were just three, I think." Will's dad told him the story. He left out no violent detail. When his dad was done telling the story that Will had visited several times in his dreams, Will was speechless. His dad just sat there in his recliner, staring at him blankly, rotating his crystal highball glass, ice cubes clinking.

"You were an impertinent little bastard. Sure, he was fat—obese, in fact. He was a glutton. That's why he's dead today. You deserved a good spanking for that. But it wasn't his right to discipline you physically. When I saw all that blood, I snapped and lost my temper. I put him down on the ground. He deserved it. So now you know. The mystery is solved." He held up his glass. "A toast is in order. Here's pissing on his grave." And he tossed back the remaining booze in his glass.

Will didn't join him.

SIX

Will's ability to differentiate truth from fiction vacillated like the rise and fall of the *Darby*'s hull. He had all of these richly embroidered memories. Was he an embroiderer of the truth, decorating it with his fantasies so that it loomed larger than reality? He knew that he was guilty of enhancing some events from his past to make them replay more poignantly on the screen of his memory.

There were memories of his youth that were inexplicable. When the events were happening, they were disturbing and scary but not bizarre. The few times he attempted to share with others what had taken place, his friends either laughed at him, didn't believe him, or told him he was crazy. So he began to doubt his strange memories, thinking he might have fabricated them. Until strange things started to happen all over again. Then he would start to question his sanity.

Before the onset of puberty, when he was ten or eleven, Will would sometimes spend hours daydreaming. He would fall into a trancelike state with eyes wide open. His mother would call him, and he wouldn't answer. Sometimes she had to shake him to pry him back to actual consciousness. She always said something like, "Boy, does that make me crazy when you do that, Will. It gives me the creeps. It's like you're not there. Never do that again." The first few times it happened, Will apologized to his mom and told her he would never do it again. But he was sure that it was something he had no control over. And he was right, because it kept happening—a lot.

Most of his indelibly imprinted traumatic experiences revolved around tantrums so extreme that he lost consciousness. While he was out he'd experience a sense of falling through a hole into an alien, unrecognizable place. At first, almost all of these extreme tantrums resulted from a confrontation with his father. He finally grew out of the tantrum stage, and the blackouts disappeared for a while.

During the fourth, fifth, and sixth grades, Will had enjoyed a normal kid's life. He excelled academically. He had a lot of friends and was considered one of the "cool guys." He was of average height and weight for his age. He was good at sports and always one of the first chosen for teams. This idyllic period ended dramatically when he graduated from Evergreen elementary school and moved on to East Whittier junior high. When he entered junior high, there was a new population of boys, most of whom he didn't know. In the seventh grade, he first encountered bullies up close and personal.

There were many glaringly obvious things about Will that were beyond his awareness as a twelve-year-old starting the seventh grade. Looking back, his blind spots were puzzling. By the second half of the sixth grade, most of his friends were going through hormonal growth spurts that were in a holding pattern in Will's body. When seventh grade started, most of his friends were three or four inches taller. It seemed that all of the eighth graders, including the girls, were taller than him. Another peculiarity of Will's that drew the attention of bullies was his hypersensitivity to acts of unkindness. When he noticed someone victimizing a helpless kid, he was incapable of ignoring it. He had an overdeveloped sensitivity to injustice. His body language, facial expression, and prolonged stares allowed the bullies to become aware of him inviting them to add him to their target list.

One of Will's classmates in the seventh grade was a tall, muscular kid called Ernie Neely. Ernie was a pretty good kid most of the time, but he had this mean streak that came out when things weren't going his way. It manifested in a tendency to punch smaller kids in the center of the deltoid muscle with the second knuckle of his middle finger extending out from his fist. It hurt like hell and left an ugly bruise. During the first weeks of school, Ernie nailed Will a dozen or so times on the playground during recess or PE. The punch always seemed to come out of nowhere when teachers were looking the other way.

One day during PE when the class was doing jumping jacks on the grassy area of the playground, Will's hackles rose. Out of the corner of his eye, he saw Ernie moving into position and starting to swing at his shoulder in a state of rage. Just before Ernie's fist smashed into his shoulder, it appeared to come to a dead stop. Will got that old feeling like he was blacking out, then falling through something beyond description, incomprehensible. And then he was back in the same instant he'd departed, and the rage was suppressed. The fist was still there, inches from his shoulder. He didn't exactly remember, but he knew he had reached out with his open palm to block it, just making contact with Ernie's hand. He could feel a pulse of energy bursting through his hand and see Ernie catapult backward several feet in slow motion. The bigger kid hit the ground hard and started howling in pain.

It happened so fast that none of the other kids saw it. Ernie was cradling his hand and wrist and yelling, "You broke it! You broke it! You broke my hand. You broke my wrist. Why did you do that?" Then he vomited. The other kids were all staring at Ernie now with shocked expressions on their faces. Will wanted to run and hide, but he couldn't move. He was stuck to the ground. The PE teacher came running to Ernie, who was writhing on the grass. He helped him up and took him to the nurse's office. All of the other seventh graders gathered around Will. Now he could move, but running wasn't an option. Thirty kids were asking him all at once what happened. He finally got his voice. "I don't know. It doesn't make sense. He was trying to punch me in the arm. I pulled my shoulder out of the way, and he just went flying." Will knew this wasn't the truth, but he couldn't tell anyone what he thought really happened. But what really had happened, he asked himself? He had no answer. He knew he had been to that strange, dark place before. But just now he thought he was going crazy. One of his classmates said he hoped this meant he wouldn't be getting punched in the arm by Ernie anymore. Two other boys echoed his sentiment.

Will was marched to the principal's office by Mr. Fisher, the PE teacher. The principal immediately read Will the riot act. He didn't allow Will to tell his side of it. Will was suspended from school for three days. When his father found out, he went apeshit and grounded Will for a whole month.

No one ever found out the truth of what happened that day between Will and Ernie. Will wasn't going to say anything about it, and Ernie was so embarrassed that he never discussed it with anyone, even when asked. In fact, for the rest of junior high, Ernie never got closer than twenty feet to Will.

For the next few years, Will did his best to avoid bullies like the plague. He became a world-class fleeing champion. He made the cowardly lion look brave. It was almost magical the way he could disappear when being pursued or ambushed, with one very serious exception at the end of the eighth grade.

SEVEN

When Will rubbed his eyes open from sleep, he saw the plumbing on the ceiling. The rise and fall of the *Darby*'s hull brought everything rushing back, producing a hard ball of dread deep in his gut as the idea of where he was headed replaced the memory of his youth. He'd woken up from a bad dream into a very shitty reality. He wondered why his thinking was so fuzzy and his eyes so full of goop. He thought about the Dramamine and how he had tripled the recommended dosage.

"Get the fuck out of bed, Will! You have ten minutes to get to the formation and PT," Rob shouted in his face.

Will slid out, almost crashing into the other bunks across the aisle. He grabbed his fatigues and boots and got dressed in a hurry. He had barely enough time to rush to the head, take a piss, and wash the sleepers out of his eyes. His hair looked like a dried-out, twisted mop. Damn, the captain's going to be all over me like stink on shit, he thought. He wetted his hair thoroughly and plastered it down close to his scalp and behind his ears. It *almost* looked like he had gotten a haircut. No time for breakfast. He sprang up the steps and made the formation with seconds to spare.

Captain Dick Royce, a.k.a. Dickwad or Dickless, was already standing there on the deck. He watched Will line up and stared at him way too long for Will's comfort. He called the detachment to attention and started toward Will but broke stride when Major Charles called him from the officers' dining deck. As he headed over to Charles, Royce shouted, "At ease!" over his shoulder. He and the major had a short conversation out of earshot. He returned and ordered, "Everyone spread out, extend your arms, fingertips to fingertips. Parish, front

40

and center—you're leading PT today. Move it, soldier!"

Will moved up, but not quite enthusiastically or fast enough.

"Look sharp, soldier. Jump to it. Start with fifty jumping jacks, now, Parish, now."

Will turned toward his classmates and placed his hands at his hips. He spread his legs a little, shoulder-width apart. He paused for the others to mirror his position. As he did, a shit-eating grin slowly emerged and spread across his face and continued to spread to the faces of his classmates.

"Wipe that stupid grin off your face, Parish. That goes for the rest of you too. You think this is fun and games, Parish? You think this is some kind of joyride? Well, it isn't. This is deadly serious shit. We are going to war. You are going to take these PT sessions seriously, all of you. You are going to land in Vietnam in a state of fitness, not flabbiness. You understand me, Parish?"

Will nodded.

"I didn't hear you, soldier!" he barked.

"Yes, sir!" Will shouted back at the top of his lungs, causing Royce to flinch. Then Will started counting off the jumping jacks, bellowing much louder than needed. He was way out of character playing the role of a gung-ho soldier. His closest buddies, the ones who knew him best, were cracking up and exercising like spastics. And Captain Dickwad was doing an intense slow burn.

Will was a little winded when he got to number fifty, but he felt he could jump jacks with the best. "How about fifty alternating toe touches," he hollered in Royce's direction. When Royce didn't respond, he began calling out the cadence and bending, touching, and rotating from side to side, shouting out the numbers.

At the count of four Royce yelled, "Stop, stop! Enough of these pussy warm-ups, Parish. It's time for some real exercise—eight-count burpees. Let's go, Parish. Give me fifty, all of you. Hit it. We'll see who still thinks this is funny."

Will started counting and dropped to the ground, did two pushups, then got back to standing. After ten or twelve reps Will's ass was dragging. Most of his classmates were falling behind and getting sloppy. Will dropped the cadence, slower and slower. Royce yelled at him to speed it up. Will took it slower still.

"Hold it, hold it. Get back in formation, Parish. You're fucking this up completely. I'm taking over. I'll show you how it's done." Will retreated, relieved, to the rear of the formation with a grin on his face that Royce couldn't see. Then Royce threw himself into it at a breakneck pace that no one could keep up with.

The captain was so absorbed in the execution of a perfect burpee that he didn't see the formation breaking down into total chaos in front of him. As Dickwad completed his set, Major Charles approached and spoke softly to him for a moment. Royce nodded obsequiously several times, then turned to the formation and called, "Ten-hut. All right, ladies, in single file, ten laps around the *Darby*. Follow me. No lagging." The asshole took off like a goosed rabbit. No one made the slightest effort to keep up with him. The entire class hung together at an easy jogging pace, including Staff Sergeant Perry. Near the end of lap number four, Royce lapped the group without saying a word. When the pack was nearing the end of its eighth lap, Will became aware that Dickhead was on his tenth and final lap and sprinting toward the finish to make it a double lapping. Then an amazing thing happened. Just seconds from the finish line, the captain, quite unfortunately, tripped over his own boots and skidded into a face-plant on the rough steel plate of the *Darby*'s deck.

After the morning debacle, Will and his closest classmates dined together at lunch in the ship's mess hall. Will was starving because he had slept through breakfast and had burned off a lot more calories than usual. He pigged out on meatloaf, mashed potatoes, gravy, and several slices of Wonder Bread. It wasn't home cooking, but he was so freaking hungry that with enough salt and pepper, he barely noticed the difference.

He and his fellow diners spent most of lunch reviewing their gung-ho captain's spectacular face-plant. They relived it in great and exaggerated detail many times during the course of their meal. It provided a powerful, almost narcotic distraction from thinking about where they were headed.

Will thought about how Royce had chosen to behave in a mean-spirited way. His natural inclination had been to abuse and speak down to those below him. Why would a human being choose to treat other humans like that? Were his injuries the result of his unkind treatment of others? Is there really karmic retribution? This continued to be one of life's great mysteries for Will. He thought about Major Charles. The major just seemed to be disconnected from it all, content with having Royce play the heavy. His role was mostly passive, a behind-the-scenes milquetoast. The major was not mean-spirited like Royce. He did have a bit of human kindness in his bones.

EIGHT

After lunch Will made his way to his whaleboat hideout, where he had stashed his copy of *War and Peace*. Before allowing himself to slip away into the world of nineteenth-century Russia, his mind circled back to his dream state of the previous night. His thoughts just kept drifting, drifting, aimlessly. No focus, no discipline. He realized that escaping into the world of Tolstoy was not an option. Will knew that he had to rise to the occasion and fight off his self-destructive tendencies—not an easy assignment. His hardest task would be overcoming his knee-jerk reaction to authority. He needed a strategy to help him suffer fools gladly, whether they be fools in the form of officers or NCOs.

He climbed out of the whaleboat legs first to get some fresh air. On deck, he backed into someone and was immediately body-slammed, knocked to the ground. Now standing over him with raised fists was someone Will had never laid eyes on. Will stood up and backed away from his much taller and wider aggressor.

"What the fuck you doin' in my boat, man?" the angry combat engineer demanded. He had a sidekick, not quite as big or mean looking.

Will didn't answer at first, still trying to make sense of the attack. He sized up the guy and his understudy. They were younger than him, probably nineteen or twenty, draftees for sure, angry about being on a slow boat to China with a stop in Vietnam. They were probably angry most of the time, always looking for a fight. Classic bullies, Will thought.

"I asked you a question, asshole," he said.

"Yes, yes, you did, but my name's not asshole and what's with all the anger?" Will said. "Why don't we start over. I apologize for not being more careful about exiting the whaleboat. I didn't mean to kick you. My name is Will," he said, extending his hand.

"I don't give a shit what your name is, asshole," the combat engineer said, swatting Will's hand away with the knuckles of his fist.

"Oww, that fucking hurt," Will said, grimacing.

"You got to be kidding, you pussy. How can a tough badass spook like you feel pain from a tap on your hand? They say you secret agent guys are like James Bond, real tough motherfuckers, and your hands are lethal weapons, and you're licensed to kill. Come on, James Bond, let's see how tough you are."

The combat engineer grunted as he launched a karate kick at Will's head. It was incredibly fast and came out of nowhere. But it came to a sudden stop amid a swirling vortex of purples. Will's mind was swept far away to that strange place beyond his understanding. Then he came back in a burst of energy and rage. He was staring at the toe of the engineer's combat boot as it millimetered toward the side of his chin. He marveled at the accuracy of the kick. This guy has to be a black belt in some form of martial arts, Will thought. He pulled his head back slightly and watched as the kick continued its slow-motion trajectory, passing by him without contact. The kicker pirouetted backward in that same otherworldly slow motion. His face registered shock that he had failed to hit his target. He leapt forward to thrust an elbow into Will's face.

Will perceived it as a barely moving object. He caught the elbow a little too aggressively and pushed back as a pulse of energy shot out of his palm. He could feel and hear the horrible snap and tearing of tissue in the attacker's upper arm and shoulder, the slow shriek of pain, and the thud as the guy's head bounced off the bulkhead. The combat engineer's friend had produced a leather sap that was now arcing toward Will's forehead. Will responded by placing his palm on the hand of the attacker, redirecting the sap back at the guy's head at extreme speed. This created a second thud when the sap made contact with his skull. There was blood oozing from the engineers' ears and noses and other wounds, and all was calm. Will came back to almost normal and moved quickly away from the scene of the violence.

He went toward the mess hall and found his mates just outside standing in a circle looking at Wolfe and Bacigalupi, who had bloodied faces.

"What the hell happened to you guys," he asked, already knowing what the answer would be.

"We got bushwhacked by two combat engineers," Wolfe said.

"Yeah, a couple of big fucking assholes, they wanted to kick our asses because they were catching all of the shit details while we were fucking off," Bacigalupi said.

"Ah, shit, I'm sorry that happened to you guys. Are you OK? No broken noses, I hope," Will said.

"Nothing serious, just bloody noses, a loose tooth, maybe a black eye coming. I think they would have worked us over a lot worse, but someone was coming, and they took off fast. Now we have to watch out for these guys. They're really pissed off. They like to fight, and there's one hell of a lot more of them than there are of us," Wolfe said.

"I think it's going to be OK. I've got a feeling somehow that those two guys aren't going to be bothering us again," Will said.

"Yeah, you and your strange feelings aren't making me feel all that secure and comfortable, Will," Rob Landau said. "I've had a few years of your weird and strange feelings, but I don't see how your feeling is going to keep us from getting jumped."

"Oh, ye of little faith, Robby, come on. We'll all hang together, safety in numbers, and stay in sight of officers and NCOs. That should work until we can come up with something better. I'm hungry as a bear. It's got to be time for chow. Let's close ranks and head for the mess hall. Who's with me?" said Will. They all started moving en masse toward the mess hall entry. No one was there yet, but the smells were strong, and it looked hopeful: pork roast and mashed potatoes with gravy and green beans. They dished up and went to the far corner of the hall away from the door and the serving line. When they had all finished their meals, they left the mess in a tight pattern, jumpy at the possibility of running into the engineers. When they came out into the open, they saw the engineering company standing at attention thirty feet from the mess hall entrance with their officers and NCOs standing in front of them looking seriously pissed off.

Will's group moved sharply toward the other end of the *Darby,* away from the engineering company. When they got to the stairwell leading to their sleeping quarters, they were intercepted by Major Charles, Lieutenant Frasier, and Sergeant Perry. They were ordered to the other side of the ship, out of sight of the engineers. Frasier called them to attention, and the major took over.

"A disturbing and violent incident took place on the deck of the *Darby* about an hour ago. Two engineers sustained life-threatening injuries. They are still unconscious with concussions or possible skull fractures. They cannot be properly treated on the *Darby.* The captain of the ship has called for a coast guard cutter for medical evacuation. If you were involved in this altercation or were a witness or have any information about it, I need you to come forward now." The major's stern gaze fell upon each man in the unit, one at a time, making eye contact and holding it.

He locked eyes with Will, who held the major's piercing gaze steadfastly but not without effort. *The major somehow senses it's me but can do nothing to prove it,* he thought. Finally the major relented and shifted his eyes to the next man, Wolfe.

"Wolfe," the major called. "Front and center. What happened to your eye, private? Have you been in a fight? Your face looks swollen. How did this happen?" he asked.

"No sir, I haven't been in a fight."

"Tell me, then, what happened?"

"I was running up the stairs from the bunk room, taking three at a time, and my hand slipped on the banister rail, and I landed on my face. That's it. No fight."

"Do you have any witnesses to this event?"

"Well . . ."

"Sir, I saw it happen," said Will.

"Oh, you did, did you, Parish? How convenient!" The major studied Wolfe and Will for a moment, looking back and forth. "Hold your hands out in front of you, palms down," he said to Wolfe. He grabbed the outstretched hands roughly and rolled each one into a fist while reading his face. Wolfe gave no reaction. "OK, get back in formation. Come here, Parish."

Will moved to where Wolfe had been standing, and the major asked him to present his hands. When it was obvious that Will's fists bore no sign of a fight, the major walked on through the formation, inspecting each man's hands. When he finished, he returned to the front of the formation and continued to study the men. He paused on Bacigalupi and stared intently at him. It was fortunate that Baci was wearing his baseball cap pulled down very low on his forehead and it obscured the damage on his face. Then the major turned to the lieutenant and spoke quietly to him. He turned back to the formation and said, "If any of you have anything to say to me in private, I want you to contact Lieutenant Frasier or Sergeant Perry to arrange for a meeting." He turned the unit over to the lieutenant, who promptly dismissed the men.

When they all gathered back in their sleeping quarters, Landau spoke first. "What the hell is going on around here? First Wolfe and Baci get beat up by some engineers. Next thing we hear two engineers get beat up even worse. It's obvious that none of us is beating anybody up. How about the assholes that laid into you guys—had you ever seen them before?"

"Never saw them before they attacked us," Baci said.

"I never saw them before, either," Wolfe added.

"Would you recognize them if you saw them?" Landau asked.

"Yeah, I would," Wolfe said. Baci concurred with a nod.

"What if there are some badass crew members going around beating people up? What if they aren't engineers at all?" McQueen said.

"No, they were definitely engineers. We saw the unit patches on their sleeves," Wolfe explained.

Will sat there on the floor at the edge of the group with his lips sealed, wondering where this was going. He imagined himself cutting through the bullshit, clearing it all up, and explaining to them that he was the one who had kicked the shit out of the two engineers. He would describe how they were at the point of fucking him up when he merely conjured a little magical power out of thin air, nothing special, just the kind that brings the local universe to a screeching halt and turns a love tap into lethal force. And he could see them all nodding, patting him on the back, saying, "Attaboy, Will, attaboy," and thanking him for explaining it all to them.

"You're pretty damned quiet all of a sudden, Will. What about that strange feeling of yours about how everything's going to be OK?" Landau said.

"Call it a hunch, intuition, whatever. It's possible that the guys who got beat up so badly might have been the same assholes who attacked Wolfe and Baci. Maybe somebody decided to teach them a lesson. Could have been other engineers. Or better yet, it was an avenging angel sent down from heaven to dole out some divine karmic retribution."

Around noon the next day a coast guard cutter appeared next to the *Darby*. Everyone from both units was on deck to watch the difficult medical evacuation by helicopter. There was little wind and a light swell, which made the evacuation possible. When the two engineers were rolled out onto the deck on gurneys, Will quickly recognized them as the guys he had nearly killed. He watched Wolfe and Baci. Both were studying the two evacuees closely. Wolfe became agitated and grabbed Baci's sleeve and pointed at them. Will couldn't hear what he said, but he could see Baci nod his agreement. Will felt good for them because they could relax knowing that they wouldn't get attacked again by those two evil shitheads. It was a perfect outcome. The chopper made two trips to complete the medevac. Almost immediately the *Darby* corrected course, and it was full ramming speed ahead. Vietnam, here we come.

The mystery of the beatings slowly faded into the Pacific doldrums. The sea had turned glassy. Wispy winds joined wimpy swells to make it smooth sailing. Frolicking pods of dolphins appeared from out of nowhere. The members of the detachment came to a consensus that dolphins were their good-luck charms, harbingers of a safe and survivable tour of duty in Vietnam. The *Darby* barely bobbed. No rolling. No yawing or pitching. No retching or puking. Forget the Dramamine.

Half of the men of the intelligence detachment spent a giddy evening on the *Darby*'s deck. One of the crew members from the mess had smuggled a case of vodka on board. De George had purchased two bottles at a highway-robbery price. The bottles were discreetly handed back and forth among nine of the classmates. No one was getting shit-faced; they were just taking the edge off things and lightening the mood. By the time the second fifth had vanished, the laughter had grown raucous. It reminded Will of being back at his old fraternity house with all of its good-natured horseplay and taunting, rat-fucking craziness.

NINE

By midafternoon of their seventh day at sea, the detachment had been ordered off deck. The *Darby* was in gale-force winds, waves coming from all directions. Hundreds of small but jarring movements were packed into each heave and roll of the old destroyer escort. At least half of the guys in the detachment were puking their brains out—or more correctly, performing the dry heaves because they had nothing left to barf up. Somehow—Will credited the Dramamine—he was holding his own through the unabated raging of the storm, the sounds of retching, and its violent aroma. The thrashing of the *Darby* was still hard to believe—how could an object so large and heavy be tossed around like a rubber ducky in a baby's bathtub? It seemed to defy the laws of physics. He hung his head over the edge of his bunk to peer down at Rob and Bobby. Both were lying on their backs with eyes closed.

"Psstt," Will whispered loudly, competing with the howling storm and his groaning shipmates. Both opened their eyes quickly.

"How are you guys doing? You hanging in there?" he asked quietly.

"Fighting it off so far," Landau said through gritted teeth.

"Same here," McQueen answered.

"How much longer is this shit going to last?" Landau asked.

"I don't know. How long do typhoons last? It's got to be over pretty soon, doesn't it?" Will said.

"It's supposed to be the same as a hurricane in the Atlantic. How long do they last?" McQueen said.

"Maybe a day or two, I think," said Landau.

"This isn't really a typhoon," De George pitched in from the other side of the sleeping chamber. "It's just a tropical depression. That's what a crew member told me. He said they usually last twenty-four to thirty-six hours."

"Maybe it'll end in time for breakfast in the morning. I'm getting pretty hungry. I don't think anyone ate lunch or dinner today. I know I didn't. Did any of you?" Will asked.

If anyone answered, it was inaudible behind the chorus of retching Will heard rising from the bunk chamber and beyond.

Early the next morning the storm was starting to back off. The *Darby's* lurching was dramatically diminished. The winds were reduced to sporadic stiff zephyrs, the pounding rain replaced by fleeting squalls. Though the ride was still anything but smooth, at least it wasn't beating the shit out of them. Still, in the aftermath of the storm, everyone in the detachment was experiencing agonizing soreness in every muscle, the result of a full day of bodily struggle to keep themselves steady and—worse for the dry heavers—their stomachs whole.

Somehow, the monumental pain and lingering vomit in the air had done nothing to kill their appetites. When the lieutenant finally released them for breakfast, they almost crippled one another in a rush to get to the mess hall. Once there, they stuffed themselves like pigs. Will ate a giant stack of pancakes and at least a pound of bacon. He was so focused on his meal that he didn't notice the bucketloads of shit on a shingle the rest of them were gorging on.

After their meal, they all went out on deck to be greeted by full sunshine and calmer seas. PT had been canceled, probably, Will figured, because the officers couldn't be in any better shape than they were. Will figure-eighted the *Darby* a few times before he found an opportunity to enter his whaleboat unseen. Inside he found *War and Peace* and his flashlight unmolested, miraculously, by either combat engineers or shifting seas. He was able to discorporate easily into Tolstoy. The excessive partying and drinking of the book's putative hero mirrored Will's behavior as a student at UCLA, though Will hadn't had the abundant financial resources of Pierre to support it. As he lived through Pierre's dalliance with the masons and the liberation of his serfs and going off to assassinate Napoleon, he saw a kindred spirit, a guy who was confused about where he was going in life and what it was really all about.

Eventually Will's eyelids fatigued and blinked closed, and the book slipped from his hands.

Will awoke with a severe kink in his neck. Most of his right arm was asleep, with a fast-spreading pins-and-needles effect. He lifted the whaleboat's canvas cover, making sure to check no one was standing under his exit point, and slid out of the boat. The sky was clear, with a light, balmy breeze. The ride was smooth as glass. He spotted Landau, McQueen, and De George sitting on the deck all in a row reading books with their backs against a bulkhead.

"Nice reading lounge you guys have established here," Will said, massaging his neck.

"Oh, you finally came out of your hideout. Ready to deal with reality, huh?" Rob joked.

"The present reality, yes. How about this weather, you guys? We just need some beautiful naked native dancing girls to complete the picture. This is such an improvement over that freak-out storm. At breakfast I heard one of the crew say we actually went backwards at full rudder for over fifteen hours."

"No complaints from me," said McQueen. "Going backwards when you're going to Vietnam is not a bad thing."

"I'm not sure I agree with you, Bobby," De George said. "That storm literally beat the shit out of me. I'd rather be safe on shore in a backwater like Saigon than go through that again."

"Yeah, well, they could send you anywhere, safe or not so safe," Will said.

"It's a crapshoot," Landau said. "I was talking to Lieutenant Frasier about this 525th MI Group in Saigon we're going to. He says most of us won't stay with that unit for long. We'll be farmed out to the other corps areas to do field intelligence. Some of us are bound to wind up in combat zones."

"Remember back when we believed we weren't going to Vietnam? What a bunch of wishful thinking," Landau said.

"Ignorance was bliss," McQueen added.

"Let's face it. We're all fucked either way, whether we're on this ship or in Vietnam. My way of dealing with it is don't obsess over it. Try to control your thoughts. Because, you know, the only thing we have to fear is fear itself," Landau said.

"Ha, ha, ha, thank you, FDR. Actually, I have an intense fear of machine gun nests," Will said.

"I don't think we have to worry about machine gun nests. More like mortar rounds, sapper attacks, land mines, and trail ambushes in our line of work," McQueen said.

"What a relief—I would so much prefer to get greased by one of those than by machine gun," Will said.

"It is better," Landau said. "At least the angel of death arrives without notice. You're dead in an instant. You don't even have a chance to get scared."

"That's if you're lucky enough to die instead of being turned into a vegetable," Will said.

"The best way to look at it," De George said, "is we're all going to die when our number is up. It's obvious to me that at the moment you pop out of the womb the time of your death is already established. You can't do anything to change it. Basically, you have a date with your destiny. Whether it ends on a battlefield in Vietnam or crossing a street in your hometown, it was fated to be, no matter where you are. So don't worry about it. Be happy with the time you have left."

"I didn't know you were a Buddhist, Jack," McQueen said.

"Predetermination of death is more of an Islamic thing, I think," Will said.

"I have no religion. It's just what I know to be true for me," De George said.

"Well, you should start a new religion based on your system of belief," Landau said.

"I think everyone should start their own religion," Will said. "Then the world might be a better place without the evils of organized religion. We wouldn't have somebody like the Pope saying he had a little chat with God last night and now it's time for another Inquisition to root out all the heretics and infidels. I say either everybody talks to God or nobody talks to God. If you don't want to talk to God, you don't have to talk to God. And I won't take it personally if you don't want to talk to me."

"Stand back, everyone, God's about to strike Will down with a lightning bolt," McQueen said.

"Now why would I want to strike myself with lightning?"

"You're pushing your luck."

"Ah, come on, God's right here inside me. Don't you feel him inside you? I know that God loves anyone with a good sense of humor—otherwise he would die from the boredom of it all."

"Enough with the religious studies taught by a heathen," Landau said.

"Fair enough, Rob, fair enough," Will said, holding his palms out in surrender.

They had been at sea now for twelve days, or was it thirteen? The last few days had been utterly mellow. Now the *Darby* was rising and plunging dramatically. Monstrous whitecaps started slugging it out and knocking one another silly. One of the ship's officers came through their bunk notifying them of the skipper's order to stay in their quarters.

"This one will make the last storm seem like child's play. The captain tried to set a course around it, but it's impossible to avoid now," the officer said. "So batten down the hatches. Use a bedsheet to tie yourselves into your bunks. Make no attempt to go outside." As if to punctuate his warning, the *Darby* made a violent lurch to starboard, knocking the man to the floor.

"See what I mean? Take this very, very seriously. I have been through several major typhoons. This one dwarfs them all. And, yeah, I'm scared," he said.

"What the fuck," Will said. "Riding on the *Darby* is like bareback riding with the Four Horsemen of the Apocalypse. This ship is cursed. What the hell is going to happen next?"

Then the *Darby* made a violent pitching motion that took everyone's breath away. The explosiveness of the movement made this suddenly feel very different from the last storm. Then the typhoon set loose on them. The *Darby* came close to capsizing sideways in both starboard and leeward directions. In fact, they rolled so close to the horizontal axis in each direction that Will couldn't figure out how they came back to upright. When the *Darby* climbed up and up and up a wave to near vertical, he thought the waves must be well over two hundred feet high to force the ship into that angle. The ship continued to be tossed around like a cork for the next several hours.

Will had tied and belted himself tightly to his bunk, yet he was still being racked and pummeled. He couldn't keep himself from clinching and bracing and anticipating the next onslaught of opposing physical forces. He reached up over his head to grab the pipes to help stabilize his movement. After only minutes, his arms and shoulders started aching from the effort. The sound of the wind and the waves blasting the hull and superstructure was horrendous. Lying there in his bunk like a tortured sardine, Will came to the conclusion that he was being tested. He couldn't get a rational grasp on what the test was supposed to accomplish. Did God want to give him a taste of what hell was like? Then he decided no: God wouldn't waste his time with nonsense like hell. Man had already created that for himself on earth without need of God's help. Maybe God was merely trying to toughen him up for what was ahead. The typhoon continued to hammer the *Darby* mercilessly for another eight hours. Several of the men of his unit were actually crying, their pillows wrapped around their faces to muffle, unsuccessfully, the sounds of sobbing. Will's fear had advanced through several stages, from severe fright into paralysis, extreme panic, and a state of numbness. The final stage was one of total surrender, he gave in to the inevitability of death and fell into a state of acceptance and grace. At last he was loose as a goose. His body flopped around on the thin mattress without tensing. He closed his eyes and gave up on everything.

In the days following the storm, they slowly learned the significance of the typhoon they had survived together. The *Darby* had collided with the greatest and most severe typhoon in recorded history: Typhoon Marie. Somehow this knowledge of coming through a storm so colossal and still being around to talk about it tempered and softened the jagged edges of the memory of the experience. Now they had bragging rights, and maybe they were all made a little tougher to go on to face their next challenge.

Calm seas, gentle swells, sunny days, and beautiful starry nights were embraced by all aboard the *Darby*. The word spread that they were less than twenty-four hours from Qui Nhon Bay, where the combat engineers would disembark. Will was nearing the end of *War and Peace,* and he thought it would be fitting to finish the book upon arrival in Vietnam. He had spent less and less time in the whaleboat because everyone was tending to stay mostly to themselves. The *Darby* had become very quiet. Even the extroverts had turned introspective as the ship closed in on Vietnam and they were all visited by thoughts of their own mortality.

TEN

All of the men from both units were on deck with the call of land ahoy, and they were all frustrated by what they saw there. A major battle was being waged not far from the shore.

They were still three or four miles from the coast, and they could see tracer rounds from .50-caliber machine guns thread through the sky, then flashes from explosions of mortar rounds and rockets. By the time they finally got close enough to hear the sounds of artillery, the *Darby* swung around and moved back out to sea, dropping anchor miles away to avoid becoming a target itself. They spent the next hour with their eyes riveted on the firefight. No one could tell exactly what was going on, but it was a spectacle to behold from a safe distance. Finally word came down that they might be stuck there for a few more days until this skirmish was over and the combat engineers could be safely offloaded. Not one of them wanted to be in Vietnam, but paradoxically, they all desperately wanted off the ship.

Will finished his big read and then no longer had Tolstoy to escape into. He reached into the bottom of his duffel bag and pulled out *Stranger in a Strange Land* by Robert Heinlein, a book he'd read and reread four times when he was nineteen. He felt a surge of anticipation as he held it in his hand and studied the cover. More than any book, this one had made him disappear entirely within its pages. Years after reading the book, its themes called to him, pursued him, and played out in the fantasies of his imagination. He had never stopped wishing for the powers held by its hybrid earthling-Martian hero. Now, he opened the book and was instantly swept away.

Three days later, after a series of sporadic firefights, the First Cav had finally driven the VC and the NVA out of the Qui Nhon highlands. The *Darby* eased into dock, and the combat engineers completed a painfully slow disembarkation. Then the ship's captain set a course for Cam Ranh Bay, where they arrived within hours. But there was one more setback in store for Will and his compatriots. They had misunderstood their port of call in Vietnam: it wasn't Cam Ranh Bay after all, but Vung Tau, another hundred-plus miles south. Cam Ranh Bay was just where the *Darby* needed to refuel and pick up supplies. "Oh, God, no, not another night on this tub," Will moaned aloud. They didn't escape the ship until late the following evening, well after dark.

It was almost midnight when they boarded an aging olive-drab-and-rust-colored bus for the two-and-a-half-hour ride down Highway 51 to Saigon. There was nothing to see and little to hear, save the roar of the bus's diesel engine, all the way to their destination. The windows were open, though enclosed by steel mesh, and most of what Will sensed through them was a fecal-scented, oppressively hot and humid blast of night air.

Finally the bus pulled up in front of an overlighted, sprawling French belle arts–style villa. The periphery was heavily sandbagged and crowned by waves of concertina and razor wire. Reinforced walled sentry boxes rose up from the outer security perimeter every fifty or sixty feet, giving the impression of a scaled-down prison. The place appeared impenetrable. Every man in their detachment had to present his orders to the officer of the watch, and then they passed like zombies through the triple-gated system into the courtyard of the compound. The lieutenant directed all of the enlisted men to follow him to a massive open-air pavilion. In the center of the space, there were at least twenty army-issue cots scattered randomly. He told the men to grab sheets and pillows from stacks, choose a cot, and try to get some sleep.

The officer pointed to the ceiling. Everyone looked up. Twenty or thirty ceiling fans were whirling away, creating a brisk breeze. He said, "Try to position your cot under a fan. It will keep you cool and make it easier to sleep, but more importantly, it'll keep the mosquitos off you."

Will followed his instructions and flopped down on a cot. He was asleep in less than thirty seconds. It was 3 a.m. Saigon time.

At 6 a.m. Will was torn from his slumber by a screeching, worn-out recording of reveille playing through the compound's PA system. Once he got his feet on the floor and started coming to his senses, he realized that something was really, really, really wrong with his face. It was stinging and itching, itching, itching something terrible. He put his hand on his forehead and yelled, "Shit, what the fuck!" He had hundreds of stinging bumps all over his face—mosquito bites. He had mosquito bites on top of mosquito bites. There were so many on his eyelids that his eyes were almost swollen shut. He started rubbing all over his face. The more he rubbed, the worse the itching got. He jumped off the cot and ran to look for the latrine so he could soak his head in water. He got to the sink, turned on the tap, and started splashing water from both hands onto his face as fast as he could. It soothed the itching, barely, as long as he kept splashing. The moment he stopped, though, it itched like hell, like stark-raving-mad hell. He filled the sink and buried his face and swirled the water violently, getting a little relief.

He lifted his head from the bowl and focused on his reflection in the mirror. His face was contorted. He looked like the elephant man. He had bulbous cheeks and a second supraorbital ridge across his forehead. By now every member of his unit was in the latrine staring at him like he was a freak in a circus sideshow. He saw their eyes gazing in wonder, in horror, in pity. Then came the itch, the mind-altering, shit-kicking, killing itch pushing him over the edge, way over. Landau came out of the group and said, "Will, you have to do something about your face. You're having an allergic reaction, man. You're swelling up all over."

Then McQueen came up to him holding a bottle of calamine lotion and two Benadryl pills. "Here, Will, take these and rub the lotion on your face. It will help with the itching and reduce the swelling."

Will popped the two pills then grabbed the bottle, unscrewed the cap, and filled his cupped hand with the pink stuff. He rubbed it into his face with eyes closed and repeated it again and again. He looked at himself in the mirror and saw a grotesque pink minstrel staring back.

"Come on, Will, we're all going to be late for formation. You've got to get dressed fast," Rob said. Rob grabbed his arm and rushed him down to his cot. Will dressed and booted up as fast as he could. They ran to the courtyard and joined the ranks of their detachment in a formation of fifty or sixty men. Every pair of eyes was locked on Will's swollen pink face. A staff sergeant in front of his unit called "Attention!" Then a banty rooster of a man, wearing crisply starched fatigues with sleeves proudly presenting the three chevrons, three rockers, and star of a sergeant major, walked to the front of the formation and growled, "At ease."

Command Sergeant Major Turk Coyle had a buzz cut with white sidewalls. His coal-black eyes were set way too close together. The inside corners of his eyelids sagged down, making him look like a snake. The point of Coyle's chin was dagger sharp. His eyebrows formed a continuous hedgerow across his overly prominent Neanderthal ridge and gave the impression he was peering out from inside a cave. The closeness of his shave made his rosy cheeks shine glossy. The brightest source of light in the courtyard was the reflection from the shine on his boots and belt buckle. Will could see that he was hard-core, old-school, brown-shoe army all the way. The sergeant major surveyed the men in the formation from right to left. When his eyes fell on Will, his chin sharpened and his body braced as if preparing to be physically attacked. He studied Will for what seemed like an eternity. He walked very deliberately over to stand squarely in front of Will and continued to stare with the cruelest smile Will had ever seen.

"You got a name, boy?"

"Yes, sir, I'm Will Parish."

"You are a disgrace to your uniform, boy." The sergeant major's baritone voice rose to the hundred-decibel level as if he had a built-in megaphone. "How dare you show up in my formation dressed like a clown, like a fucking faggot mime. You make me want to puke. You are out of uniform, boy. Now get out of my formation and wash that shit off your face on the double."

"Mosquito bites, sergeant major, I must have got a thousand mosquito bites last night when the fan turned off. That's why the lotion . . ."

"What? What? Are you mistaking me for someone who gives a shit? You must think I'm your mommy. I don't give a shit about how many goddamned fucking mosquito bites you got, boy. Now you get your sorry ass out of my formation and my sight before I slap you with an Article 15," he bellowed.

Will moved in haste back to the latrine, wondering if this place could possibly be even worse than the fucking *Darby*. He ran the water into the basin and scrubbed the dried pink lotion from his face while he rubbed intensely at the impossibly itchy areas. He toweled off and continued to rub like a wild man. When he returned to the formation, the sergeant major was gone. As soon as he queued up, the formation was dismissed. De George and McQueen told him that the three of them had been assigned to a work detail moving furniture and gear starting in about an hour. They explained to him that the 525th MI Group was the headquarters and processing unit for all new intelligence arrivals in-country. All of the enlisted men in the detachment would get their orders within a day or two. Will listened and nodded while the two of them briefed him on what was next, but he couldn't stop pawing at his face. He went back to the latrine to retrieve the bottle of calamine. McQueen followed him and watched him swab his face pink.

"I found out how you got all of those mosquito bites," McQueen said. "The power went out, and the backup generator was out of fuel, so the fans were off for an hour or two. What I don't get is how you got bit hundreds of times and nobody else got bit more than a few times."

"It's the story of my life in the great outdoors. I am a fucking mosquito magnet. The evil little bloodsuckers love me. People who always get tons of bites in mosquito season almost never get bit when I'm around. DEET bug spray's the only stuff that'll keep them off me. And I didn't bring any. I got to find the PX and buy some before tonight."

"Don't worry. I've got some you can use. But you better pray you don't run into the sergeant major with your face all pink. I think he's got a real hard-on for you."

"Nah, that was just in the formation, something about being out of uniform. Besides, fuck him if he can't take a joke."

"I wouldn't take the chance if I were you. He might go ballistic and give you an Article 15."

"What's this Article 15 bullshit?"

"I think he can bust you down to a private E1 and dock your pay for six months."

"Big fucking deal. What can I spend money on in Vietnam anyway?"

"You're pushing your luck, Will."

"Always, and fuck that little cocksucker with the Napoleon complex. I'm so sick and tired of these abusive power-trip assholes being in positions of authority everywhere we go in the army. That's why they're in the army—"

McQueen interrupted him, saying, "Hey, it's time to go on our work detail. Hustle up or we'll be late. We go to room seventeen on the other side of the compound. We have to help a specialist four by the name of Billy Joe Dubois move his quarters back to this side of the compound. He's the sergeant major's clerk."

When the three-man work detail got to room seventeen, the door was open and Billy Joe was waiting for them. He was smoking unfiltered Camels—chain-smoking, judging by how thick the smoke was in his hooch. He had a nasty case of acne and desperately needed to pop some white-headed specimens on his cheeks and chin. He was jumpy and twitched involuntarily like a guy on amphetamines. His sandy colored hair was pomaded into a flat top. He wore his fatigues skintight with sleeves rolled high into his armpits. Asshole was written in boldface font across his forehead.

"Y'all shitheads three minutes late. I'm puttin' y'all on report," he said with a serious twang straight from the bayou. Then he frowned at Will and said, "Shit, not the pink-faced freak. You stupid or what? Didn't hear a word the sergeant major said at formation? He's gonna fuck you up one side and down the other."

Then Will, with his best Southern drawl, said, "I guess if y'all think he's gonna fuck me all over, I best get to shakin' in my boots and shittin' in my skivvies, y'all." Will was grinning broadly.

"Y'all think you're pretty fuckin' funny, huh? Now get in here and start to movin' my things out in the hall. And you, pinky, pick up that chest on the floor and put it outside."

Will tried to lift the chest, but it must have been full of boulders, because he could barely budge it. "Hey, y'all, it's too heavy to lift. I need a handcart or four people to move this fucking thing."

"Lift it by yerself. I'm givin' y'all a direct order."

"Speedy fours don't give direct orders, kid. You got to have some stripes or some bars to give orders."

"Pick that fuckin' chest up now or y'all gonna be in big trouble for insubordination." Billy Joe was gesturing at the chest with a small metal case in his hand.

"Pick it up yourself, numbnuts."

The speedy four lost his cool and flung the case at Will's head. The corner of the case struck Will just above his eye, and blood started to flow from the gash.

Will's head began to purple up inside, but he didn't go away. He grabbed a duffel bag lying at his feet and thrust it at the speedy four, who went flying hard into the wall and slumped to the floor.

"Goddamn it, Will, now you've really gone and done it," De George said. "That's the sergeant major's boy. He's really going to be pissed." McQueen went over to Billy Joe to see if he had a heartbeat, and when he nudged him, the speedy four rolled over and came out of it, moaning and holding the back of his head. He pushed himself up from the floor and pointed at Will.

"Yer in for it now, asshole. I'm reportin' you for assault and battery and insubordination against a ranking NCO. You'll be doin' time in the stockade."

"Bullshit! You started it when you threw the metal case at my head. I've got blood gushing out, and I've got witnesses."

"Don't matter, sergeant major'll believe me, not y'all peckerwoods." He scuttled away.

"It looks like you need a few stitches for that gash over your eye, Will," McQueen said.

"Yeah, that looks pretty ugly," De George added.

"Fuck it. It'll heal," Will said. "You guys are going to back me up? You saw what happened, right?"

They both nodded. The three went back to the pavilion, and Will replaced his bloodied shirt with a fresh one. He washed the blood and calamine off his face then pulled a large bandage out of his kit and covered most of the gash on his head. When he came back to his cot, two staff sergeants were waiting to take the three of them to the command sergeant major's office. When they got there, they were taken to a reception area and told to wait. They came for McQueen first. He was gone for twenty minutes. When he came back, they took De George. While he was gone, McQueen whispered softly to Will.

"He's threatening all of us with a court-martial for attacking his asshole clerk. He said it will be stockade time for all of us. I told him what happened, but he accused me of lying to protect you. He said if I say you started the fight, he'll go easy on me. I told him no way. I wouldn't lie even to keep myself out of the stockade. He got furious. I'm sure he's giving De George the same treatment."

"Thanks, Bobby," Will replied.

When De George came back, they took Will in to stand before the sergeant major. Will felt as if he was in the presence of a serpent readying his coils to squeeze the life from him. The E9 looked down at an open file on his desk and then back at Will.

"Now this is all starting to make sense," he said in a loud, booming baritone designed to intimidate. "I see what we have here is a goddamned prima donna on our hands. You got the Joe College secret-agent-man syndrome; must have caught it at that communist brain-washing joint UCLA, huh? So you think you're too good for the army, too special to be an enlisted man, too fucking smart to have to go to Vietnam. Yeah, too fucking smart for your own good. Or more likely, you're a cheating son of a bitch. Nobody but nobody gets a perfect score on the army GT test. Yet you did it twice. How did you do that? You should be spending the rest of your enlistment in the stockade. But your asshole buddies say Billy Joe started the fight. Well, this old sergeant major has a couple of tricks up his sleeve for you and your pals. By the time I get done with you, you might be wishing you were in the stockade." He turned to his staff sergeant and said, "Put all three of them on sandbag detail, standard protocol." He looked at Will again for a few seconds. "Good luck out there on the Bien Hoa Highway, Joe College. Now get the hell out of my sight." He let out a cackle before he broke eye contact with Will.

The staff sergeant, name of Colby printed across his fatigues, escorted Will, Bobby, and Jack to the armory and issued each of them a holstered and belted .45-caliber army-issue Colt pistol. From there he took them to the motor pool and signed them out in one of the unit's deuce-and-a-half trucks. He pulled three shovels out of a tool bin and threw them in the back of the truck. He picked up several bales of burlap sandbags and tossed them in as well. He turned and faced the three of them with a pained expression. "Has anyone driven one of these before?" Jack raised his arm. "OK, get loaded up. De George, you follow me. I'll be in that jeep," he said pointing at a jeep with a Browning Automatic Rifle mounted in the back loaded up with sandbags. I'll lead you to the pit."

He walked over to the jeep and pulled out a steel helmet and a flak jacket and put them on. He was joined by a private carrying an M16 who was wearing the same gear. The jeep pulled out. The three amigos followed in the deuce and a half. The two-vehicle convoy proceeded to the Bien Hoa Highway. The ride took twenty-five minutes. The private draped himself over the BAR mounted in the back of the jeep during the last ten minutes of the ride. They pulled off the road into a hollowed-out sandpit. Every inch of Will's skin immediately started crawling. They were in the middle of nowhere. Dense jungle surrounded them on three sides. This looked like a very dangerous place to be filling sandbags. Then he got it, the sergeant major's maniacal laughter.

Colby made a radical U-turn and pulled up next to them. "When all of the sandbags are filled and loaded in the truck, drive back to headquarters." Then he peeled out, the jeep throwing a shower of sand against the side of their truck.

"Guys, I think I have got us into some very serious shit here," said Will. "It's all my fault. I'm guessing this is Coyle's way of punishing grunts who don't go along with his shit. This has got to be Viet Cong turf. We have to get out of here."

"I think we have to fill up enough of these bags or we'll just be back out here tomorrow," McQueen said.

"Bobby's right," De George said.

"As much as I hate this, I guess I have to agree," Will said.

They set up a rotating assembly line under the best cover they could find and started filling and tying the bags. It was stifling hot, with barely a breeze. They were all sweating profusely.

After four or five hours, they had assembled a massive pile of stacked sandbags. The sun was getting lower, and they decided to start loading the jeep as fast as they could. The bed was almost full, and they only had seven or eight bags left on the ground when Will's radar went wild. Every hair on his body stood straight up and out. He dove at his buddies, knocking McQueen off his feet just before the first sniper round went *ka-ching* off the side of the truck, right where he'd been lifting and loading bags. The report of the rifle followed quickly.

Will heard McQueen's voice in a strange slow-motion. "*Whaaaat thee fuuu-uuck!*"

"Stay down! Don't move!" Will called out.

"*Oooooooooooooooh, shiiiiit!*" shouted De George.

Then Will went far, far away for a while. He saw the swirling purple clouds, the strobing lights, the eerie forms; he heard the sounds, smelled the scents, felt the textures. He was enthralled, beyond fear. He lifted his head from cover and was immediately aware of the sniper and his exact location. He could see the sniper aiming at his forehead and squeezing the trigger. Will was unfazed. He saw the round as it spiraled toward his head, and simply leaned out of its path. He jumped up and ran toward the sniper's position. It seemed to him he was running quickly, but his movements were strange and effortless, like he was floating.

He was on the sniper in less than a heartbeat, which didn't seem possible, because the sniper was at least five hundred yards away from the truck. But here he was somehow above the sniper, who was twenty feet off the ground in a tree. The sniper was just sighting his next shot through the PSO scope of his Russian Dragunov rifle when he sensed Will above him. He'd barely begun to raise his head to look up, but Will met his eyes at once. In those eyes, in that instant, Will saw pure evil, a casual murderer who had killed hundreds of unsuspecting South Vietnamese and American soldiers. Will's body convulsed in a fiery fury. He lashed out with a pulse of energy and watched the gunman disintegrate in a pink cloud. Then he was gone, gone, gone.

Down from the tree, Will jogged back to the deuce and a half in a highly agitated state. Bobby and Jack were still hugging the ground tightly. "OK, time to get out of here," Will said.

"Where the fuck did you go?" De George said.

"I tried to circle around behind him. He must have spotted me and took off. Come on, let's hit the road."

"Are you insane? You circled around behind him?" De George asked.

Will didn't answer. They left the remaining sandbags on the ground and leaped into the truck. De George fired up the deuce and a half and took off as fast as it could go. He ground his way through the gears with the pedal to the metal until they were out of the jungle. Will was all for it—the faster the better. As they worked their way back through the confusing matrix of Saigon, he and McQueen were amazed at De George's sense of direction and how few errant turns he made finding his way back to the 525th. When they pulled into the motor pool, Staff Sergeant Colby was standing there with mouth agape, a look of astonishment on his face.

Will got out of the truck and marched up to him threateningly, with his hand on the grip of the .45. "Surprised to see us make it back with all of our body parts intact, sergeant?" Colby shrunk back as if he expected to be attacked. "Filling sandbags in sniper alley? How wonderfully sadistic of you and your command sergeant major," Will said. "There has got to be a special place in hell just for the two of you."

Colby didn't say a word. Will unhitched the web belt from his hips, wrapped it around the holstered .45, and tossed it hard at Colby's chest. It bounced off him and fell to the ground. McQueen and De George removed their belts and .45s and set them down on the hood of the deuce and a half and followed Will back to the pavilion, where most of the rest of the detachment members were hanging out. They shared their day's adventures and learned that most of the unit had already received their orders for assignments in all four corps areas of Vietnam. Landau was heading to the boondocks in Tay Ninh province. It seemed that the three of them were the only ones left without orders.

They descended together on the mess hall in a show of force. Will was on guard, expecting a confrontation with the sergeant major and his minions, but there was no sign of Turk, Colby, or Billy Joe. Will had already missed breakfast and lunch, so he was famished, especially after the sandbag-filling-and-lifting workout. The meal was delicious, one of the best served in an army mess hall since he had enlisted: roast beef, sticky rice, peas, and dinner rolls. He went back for seconds and thirds.

The rest of the night was strangely uneventful. They hung around the pavilion, smoking, sitting and lying on their cots, bullshitting each other about what came next, where they were going. It was all smoke and mirrors. No one had the slightest fucking idea of what would happen next. Will borrowed McQueen's insect repellent and slathered it on his face and neck, then he swirled a sheet around himself and dropped on his cot, falling asleep as his head hit the pillow.

When he finally awoke the next morning, everyone was gone. The sun was already several hours high above the horizon. His internal clock said it was almost nine. "Why didn't anyone wake me?" he said aloud. He sat up on the cot, got his feet on the tile floor, and put his hands to his face to try to rub the sleep from his eyes. I must have slept for twelve hours, he thought.

"Well, Sleeping Beauty has awakened. Good morning, prima donna."

Will's hackles didn't just go up, they freaked out at the sound of the sergeant major's gnarled voice.

"Was Joe College all tuckered out from fun and games on Bien Hoa Highway?"

"Where the hell did everybody go?" he said, standing up and turning toward the sergeant major's voice.

"Your buddies have all flown the coop. They went to meet their destiny. You're the last one to get orders, Joe College. Clean your sorry ass up and report to my office in twenty minutes."

He made his way to the latrine and pulled his razor and shaving cream from his kit. He hadn't shaved for three days. His blond whiskers allowed him to get away with it. When he finished shaving, he examined his face in the mirror and realized that all of his mosquito bites had mysteriously vanished. He pulled the bandage from over his eye and was stunned to see that the gash that had seemed to need several stitches was now only a thin line on his face. No way, he gasped, this is crazy. OK, OK, get over it. Save it for later. Right now, go deal with the devil.

He walked to Turk Coyle's office. In the reception area, Will found speedy four Billy Joe Dubois, leering at him with that face that not even his mother could possibly love. "Wooee, boy, you got yourself in a deep bucket a shit this time. Where yer goin' yer never comin' back. 'Cept maybe in a body bag," Billy Joe squeaked.

"Hey, Billy Joe, here's some friendly advice for you. You should try to get some help for that psychiatric disorder before the orderlies in white jackets come for you and throw you in the padded cell," Will said with a fiendish grin.

"Yer gonna get yours right now, motherfucker."

Will ignored him, knocked on little Napoleon's door, and barged in. The tiny tyrant was sitting there on his make-believe throne. The look on his face was what Will might have expected had he just passed through the gates of hell and into his satanic majesty's private office to have the horned beast himself break some bad news. Will wished he could wipe the grin off Turk's face.

"Now this is perfect, so fitting, for someone who is such a discredit to the traditions of the United States Army, Parish." His gravelly voice got higher, and he squeaked with excitement. "Everything about you is an insult to men in uniform. A hundred years ago I would have had a detail take you out and hang you by the neck from the nearest tree. No questions asked."

"Let's just cut through the bullshit, sarge, and give me my fucking sentence."

"You shut your insubordinate mouth you despicable ball of slime. How dare you address me that way!" Coyle shrieked, his face twisting grotesquely.

Will was standing at the abyss of rage. "Just give me my fucking orders!" he roared into Coyle's face, leaning over his desk.

Coyle jumped up as if to leap across his desk, but he stopped short when he saw the depth of rage in Will's eyes. He recoiled into his chair and curled his lip into a sneer.

"OK, Parish, you're just heightening my pleasure. Here's your bad news," he said, too joyfully. "You are now a proud member of the Fifth Special Forces. You have earned your place with the most dangerous unit in all of Vietnam. Can I have a drum roll, please? You are hereby officially assigned to the nearly always fatal Detachment B-57 of the Fifth Special Forces. For a fuckup like you, this is a more just punishment than hanging from a tree because you might have been able to survive the tree. So get ready for lots of jungle time with the bug and snake eaters in green beanies. Ha, ha, ha, ha!" He handed Will his orders and continued laughing convulsively.

Will was completely knocked off balance. Me a Green Beret? he thought. No fucking way. I don't have the training. This has got to be a mistake. But he kept his mouth shut. He refused to give Coyle the satisfaction of protesting, appearing frightened.

"Where's your smart-ass bullshit now, Parish? I can see it in your eyes: you're scared shitless. You know you're *really* fucked."

"Looking forward to it, sarge. Can't wait to join up with my Special Forces brothers. Once I get out of this chickenshit outfit, I'll be happy out there in the jungle kicking VC ass with the Green Berets. You just made my day. Thanks a lot, sarge," he said with faux bravado.

"Bullshit, bullshit, bullshit, Parish. You can't fool me: you know you're going to die out there in the jungle ten thousand miles from home. And no one will give a shit."

Will turned his back on him and walked out of his office, bumping hard into Colby. The sycophant staff sergeant stepped away from him and said, "There's a guy sitting in a black jeep waiting for you. He's your ride to B-57."

ELEVEN

Will walked outside to look for a guy in a black jeep. He spotted the jeep at the outside edge of the porte cochere and walked over. Behind the wheel was a handsome lad who looked a lot like a young Humphrey Bogart. He wasn't wearing a beret or fatigues but was decked out in a Panama hat, aloha shirt, khakis, and huaraches.

"Hey, I'm Will Parish. Are you waiting for me?"

"Sure as hell am," he said, jumping out of the jeep. "Good to meet you, Parish. I'm Brad Stall, advance man for the Detachment B-57 welcoming committee," he said, extending his hand and pumping Will's vigorously. "Let's go get your gear. I'll help load you up and get us both the hell out of this sorry-ass place."

Brad's words brought the first real smile Will's face had held in many days. They walked up to the pavilion together. Will grabbed his pile of dirty laundry from the end of his cot and crammed it into his open duffel bag along with his Dopp kit, before folding and cinching the duffel's top and slinging it over his shoulder. Brad had already performed the same maneuver with Will's other bag. They moved to the jeep with a sense of urgency, threw the bags under the canvas top, and hopped in. Pulling out from the porte cochere, Brad jacked the steering wheel sharply and laid some serious, noisy rubber while peeling out of the compound's driveway. In near unison, they exploded in laughter. Will had no idea what he was getting into, but so far, so good, he thought to himself with an ear-to-ear grin.

Brad drove the jeep through the streets of Saigon like a wild man. He weaved his way through masses of pedestrians, pedicabs, cyclists, carts, cyclos,

Lambrettas, and old Citroën taxis like there was no tomorrow. They must be on a tight schedule, Will thought. He braced his body and steadied both feet against the floorboard again and again in anticipation of a violent collision, but it never happened. It was Mr. Toad's wild ride and then some. Then he skidded the black jeep to a stop in front of a turn-of-the-century château on Louis Pasteur Street, right across the street from the Louis Pasteur Institute. The machine-gun-bearing security force rolled the gate open for him, and he drove inside.

"You have your orders, right?" Brad asked.

"Yeah, right here," Will said, pulling the crumpled sheet from his fatigue shirt pocket.

"Now we have to go in and get you processed. Big waste of time. Come on," he said, waving Will to follow him inside the fancy French colonial courtyard, where they were greeted by a squad of fierce-looking Nung security guards. They went through a large hall into a recreation room with a couple of pool tables. Will followed Brad into a clerk's open office, where Brad handed the clerk Will's orders. The clerk nodded at Brad, xeroxed a copy, and handed the orders back. They were out the door and back in the jeep in minutes. Brad took off down Pasteur Street like a bat out of hell, barely missing a stylish, nubile young woman in an ao dai riding a bike.

"Aren't you worried you're going to kill someone?" Will asked.

"Not a chance," Brad answered. "Doesn't matter anyway—life is cheap in the Orient, and they're just slopes." He roared with laughter. "Hell, don't worry. I'm just fucking with you. I never hit anyone. It's just a fast game of chicken."

He made the jeep's little four-banger engine whine and scream with high RPMs all the way down Tran Hung Dao Street. Approaching an intersection with a green light in his favor, he sped up to try to run down some scofflaw red-light-running jaywalkers. They sprinted out of his way at the very last instant. He repeated the kamikaze scenario one more time as they drove through an intersection in Cholon. This time he veered purposely to clip the back wheel of a pedicab operator who dared to run the red light in front of him. The pedicab rotated a one-eighty at the edge of the intersection, and

Brad sang out in delight, "Round eyes one, slopes zero, hurrah, hurrah," in rough imitation of "When Johnny Comes Marching Home."

Will winced and thought, Uh-oh, what the hell have I got myself into this time? Does this guy have more screws loose than me?

"Hey, Parish, I saw that flinch. Don't be a pussy. The rules of the game are no harm, no foul. You'll see how things work around here. You'll figure out you don't have to take any shit from these sorry slopes. It'll take a few days, but you'll get it."

He threw one last wild maneuver, making a sharp, squealing left turn at speed on two wheels and almost rolling the jeep as they skidded into the driveway of a heavily fortified and sandbagged four-story structure. He almost crashed into a massive reinforced-metal-pipe gate, the jeep's bumper kissing the gate's edge as it came to a stop. Lined up on both sides of the jeep, three to a side, were six menacing Nung security guards pointing automatic weapons at them with scowling faces that turned very slowly into wide, toothy grins. One more big game of chicken, Will thought. He pulled off his cap and rubbed his forehead with both hands. He felt Brad's hand patting him on the shoulder.

"OK, OK, that's it, Parish, end of hazing. If you didn't shit your pants, you done real good. I just had to give you a little baptism under fire, and you came through with mostly flying colors. It's all part of our Special Forces welcoming ritual," he said, extending his right hand and grabbing Will's in a vigorous handshake.

"How do you know I didn't shit my pants?"

"Because I'd have smelled it by now," he chortled. Will had to laugh too, because he had come awfully close.

"And give me that stupid-looking ball cap. I'm throwing it in the garbage. You're Special Forces now. You wear only a Green Beret in this outfit. I'll get you one later."

By then the guards had rolled away the metal gate, and Brad drove into the compound and parked the jeep in the courtyard. They got out of the jeep, and Will started to reach in the back for his duffel bags. "Leave them there, Parish. One of the houseboys will take them to your suite."

"Ha, ha, ha, that's very funny, Brad. I thought you said the hazing had ended."

"I'm not shitting you, Parish. We have houseboys, and you have a luxury suite. That's SOP here at B-57. Don't be such a goddamn doubting Thomas."

"Well, I've been jacked around enough during my brief army career to have grown a thick layer of skepticism. I'll believe it when I see it."

"Come on, I'll show you." He led Will through a back entrance, down a hallway, to a generously proportioned and appointed bedroom. He opened the door to a bathroom with a tiled shower.

"Wow, you got to be kidding me. This is my room?"

"It sure as hell is, buddy. This is how we live in B-57, only the best for our case officers."

"My God, who do I thank?"

"You can thank me for all of this, young man," said a smiling, tall, handsome man with kind brown eyes who was standing in the doorway. He was wearing the new lightweight jungle fatigue tunic with the chevrons, rockers, and star of the sergeant major of the unit.

"Welcome to Detachment B-57, Will Parish. I'm your sergeant major, Jim Todd. We are delighted to have you join us in our mission, son." He extended his hand to Will, who shook it firmly.

"It's great to be here, sergeant major," he said earnestly.

"Just call me Jim, son. Now let me take you in to introduce you to the old man, the CO. He's been waiting all morning to meet you."

As he followed the sergeant major down the hall, Will wondered if he had died and gone to heaven or if he was dreaming. Waiting all morning to meet him? That's pretty hard to believe. When they got to the commanding officer's private office, the CO was standing with his back to them, studying an oversize map on the wall that had markings and symbols on the border area between Vietnam, Cambodia, and Laos.

"Beg your pardon, colonel, you asked me to bring Case Officer Parish in as soon as he arrived," he said.

The CO spun around with a kind and mischievous smile on his face. He had a high forehead and prominent cheekbones. His clear blue eyes radiated intelligence and energy.

"Well, well, well, now what a pleasure it is to meet you, young Will Parish. I'm Lieutenant Colonel Patrick Mahoney," he said with a hint of an Irish brogue, as he grasped Will's hand between his two and shook it warmly. "Welcome to our Detachment B-57, the finest intelligence unit in all of Vietnam. Our sources at the 525th told us that some low-integrity players over there tried to give you the shaft. I understand you had a little run-in with that abusive command sergeant major. Well, that's all behind you, and it's our good fortune that we were able to intercede and arrange for you to be transferred to us. We can use a bright young man like you. Now, why don't you go get settled in, and we can all meet in the dining room and take lunch together. Half an hour?" Colonel Mahoney said.

"Yes, sir," said Will. He stepped out of the CO's office and walked back to his room. He sat down on the edge of his bed, trying to make sense out of what had happened during the last thirty hours of his life. It had been a roller-coaster ride with breathtaking highs and lows. He couldn't make sense of the reception he was getting here at B-57. What was next, a ticker-tape parade down the main drag of Cholon? Why were they so thrilled with his arrival? No matter how joyful he felt, he continued to get that early warning tingling sensation at the base of his brain stem.

After unpacking, Will made his way into the main office area, where Brad, who had changed into jungle fatigues, was sitting behind a desk, banging away on a typewriter. He was surprised to see that his wild, death-defying chauffeur was wearing the eagle insignia patch of a specialist four. The sign on his desk read Spec. 4 Bradley J. Stall, Det. B-57 Chief Clerk. Will had thought he might have been a case officer with a rank of lieutenant or sergeant.

"Ah, there you are, Parish. Time for chow—come on," he said, rising from his swivel chair. "I'll show you where we take our meals." Will followed him to the stairwell and up to the fourth floor of the villa.

What he saw took his breath away. The space was beautiful, elegant. There was a long bar crafted of exotic hardwood exquisitely carved. The barstools were of matching wood. Behind the bar were beveled-glass mirrors and a series of glass shelves with an astonishing abundance of booze beyond any souse's imagining—whiskeys and scotches, vodkas and gins, tequilas and grappas, ports, liqueurs, and cognacs. The dining tables were layered in fine linen and fine china and sterling silver flatware, with glasses of leaded crystal. The draped room opened onto a spacious, canopied patio offering a panoramic view of the cityscapes of Cholon and the rest of Saigon beyond it. Hung from the dining room's high ceiling were chandeliers with clusters of dangling crystals that dazzled in the light of the midday sun. Will bowed his head slightly, closed his eyes, rubbed them with his knuckles, then slowly reopened them.

"No, Parish, you're not dreaming. And you're not in Kansas anymore. This is very real. This is life in Special Forces. That's why it's called special," Brad said with a chuckle.

"You're laying it on a little too thick now, Stall," said the sergeant major, easing in behind them. "Poor Parish is going to have a distorted image of what life as a Green Beret is like. So, tone it down a bit."

"Will do, Jim. Sorry about that."

"Forgive me, Jim," said Will, "but I'm having a hard time with the transition. I just came from a place where I was lower than whale excrement. Now I'm here and, and, and, and I'm . . ."

"Yeah, I get it, Will. You and Turk Coyle, must have been the worst-case scenario, like matter and antimatter. But this is the happy ending. Now you are where you belong, among kindred spirits. Here you will thrive. Forget all of that unpleasant crap with the command sergeant major. He will meet his destiny in time. Now is anybody hungry? I'm starving. Let's eat."

Then Colonel Mahoney emerged from the stairwell, followed by a captain and a lieutenant. We're eating together, officers and enlisted men in the same dining room, how egalitarian for the army, Will reflected.

"Ah, here he is, our newest star recruit," Mahoney said. "Will Parish, I would like you to meet the real brains of the outfit, the ones who make me look good, my brilliant staff, Captain Bert Michaels and Lieutenant Jim Kavanaugh." Each officer came up to him and grasped his hand in a warm and welcoming handshake. Will had to restrain himself. After the other officers he'd been dealing with, he was shocked to find that a gesture as warm as a mere handshake from one was almost enough to bring him to tears.

"Here, Will, sit with me," the colonel said, pulling the chair next to him out from the table. Will was struggling. What the fuck was happening? He had started to open his mouth to ask just that when a squadron of servers in white jackets appeared. The first filled crystal water glasses. The next placed rolls on their bread dishes with sterling-silver tongs, and the third set a perfect Waldorf salad in the middle of their chargers. Each officer at the table snapped up his linen napkin and almost aristocratically shook it open and allowed it to fall gently into his lap. Obvious devotees of Emily Post, Will thought, as each picked up his salad fork with his left hand and switched it to his right and started on his Waldorf. Will had to work at emulating their perfect manners. He pressed his fork into apple, celery, grape, and, with effort, a walnut, then placed it all into his salivating mouth.

Between bites, Colonel Mahoney explained to Will the two officers' roles in B-57: Lieutenant Kavanaugh was the S2 in charge of intelligence; Captain Michaels was the S3 in charge of operations.

The servers were back now; a first set collected the salad plates, followed by a second group who placed a beautiful lobster cocktail on their chargers. Will squeezed a little lemon from the wedge on the plate and dug in. It was exquisitely delicious. It had to be fresh lobster. The colonel must have been reading his mind.

"From the look on your face, Will, you are probably trying to figure out how we can be eating fresh Maine lobster so far from home. Suffice it to say that when you're in a Special Forces unit, special things always seem to come your way. We have a masterfully skilled supply officer who has a knack for providing us with delicacies and imbibements beyond all expectations. Now you need to understand that we do not dine like this at lunch on a daily basis. I asked our chef to show off a little in honor of your first meal here at Detachment B-57," Mahoney said.

"I'm overwhelmed by all of this, sir. It's like I died and went to heaven. I keep pinching myself under the table, and I haven't woken up yet."

The main course arrived. It was prime rib done medium rare, horseradish cream, Yorkshire pudding, baked potato with sour cream and chives, and steamed asparagus. Will struggled not to drool. He dug in. It was fabulous, a meal fit for a king. By the time he cleaned his plate, he felt like his gut was going to burst, shades of Thanksgivings past. But it wasn't over yet. Dessert appeared in the form of oversize ramekins of crème brûlée. He found more room. A French press, plunger up, with piping-hot fresh-ground dark-roast coffee was placed next to the dessert at each table setting. My God, what a meal, he thought. He might never need to eat again.

Sitting at that table in a blissfully gluttonous stupor, Will kept hearing the colonel's words replaying—the "expecting great things from you" part—and wondering when the other shoe would drop. What "great thing" could he possibly do for B-57? He was worried about the answer to that question.

Right on cue, the colonel said, "Well, young man, I'll bet you are in a state of great anticipation waiting to learn what assignment awaits you in our unit. Let's meet in my office in fifteen minutes, and I will brief you on our mission and describe what you will be doing in the field." He stood up from the table, and everyone in the room, including Will, followed suit.

By the time he reported to the CO's office, he had worked himself into a state of dread. When he was called in, he saw Captain Michaels, the operations officer, standing next to the CO. They both smiled warmly at him, and he reciprocated. Colonel Mahoney was sitting at his desk. When he started explaining the nature of B-57's mission, he reminded Will of a kind college professor.

"Please sit down, Will, and make yourself comfortable. Captain Michaels and I will fill you in on the mission of B-57 and how you will play a vital role in helping us fulfill our goals. B-57 was created about a year ago in 1965 by General Westmoreland himself. He was very concerned about the lack of quality reliable and verifiable intelligence data on North Vietnamese Army divisions' activities and movements in Cambodia and Laos. There was evidence that the NVA had created several divisional headquarters within a mile or so of the border area where it coincides with the Ho Chi Minh Trail, their main supply route. General Westmoreland came up with the idea to place teams of case officers in ten A-Teams in this triborder area for intelligence collection. As you are no doubt aware, the president has declared Cambodia and Laos off-limits to all US military forces, so we are forced to make use of the Montagnard indigenous people—the men call them 'Yards'—to help us collect intelligence on the enemy."

The colonel stood up and walked over to the large map of Vietnam, Cambodia, and Laos. He grabbed a pointer and turned back to Will. "Initially our mission targeted six major hot spots in this area," he said, pointing at several places from the top of II Corps to near the bottom of IV Corps. It looked to be more than three hundred miles long. "Now it has been expanded—or I should say in-filled—to ten hot spots. We started out with a need for a minimum of six case officers recruiting and deploying Montagnard tribesmen to penetrate the target areas. Now that has expanded to ten, although fifteen or twenty would be preferable. B-57 is represented in all ten of these A-Team locations," he said, quickly tapping locations on the map. "But some of our locations lack case officers. Without case officers, the quality of our intelligence product is lacking. I have a hot spot that is particularly problematical," Mahoney said, thrusting the pointer at a place close to the Cambodian border. "Here is where I need your talents, Will. You'll join Special Forces Alpha Team Detachment A-239 in Duc Lap. I have a cowboy there, a good man, an old Special Forces NCO who went to Officer Candidate School and came back to Vietnam a lieutenant. He is our man in Duc Lap now, First Lieutenant Aramis Healy. He is doing the best he can, but intelligence work is not his strong suit. So, Will, I am sending you to Duc Lap to create a complete, professional intelligence-collection team."

Now Will thought he understood the opulent lunch he'd been treated to: it was his last meal before he was sent to die in the fucking jungle. He wanted to say something to the good-hearted colonel about how he probably wasn't the best possible candidate to send to an A-Team owing to his lack of jungle warfare training and his preference to avoid any and all forms of violence that could result in his being sent home in a body bag.

Captain Michaels seemed to have been reading his mind. "We don't expect you to go out there and pretend to be a Green Beret without proper preparation and training, Will. So, we have prepared an intensive thirty-day training program to get you ready for your field work."

Uh-oh, uh-oh, uh-oh, said Will's inner wimp.

"During the next month you will train in light and heavy weapons, infiltration/exfiltration, contour-map reading, jungle survival, Montagnard tribal customs and beliefs, the basics of civic action and psychological operations—what we call CA/PSYOPS— which will be your cover, the history and lore of Special Forces, hand-to-hand combat, and to top it off, jump school. Your cover needs to stand up to the test of close scrutiny. This will be accelerated training, like cramming for a final in college. But it should be child's play for someone with your credentials and your intelligence, Will."

Will was speechless.

They smiled at him. They thought very highly of him. He couldn't cry out in protest, couldn't resist their kind thoughts and intentions toward him. They were good men, the best he had encountered in the army. He couldn't let them down no matter how badly he wanted to. He smiled back and nodded.

That evening, when the sun was starting to set spectacularly over the ethnic-Chinese quarter of Saigon called Cholon, Will joined the rest of the B-57 headquarters contingent for another feast in what he learned was called "the club." He was still a private E2 and technically wasn't allowed to be fraternizing in such a club, but that afternoon the colonel had summarily promoted him to sergeant E5. When Will got to the bar, the colonel and his staff officers were already ordering drinks from a Nung member of the team's security force moonlighting as a white-jacketed bartender. The colonel saw Will and motioned him over.

"What are you drinking, soldier?" the colonel asked him.

"I'll take whatever you are having, sir."

"So, you like Manhattans, do you?"

"I've never had one, sir. I have been pretty much a beer drinker in my misguided youth."

When everyone had a drink in his hand, the colonel hoisted his Manhattan and said, "Gentlemen, a toast to the team's newest case officer and the US Army's newest sergeant, William Banyan Parish. Welcome to the team, son."

They all raised their drinks and shouted, "To Will" and imbibed.

"I don't know how to thank you, sir, for the promotion and the confidence you have shown in me. I'm still trying to figure out how all of this good fortune has come my way."

"Just take it in stride, Will. Try not to overthink it. Come sit at my table again. This is your night to be honored."

The meal was sublime. It began with the best Caesar salad Will had ever had, not too heavy on the garlic and anchovies. The entrée was duck à l'orange with Gruyère scalloped potatoes and green beans. The colonel told Will that he was pouring several ounces of a 1962 Louis Latour Corton-Charlemagne white burgundy into Will's crystal wineglass to accompany the duck. The moment Will tasted it was an epiphany for him. He had never experienced any wine other than the Red Mountain rotgut jug wine poured at Monday night meeting dinners in the Phi Kappa Sigma house back at UCLA. He watched everyone at the table swirl, sniff, and take small sips from their glasses. He tried to emulate the ritual, but once the exquisite liquid was flowing on his palate, it was all he could do to keep from chugging it down. It was incredibly delicious. So, he wondered, is this what wine is supposed to taste like?

There was no backing off at dessert. The pièce de résistance was a triple-chocolate-mousse cake with a hot-fudge drizzle that Captain Michaels called Death by Chocolate. The confection actually brought tears to Will's eyes. The dessert was accompanied by more rich, dark coffee in French presses. After the tables were cleared, the bartender placed crystal brandy snifters at each setting and poured a generous shot of a thirty-year-old Courvoisier Napoleon Cognac. Once again, Will was in an exalted state.

Soon, they brought out the Cohibas. "Here, Will, allow me," the colonel said as he saw Will's eyes light up at the sight of the cigar. He took Will's Cohiba and deftly snipped the mouth end of the cigar with a small tool and handed it back to him. Captain Michaels produced a Zippo and snapped out a flame for Will while he drew his cigar into a large ember, generating an aromatic cloud of smoke. It was glorious. He couldn't stop puffing. Everyone at his table, including the colonel, was doing likewise. Faces soon started disappearing in clouds of fragrant smoke. Wow, he thought, can it get any better than this?

TWELVE

Will woke up the next morning, his first as a member of B-57, with a moderate hangover. He popped a couple of aspirin and gulped a few handfuls of water from the tap in the bathroom. He sat there on his bed for a few minutes thinking about what was yet to come, and he felt a few butterflies of apprehension flutter in his gut. A knock on his door interrupted those butterflies, and he said, "Come in."

"Good morning, Parish," Brad said, as he set down a stack of lightweight jungle fatigues. He grabbed a tunic from the top of the pile and held it up for Will to admire. There on the sleeve were the three chevron stripes under the Special Forces insignia that bore an upright sword crossed with three lightning bolts and "airborne" spelled out on top. He saw his name embroidered above the right pocket of the tunic. He fingered the airborne patch.

"But I'm not airborne, Brad."

"Doesn't make a damned bit of difference—the unit is airborne, so you are too. And you'll be going to jump school up at Dong Ba Thin soon enough."

"Wow, lucky me, I just can't wait."

"Now don't go gettin' sarcastic. Today starts your training exercises. So, get dressed and meet me upstairs. I'll introduce you to your training team over breakfast."

"Swell, just swell. I'll be right there."

He put on his new uniform and looked at himself in the bathroom mirror. The lightweight fabric was cool on his skin, and he liked the way he looked. It brought a little something into play that he had never felt in his army experience until now. He felt a little swagger coming on. It must have been that elusive thing they called esprit de corps. He rolled his deltoid toward the mirror and got a little rush from the patch and the stripes. Who knew? He walked out of his room and went up the stairs to the club level. Brad was seated at a table with four other unit members, sergeants first class and staff sergeants. They stood up to shake his hand: Jerry Wagner, Frank Lewis, Tom Pritchard, and Mike Hadley.

Wagner and Lewis were the team's communications NCOs, Pritchard was a weapons NCO, and Hadley was an engineer NCO. When the introductions were over Wagner said, "Now for the important shit—let's get some breakfast." He waved over the Nung steward and started ordering.

"Will, you must have noticed by now that we Special Forces folks are into real fine dining. You know that old saying, 'Dine well today, for tomorrow you might be dying,' or something like that," Wagner said. When the table was cleared, they finally got down to the business of planning Will's training.

"All right, Parish," Pritchard announced sharply. "For the next five days your ass is grass, and I'm the lawnmower man. You'll be with me learning about a whole bunch of weaponry. I'm going to introduce you to the full arsenal available to members of an A-Team. Come on, follow me to the armory room and we'll get started." Will followed Pritchard to the first floor of the villa and stopped with him in front of a heavy metal door with multiple locks. The roughly five-hundred-square-foot room was a gun nut's candy shop. There were rifles and machine guns galore in every size and shape imaginable. Will didn't recognize most of them, but he did notice several of the bulky, heavy piece-of-shit rifles that he'd qualified with in basic training— the M14 caliber 7.62 mm. He recognized several Russian assault rifles, the infamous Kalashnikov AK-47, in a wall rack. It was standard issue to the NVA. A lot of Viet Cong soldiers were using it as well. That rifle had killed an awful lot of young American boys, Will thought.

"Where'd you get all of those AK-47s?" Will asked.

"To the victor go the spoils," Pritchard said. "We get them by the dozens out of the A-Teams. I only keep the ones in the best condition in here—the rest of them are used by our supply officer as barter to get, among other things, all of the great food and booze we consume upstairs. So, do you recognize many of these weapons?" he asked Will.

"A few, but not most of them. That one looks like a Tommy gun from the old Hollywood gangster movies," he said.

"Correct, Thompson submachine gun," Pritchard said, walking up to a rack of mixed rifles and machine guns. "The Tommy gun, but without the circular magazine. And this one replaced it: it's the M3 Grease gun, the greaser, because it looks like the grease gun they use to lube your car. See, it's a lot lighter and cheaper to manufacture than the Thompson.

"Next in line is the Brits' early favorite, the Sten gun, with its side-mount magazine. Makes you think you have to ride side saddle or something. And here's the crazy little Uzi the Israelis came up with, very compact and a helluva weapon. And here's an exotic and obscure little number, the Czech scorpion."

Next Pritchard pulled out a weird-looking gun.

"Swedish K Carl Gustav M/45, the pride of the heavily combat-tested Swedish paratroopers," he said sarcastically as he tossed it to Will. "Still, it's a pretty damn good machine gun." Will unfolded then refolded the stock. He cranked the chamber open, inspected it, and released it.

"Nice balance, but heavier than it looks," Will said.

"And this one's the BAR or Browning Automatic Rifle, heavy and cumbersome," said Pritchard. "The Yards love this guy. You'll see a lot of them when you get to the A-Team. Here we have Hitler's storm troopers' favorite machine gun, the MP 40. Everyone called it a Schmeisser, but it wasn't. Now here's my own personal favorite, just in from Germany. It's the Heckler & Koch MP5. It's a beauty, perfectly engineered. Those goddamn krauts can sure make machine guns. If I were going out to the A-Team, this would be my first choice as a close-in operations weapon. But this is a prototype, the only one I know of in all of Vietnam. It's staying right here with me. All of these other oldies but goodies are just a bunch of fantasy throwback weapons. You may see a few of these that I just showed you in the hands of some old diehard A-Team members. But there are much better choices for you."

He motioned Will over to a workbench where he had laid out three rifles. He picked up one and handed it to Will. "This is getting real popular in

Special Forces operations. It's the new AR-15 or M16. It's a good single-shot rifle and a great fully automatic rifle. It's going to replace the M14 over the next few years as the army's standard-issue infantry rifle. It's pretty good. It should be in the running for your A-Team weapon. Next up is the commando version of the AR-15. This is the experimental XM177 version of the CAR-15. It's got a much shorter barrel—only ten inches, about half as long as the AR-15." He handed it to Will, who knew he liked it in a heartbeat.

"God, I love this thing. I can't believe how light and compact it is, and it's really cool-looking with this telescoping stock," he said.

"Well, cool can get you killed in the jungle, and cool ain't gonna save your ass in a firefight with Victor Charlie, Parish. It's a great weapon, but don't go choosing it for how cool it looks. Now here's my personal favorite of the whole damn lot." He lifted it from the bench and handed it to Will, who got a sudden rush as soon as he touched it. This is the one, he thought, the rifle I'll be taking to war.

"This is old reliable, the M2 carbine, a variation of the venerable M1 of World War II and the Korean War. This one's been tricked-up a bit. It goes single shot or auto, and it's got the folding stock to give you that submachine-gun feel."

Will loosened the strap and lifted it over his head and across his left shoulder, cradling the compact carbine with his left forearm. He looked up at Pritchard and smiled broadly. "This is the one."

"It's a great one, but don't make up your mind before you've fired it. Take these three out to the firing range and give them a thorough evaluation before you decide."

Pritchard then moved on to the bigger stuff. He showed Will claymore mines; the M60 machine gun; the .50 caliber machine gun; three different sizes of mortars, the .60 mm, the .81 mm, and the four-point-deuce. But when he pulled out the M79 grenade launcher, Will was smitten.

"Man, this is a beauty. You could do some serious damage with this baby," he said.

"You've got that right, Parish, but if you get into a firefight carrying this, you become a priority target. The VC will work hard to blow your brains out.

You need to stay away from whoever's carrying this weapon," Pritchard warned. "There's always going to be a few Yards carrying them around the A-Team. You'll need to know how to use it and get accurate with it in case you're in a situation where it could save your life, but otherwise, keep the hell away from it." All the same, Will could hardly wait to fire the M79 out at the range.

For the next four days, Pritchard and Will were joined at the hip, driving back and forth in one of the unit's black jeeps to a firing range at the edge of Tan Son Nhut airbase. Every morning Pritchard woke Will up at 4:30 a.m.

"Get your ass out of bed, Parish! I've already been awake for an hour waiting for your pretty-boy beauty sleep to end. Let's hit it. Come on: two feet on the floor." Pritchard thought Will was out of shape from that long boat ride across the Pacific, so every morning the regimen was the same—a five-mile run through the streets of Cholon and Saigon before the crack of dawn.

"You know, Parish, you've got a band of blubber around your gut with goddamn love handles, must be ten pounds worth of fucking lard. We need to burn that crap off you to make you worthy of serving in an A-Team."

"You're going to kill me off with this early-morning running before I ever get out to that A-Team, Pritchard. You could back off the pace a little."

"Shit, I'm almost walking as it is. This is only a sissy ten-minute-mile pace. You should be embarrassed, Parish, letting an old man like me run circles around you. Come on, man, dig deeper. Show me some cojones."

For the next four days the weapons NCO worked Will's ass off getting him to a halfway decent proficiency with most of the unit's arsenal, including the .50-caliber machine gun. The highlights of his training were setting up and blasting off dozens of claymore mines and firing at least a hundred rounds with the M79 grenade launcher. He got a major adrenaline rush from the M60 machine gun with all of its visceral power. He loved the CAR-15, which became his favorite toy for its combination of power, compactness, and sexiness. But the M2 carbine became his weapon of choice. He actually slightly preferred the CAR-15 over the M2 but chose the M2 for a more practical consideration after Pritchard described what it was like to go out on security patrol or an ambush in VC-controlled jungle.

"Here you are, Parish, part of a four-man A-Team unit pulling security with a platoon of thirty or forty Montagnard CIDG, meaning civilian irregular defense group, which you'll learn more about later. An hour or two after dark you leave the A-Team compound and move out to the edge of the Ho Chi Minh Trail and set up an ambush with two or three dozen claymores. About midnight along comes a company of Victor Charlie or NVA. Off go the claymores and BARs and the M60. Your ambush unit wipes out a whole platoon of the enemy. But the rest of their company still outnumbers you three or four to one. They've got you pinned down, and you can't retreat. Half your Yard platoon is dead or wounded. You call for an air strike or artillery if it's close enough. The firefight is savage. You're nearly deaf by now. You're running really low on ammo. There are three or four dead Yards close by, and they were all carrying M1 carbines that use the same .30-caliber round as an M2. Among them they have maybe a dozen unused .30-round magazines. Now my question for you, Parish, is what's in your hands? What are you shooting at the VC? Is it your M2 carbine? Or is it that really cool, sexy CAR-15 that can't shoot any of that .30-caliber ammo that's lying there all around you because it fires the new 5.56 mm NATO round? What rifle are you holding or wish you were holding in this hypothetical, Parish?"

After their last day of training. Pritchard decided to have a heart to heart with Will. "Parish, you're basically not a bad man, a little bit fucked-up by my standards, but still a person with a lot of potential. I'm worried about you getting assigned to that A-Team in Duc Lap. There's some serious bad shit going on out there in the jungle, and I don't think you're taking this very seriously. I get a kind of lackadaisical feel from you like I don't have your full attention and you think this is some kind of game. I'm worried that you are going to place the other A-Team members at risk. Because you were assigned to their team, they will assume that you are fully qualified and will be able to pull your own weight, that they won't have to compensate for your inadequacies."

"You're pretty damned observant, Pritchard. You've captured my essence to a tee. I'm not gung-ho like you and the rest of the guys in the unit.

Compared to all of you I am basically a slacker, a fuck-off, an underachiever. I wasn't cut out to be a soldier. I tried like hell to stay out of Vietnam, but here I am, and there's not a damned thing I can do about it except maybe get through it in my own way. When I get to Duc Lap, I hope I'll rise to the occasion."

THIRTEEN

Pritchard granted Will a passing grade in weapons training, and Will began his training in radio operations with NCOs Jerry Wagner and Frank Lewis. By now he had taken several meals with the two. Wagner was starting to remind him of a young Hopalong Cassidy, or the way the actor William Boyd must have looked when he was a younger man. The other half of the commo team, Lewis, had bulging, expressive eyes and thick, heavyweight upper eyelids that made him look halfway between Peter Lorre and Victor Mature.

Will had been escorted into the unit's highly restricted communications bunker. Once the escort left, Wagner laid out the plan for Will's training. "Will, baby, have we got a big night planned for you," Wagner said. "Tonight is your night to run amok. Lewis and I are taking you into the big shitty for a night on the town, Special Forces style. We are going to pop your prudish cherry in bacchanalian and licentious excess."

"Where the hell did you come up with those fancy words?" Lewis asked. "You don't even know what they mean."

"I sure as hell do. I'm just trying to impress our college boy genius here with my brilliant vocabulary. Not bad for a high school dropout, right, Will? Now go get yourself gussied up, because we are going to do some serious barhopping and hell-raising with some fine Tudo Street bar-girl pussy tonight."

After another delicious meal in the unit's elegant dining room, Wagner signed out one of their unmarked black jeeps, and the three of them set off for the bars and back-alley brothels of Tudo Street. It was nearing dusk when Wagner drove them out of the safety of the B-57 compound and back up

Tran Hung Dao Street toward the heart of Saigon. Will was amazed at the sea of humanity on the streets around them. The sidewalks were one long outdoor market with flower stands, cigarette hawkers, and food stands offering produce, poultry, and mystery meat. The flow of bicycles, scooters, pedicabs, horse-drawn carts, cyclos, and taxis dodging and weaving through the throngs of pedestrians made him feel like he was in an ant colony. Thankfully Wagner's driving was nothing like Brad's.

They reached Tudo Street, the main drag of downtown Saigon, which Lewis explained meant Liberty Street in Vietnamese and used to be called Rue Catinat during the French colonial era. Wagner made a long slow cruise of it. It was beautiful to Will. He had never been in France, but the architecture, the outdoor dining terraces and sidewalk cafés, and all of the Peugeots and Citroëns reminded him of the travel agency posters of that country he had seen when he was a student. It didn't feel like he was in Southeast Asia.

As they slowly made their way down Tudo, his guides took turns calling out the noteworthy sights. There were several classy looking hotels: the Majestic, the Continental Palace, the Saigon Palace, the Eden Roc, the Caravelle, the Astor, the Miramar. Mixed in among them were dozens of restaurants and bars, like Café Brodard, Maxim's, Princess Bar (Wagner's personal favorite), the Sporting Bar, Givral's, Keely's, La Pagode, Caruso's, First Bar, Café Imperial. When they went around the block where Le Loi and Louis Pasteur intersected, Wagner pointed out the infamous Rex Hotel on Nguyen Hue near the Notre Dame Cathedral. He explained that the Rex was the site of the US Army MACV Command's daily briefings known as the "five o'clock follies." The American media had coined the phrase to mock the army's attempts to spin the results of the war to the folks back home.

Wagner found a parking spot on Le Loi and pulled in. They got out and headed down the sidewalk toward Tudo Street and the Princess Bar. Wagner started warning Will about how the bar girls ripped off GIs by getting them to buy them Saigon tea for a buck a cup and splitting the proceeds fifty-fifty with management.

"Don't buy them a single fucking cup," he said. "Don't buy them booze or champagne, because it's mostly water. Offer to buy them a beer. If they say no, buy 'em one anyway. When they don't drink it, it's your beer. Follow me?"

As the three of them closed in on the Princess, Wagner stopped abruptly and threw his arms out to his sides to stop Will and Lewis.

"Oh, shit, here we go again," Lewis muttered.

Wagner slowly sidled over to the massive plate-glass window at the front of a fancy restaurant called Le Kim Pho Dung. Sitting just inside at a candlelit table for two were an elegantly dressed Vietnamese couple in their thirties. The man wore an expensive-looking white linen suit, and the alluring woman wore a stunning black-silk ao dai. Wagner pressed his face against the window facing their table. The couple started shooing him away with the back of their hands. Wagner began to lick the glass like a dog—Will, and the couple inside saw that his tongue was unbelievably long. The couple became very agitated, stood up, and started yelling at him. All of the other patrons of the restaurant were staring at him in amazement. Then Wagner did something unthinkable. He stuck his finger down his throat and vomited violently and profusely against the window. All of the diners near the window immediately abandoned their tables. Wagner and Lewis cracked up and started dancing around like madmen. No one came out of the restaurant to chastise or challenge them. Will didn't laugh. He was simply stunned by what he had just witnessed.

"Come on, Parish, don't be a killjoy," Wagner said. "It's all part of our fun and games with the worthless slopes. Give yourself a few weeks, and you'll learn to hate their sorry asses as much as we do. Now, let's go raise some hell."

They walked into the Princess Bar, Wagner and Lewis leading the way and Will lagging behind a little tentatively. The music was loud, Mick Jagger and the Rolling Stones lamenting their lack of satisfaction about pretty much everything. Wagner's arrival created quite a commotion among the miniskirted, high-heeled bar girls, most of it negative. There was a lot of shouting with invective like "You numbah-ten GI" and "Buku dinky dau crazy." Several kept pointing to the door and yelling, "*Di di mau, di di mau,* go 'way, go 'way!"

Wagner turned to Will, winked, and said, "They love me here. I'm a rock star. They can't get enough of me."

After a while the commotion died down, and they found a corner table. Two bar girls came over and sat on Wagner's and Lewis's laps.

"Meet Cam and Ha," Wagner said, nodding first to the girl on his lap and then to the one on Lewis's. "Girls, this is our new buddy, Will. He just got here from the land of the big PX."

Will held out his hand and said, "Nice to meet you."

Cam and Ha giggled nervously. Neither extended a hand. They were wearing a lot of makeup, kind of the China doll look. Cam had her hair braided into a long ponytail, and Ha had medium-length pigtails. Neither girl was particularly attractive or unattractive, just kind of average.

"Will here is a virgin, and we brought him down here to Tudo Street to pop his cherry nice and proper," Wagner said. "Which of you girls wants to volunteer to service good old Will here, give him your best boom-boom? Or maybe you both want to do him together, huh?"

Both girls protested loudly in Vietnamese. Cam tried to slap Wagner in the face, but he caught her hand. "We no whores. We no boom-boom friend. You bad GI, 'Agner," she said indignantly.

"Oh, come on, you girls are going to give poor Will the wrong idea about Tudo Street bar girls," Wagner said, laughing.

Will was rendered speechless, and his face instantly flushed bright red.

One of the bartenders placed five bottles of Ba Muoi Ba beer and two glasses on their table. Wagner and Lewis each grabbed a bottle and a glass and poured a half glass for Cam and Ha. Lewis handed a bottle to Will and hoisted his in the air, saying, "To round eyes." Wagner and Will followed suit, and the three clinked their glasses together over the table and chugged.

"Round eyes, numbah ten," Cam offered.

Wagner and Lewis drained their bottles in a flash. Will did not. Ba Muoi Ba was the worst beer he had ever tasted—worse than the crappy Brew 102 that his father brought home during Will's teenage years because it was the cheapest beer on the shelf. It was worse than the Brown Derby swill his fraternity brothers favored when they were almost broke.

"How the hell can you guys drink this stuff after all of the great brews we've been drinking back at the B-57 bar? It smells like shit, and the taste isn't much different than the smell," Will said.

"You'll go broke drinking decent beer in here, Parish. A Foster's might set you back two, three bucks. Any American beer would be more than that if they even had it," Wagner said. "So hold your nose and drink up. It'll start to taste better as the night goes on. Hey, girls, go find old Will here a pretty co."

Cam hopped off Wagner's lap and came back a minute later with a girl who was far from pretty. Will squirmed when she sat on his lap. He didn't want to hurt her feelings, but he wished she would dismount. She said, "You buy me one Saigon tea." Then she said it over and over like a cockatoo or a broken record. Will had an urge to say, "Polly want a cracker" each time she said it. He shook his head and said, "No Saigon tea, only Ba Muoi Ba," which he had to repeat at least ten times. When she finally figured out that she wasn't getting anything but rotgut beer, she got off his lap and left in a huff. He was relieved.

"Cam, go find Will another girl, not such an ugly one."

"No, no, Cam, don't," Will protested. "I'll find my own girl later. Maybe after I get drunk enough even the ugly ones will look pretty."

"You got a bad attitude there, Will," Wagner said. "You're way too persnickety. You need to downgrade your standards. This is Vietnam, man. You're in slope land now, not back in the old US of A where a good-looking stud like you could take your pick of all that fine coed poontang. Pretty girls are few and far between around here for us round eyes."

After the third round of beers Will had mastered the technique of not smelling and barely tasting the swill they were drinking. The jukebox came alive way too loud, and Chuck Berry started blasting out "Johnny B. Goode," which prompted Wagner and Lewis to jump up with their bar girls, scurry out to the dance floor, and start rocking out. Their dancing style was neither elegant nor skilled but highly energetic and highly suggestive of humping, animal-style. Their partners were screaming at them and hitting them in mock protest over their lewd pantomime, but the two girls were smiling, and it was clear that they were having fun. Wagner twirled Cam around explosively, and Will could swear she was not wearing any underwear.

When the last notes died out, Wagner lifted Cam on top of the bar, spread her legs over his shoulders, plunged his head between her thighs, and initiated the fine art of cunnilingus—or at least a very close approximation thereof. It must have taken a dozen bar girls to separate the two of them. It didn't help that Cam's hands were locked tightly on the back of Wagner's head. When they were separated, Cam's face was adorned with a serene smile, as was Wagner's. Will's brain struggled to process what he had just witnessed. Less than a week in Saigon, and he felt that he'd fallen into some kind of rabbit hole and slipped into a parallel universe. The couple returned to the table as if nothing had happened.

"Is that the way you finish all of your dances, you two?" Will asked.

"Always," Wagner said. Cam was sitting on his lap again, smiling coyly back at Will, then she buried her face in the crotch of her partner's neck and started working up a hickey.

Will looked askance at Lewis, who ever so slightly arched an eyebrow and nodded in agreement. Will wondered what they might do for an encore. He was challenged to make conversation.

"So, anybody read any good books lately?" Will offered.

Lewis and Wagner burst out in laughter. When they stopped laughing, Wagner asked, "Did we shock your dainty sensibilities there, Parish? Did we blow away your prudish state of mind?"

"Scarred for life," Will said, smiling.

"Good," Wagner replied gruffly, "now you'll fit right in with the rest of us."

After a few more rounds of Ba Muoi Ba, Will was starting to lighten up. He wasn't drunk, but he was getting pretty uninhibited. Some of the bar girls were beginning to look almost cute.

"OK, time to hit the road, Jack," Wagner said, as he stood up with Cam in his arms. He kissed her passionately, set her down, and said, "We'll be back before closing, girls. Now get out there and sell a bunch of that goddamn Saigon tea to those stupid-shit GIs."

Lewis and Will finished their beers and followed Wagner out the door of the Princess.

"We have to go somewhere really exotic next," Wagner said, frowning and scratching the top of his head. "I've got it. Will, have we got a treat for you. We're taking you to our favorite steam job and blow bath parlor. It's just three blocks from here." He took off down the street, and the two of them followed. They turned left down a side street, then stopped in front of a nondescript storefront with draped windows and a small blinking neon sign that read "Saigon Massage." They entered a small lobby where several young women were seated around a low table reading magazines. They all looked up, instantly recognizing Wagner and Lewis. Two girls smiled sweetly at them, and the others started laughing and chattering unintelligibly. Wagner and Lewis paired off quickly with their favorite masseuses. Wagner directed a cute girl to pair up with Will, and then he slipped away with Lewis.

The masseuse introduced herself as Edie. She was wearing children's seersucker pajamas featuring images of Donald Duck. She was all of four foot ten and ninety pounds, looking not a day over fourteen. She took Will's hand and led him into a small, dark chamber with a massage table in the middle. She reached a hand to Will's belt buckle as if to help him undress. He caught her hand gently.

"How old are you, Edie?" he asked.

"I eighteen," she answered.

"No, really, please tell me your true age."

"I true age eighteen."

"You look very young to me, Edie, too young to be working here."

"I no too young. I eighteen. You see. I give you numbah-one blowjob."

"Well, to tell you the truth, Edie, I would really like a back and shoulder massage. My back is killing me. Can you give me a massage?"

"Can do numbah-one massage."

Will nodded and smiled then took off his shirt and khakis, leaving his boxer shorts on. He climbed onto the massage table.

"You have numbah-one beautiful body."

"Why, thank you, Edie. That's very nice of you to say so. You have a very nice body too."

In the blink of an eye, Edie dropped her pajama bottoms and lifted the top over her head and stood naked before Will.

"I make love you now."

"No, Edie, I can't do that. But I would love to have a massage, OK."

"You very sexy man."

"Thank you again, but I'm going to stick with the massage. So get your clothes back on." He rolled onto his belly and stretched out. Edie slipped back into her Donald Ducks, climbed on top of his back, and stood up.

"I give foot walk massage."

She kneaded his back with her toes, the balls of her feet, and her heels. Her massage technique was nothing short of amazing. She had an uncanny ability for finding every tight nook and cranny in every muscle and all the connective tissue in his back, neck, and shoulders. She created great pain and pleasure in the same moment. She worked her way down to the muscles in his butt, down the hamstrings and the calf muscles. She never lost her balance. She could have been an acrobat or a ballerina. Nothing had ever hurt so good.

Toward the end of the massage he started hearing a lot of climactic moans and groans through the thin walls. He was pretty sure he heard Wagner's distinctive voice howling like a wild animal a couple of rooms away. Edie sat down on Will's back and slid off the edge of the massage table. When Will rolled over to sit up, Edie made one last attempt to service him. Her head darted quickly toward his crotch as her hands deftly pulled down his boxers, and she almost got her mouth around his penis before he was able to block her face with his hand.

"I make feel better. I suck you. You feel better," she said.

"No can do, Edie. You're just a child."

"I no child. I eighteen. You dinky dao crazy."

"True, I am dinky dao crazy. You're very observant for someone so young."

Their conversation was interrupted by a sharp knock on the door followed by Wagner's assertive voice. "You got your plumbing all cleared up yet, Parish? You had enough time to get your rocks off at least two or three times by now," he guffawed.

"Be right out," Will answered. He got dressed and tipped Edie several hundred piastres, ten dollars American.

"This buku dinky dao too much tip," she said as she tried to hand back most of the piastres.

Will grabbed her hands, cupping them around the bank notes. "You keep this. I should give you more for that terrific massage. It was beautiful." He opened the door and joined his comrades in the lobby.

When they were back out on the street, Wagner said, "I hope you noticed that we saved the prettiest, most virginal-looking one for you, old Will."

"I did notice that Jerry, and I really appreciate your great sacrifice in not claiming her for yourself, but I don't think she could have been older than fourteen," Will said.

"Sounds about right, but you know the old saying, 'when they're old enough to bleed, they're old enough to butcher,'" Wagner said with a lurid grin on his face. Will winced, and the three of them headed back in the direction of Tudo, with Wagner whistling a worthy rendition of the theme music from *Bridge Over the River Kwai.*

As they walked along, there was a little bit of that vague static-electricity field raising the hair on the back of Will's neck. He glanced back over his shoulder and saw two guys he thought he recognized from the Princess Bar— they had taken a table near where the trio had sat with the bar girls. He remembered thinking back then that they didn't fit in with the GI clientele of the Princess. In fact, come to think of it, they had stuck out like two sore thumbs looking very uncomfortable. They didn't come across as Americans: they had this Slavic thug thing going on. He remembered that they had quickly and unkindly rejected the advances of several bar girls.

Will asked Wagner and Lewis in a soft voice, "Hey, have either one of you noticed the two guys tailing us?"

They both glanced back over their shoulders. Wagner said, "Shit, I haven't seen those guys for weeks. They must be interested in our new blood here, huh, Lewis? Have you had your intel briefing from Lieutenant Kavanaugh yet, Parish?"

"No, not yet."

"Those guys are with the International Control Commission. It's supposed to be a peacekeeping agency with representatives from Canada,

India, and Poland, but it's really more of a cover organization for spying on American intel ops in Vietnam. Kennedy says that the CIA has identified most of the Polish members as KGB agents. They're here to try to help the NVA and the Viet Cong kick our asses and let old Ho Chi Minh turn the country commie. They always seem to show up when we get a new case officer. Kind of makes you wonder about our unit security. How the hell do these guys know about you, Parish?"

"They probably have the headquarters under surveillance and notice when someone new shows up," Will offered.

"Yeah, probably that. Well, Kavanaugh will give you the low down. You should know that we are under strict orders from the CO not to engage them. We're supposed to ignore them, pretend they don't exist."

"Now that I'm aware of them, that's not going to be easy. They might as well be wearing black pajamas and conical hats and brandishing AK-47s. This is a crazy, fucked-up war," Will said.

"I'm with you there, Parish, but there's not a fucking thing we can do about it except look the other way. You just have to cool it. They have diplomatic immunity. They're untouchable. A direct order from the old man makes me stifle my murderous impulses."

"Mine too," Lewis agreed.

Easier said than done, Will mused.

They worked their way back to the Princess. Will lost track of the KGB agents in the Friday night crowds of Tudo Street. Inside the Princess, they found three stools open at the bar, and Wagner ordered three more Ba Muoi Bas. They sat and watched the action behind them in the reflection from the massive mirror behind the bar. Cam and Ha were locked in rapt conversation with a couple of very young GIs who were in the process of having their wallets emptied on a table full of Ba Muoi Ba beer bottles and a whole lot of tiny cups of Saigon tea. Ouch, there go their first paychecks in an hour or two, thought Will. Oh, well, they'll learn. He continued to scan the bar for any sign of the KGB thugs, but they never showed their faces.

By the time they had finished their beers Wagner said, "We should probably move on and introduce good ol' Will to the beauties of 25 P Alley."

"Ah, shit, Wagner, no way. I don't think Will's ready for that experience," Lewis said.

"I beg to differ with you there, my friend. Will needs to be exposed to the dark side of humanity, and there ain't none darker than in 25 P Alley.

FOURTEEN

It was nearing midnight when crazy Sergeant Jerry Wagner fired up the jeep and the three of them made their way toward Cholon and the dreaded 25 P Alley. The street was still busy with human and vehicular traffic, but nowhere near as crowded as when they'd started their tour. They hadn't traveled very far when Wagner eased the jeep into a parking spot about a half mile from B-57 headquarters. A hundred feet or so ahead on the right stood the narrow entrance to an alley with a steady flow of foot traffic going in and coming out. They sat there in the jeep for a couple of minutes, quietly watching the movement.

"Take notice, Will, it's all slopes going in and out, no round eyes, no grunts, just lowlife slope slime. They're going in there to purge their sickest perverted fantasies, mostly with tiny children, all for the price of a quarter, twenty-five piastres. When we go in there, we need to stick real close together."

They marched over to the entrance in an uptight formation, Wagner leading the way. The first thing to assault Will's senses as he entered the alley was the putrid smell. It was a disgusting mélange of sewage, rotting fish, and body odor. The passage was narrow and crowded. Naked toddlers were wading in what appeared to be an open sewer. Will fought back the gag reflex, reached for his handkerchief, and covered his nose and mouth. What he saw was beyond his comprehension. The scene was impossibly heartbreaking. Terminal dehumanization. It was Victor Hugo and Charles Dickens in extremis. He expected to see lepers coming out of the shadows. His memory flashed on the horrific illustrations of the deepest levels of hell in Dante's

Divine Comedy. He imagined the ground opening below him and exposing the wretched and damned gnawing on human skulls.

All along the alley, large families huddled together in tiny cardboard shanties. The filthiness was unfathomable, children and adults alike wearing tattered rags with congealed food and dirt holding them together. The worst of it was fathers and mothers offering their little girls and little boys to be used as sex toys. Older women were standing in the middle of their families pantomiming oral sex. Nowhere was there a hint of shame or embarrassment, only the primal urge for survival. It was the saddest thing he had ever seen. He wished he could save these children, conjure the awesome power within to throw a protective energy field over them, but all he had was a sense of helplessness and futility. These tiny, innocent babes were being offered to passing strangers for sexual depravities, all for twenty-five piastres. Here and there he saw takers going into alcoves, behind thin, dingy curtains with a tiny girl or boy in hand to act out their sickest fantasies. Will's brain was in danger of shutting down. He needed to close his eyes and make this picture go away forever. He squeezed his eyes shut and came to a stop.

When he opened his eyes again, he realized that he had fallen far behind Wagner and Lewis. They were starting to turn a corner a hundred feet in front of him when Wagner looked back for him. Wagner's eyes bugged out, and he yelled, "Behind you," just as the high-energy static surged up Will's spine and neck and out the top of his cranium. The blackout came and went in an instant. Then all was slow. He turned to assess the threat. Less than ten feet away stood a group of seven or eight aggressive Vietnamese teenagers brandishing pipes and broken bottles, three of them wielding oversize tactical knives. There was no mistaking their intentions toward Will. They had stopped and spread out, and Will noticed the two KGB thugs standing thirty or so feet behind the teenage assault force, smiling. He had no doubts about who had sicced this gang on him.

The three with knives were preparing a frontal assault while two on each side with pipes and broken bottles started to flank him. In slow motion the nearest knife wielder launched his attack from the direction of Will's right shoulder. Will raised his left palm to strike a killing blow, but before he could deliver it the hissing sound of hollow-point bullets sped past his ear, first one, then two harmlessly missing their target, but a third finding the neck under the ear of its intended target. Will looked back over his shoulder to see Wagner sprinting in full slow motion with his outstretched arm firing rounds from a vintage .32 Colt hammerless semiautomatic pistol. Will turned back to his attackers. The would-be knife assassin had been spun around and was falling to the ground, a swirling blood pattern pulsing from the gaping hole in his neck. His sidekicks were turning and fleeing in full retreat toward Tudo Street. Will had the power to kill the remaining attackers and their KGB instigators in less than a blink of an eye. His killing lust was high, but there were too many witnesses and no chance of keeping Wagner and Lewis from seeing what he wanted no one to see. It was a crying shame to forgo such a righteous slaughter.

As the passage of time returned to normal, Wagner fired two more rounds at the fleeing attackers without success. "Shit, Will, that was way too close for comfort. A few more seconds and they would have shredded you. I told you to stay close. Why did you lag like that? Come on, there's a back way out of here." Wagner and Lewis started jogging up the alley. Will looked back at the fallen teenager who was hard on the filthy soil of 25 P alley, showing no signs of life. Then he sped after Wagner and Lewis. They worked their way back out to Tran Hung Dao on full alert. They got back to the jeep and discovered it had four slashed tires. Wagner ignored the flats, and they drove back to the villa on the rims and shredded tires. When they got inside, they went to the commo bunker and locked the door.

"OK, that's some new shit," Lewis said. "Those ICC guys, it was pretty obvious they set up the attack on Will. They've never done anything that aggressive before."

"Yeah," said Wagner, "they've been around for a long time taking pictures and tailing our guys coming in from the field, but never any violence or attacks like this. What's going on with you, Will?"

"Nothing. I'm clueless why they came after us. By the way, Wagner, thanks for saving my ass back there in the alley. I'm sure glad you had that pistol, otherwise I would have been a stuck pig," he fibbed.

"Yup, that little piece has saved my ass a few times too. I never leave headquarters at night without the .32 in my boot holster. You should get yourself one from old Pritchard now that somebody seems to want to grease your ass."

"I'm sort of a snub-nose .38 guy myself," Will said.

"A little more pop but too hard to reload in a pinch. OK, you guys, we need to agree on our story. We have to make a report to let the CO know what's happening out there. First off, I don't think the guy I plugged had a chance of surviving in that alley, so we don't say anything about me shooting him. I say our story is we were in the alley and got attacked by a teenage gang. We include in the report that the KGB guys were following us on Tudo Street. We say the fight had just started when somebody began shooting. We saw a kid with a knife take a round in the face, and then everyone, including us, took off running. End of report. Are we in agreement?"

"Sounds good to me," Lewis said.

"I agree," Will said.

"OK, Will, you're the college grad, the case officer—you write the report. We'll sign it with you," Wagner said.

"OK, I'll do it first thing in the morning."

"Listen, Will, it's probably better to leave out any mention of 25 P Alley. The truth is that the old man had put the place off limits to detachment personnel. Somehow, in my drunken stupor, I must have forgotten all about it. So you've got to make a report that tells about the ICC–KGB thugs following us aggressively and openly, but nothing about what happened in 25 P, OK? I've got enough black marks on my record around here already."

"OK, I'll leave it out. What about the slashed tires?"

"Just say it happened where we were parked off Tudo Street, and we saw them walking away from the jeep when we came back then discovered the flat tires," Wagner said.

It was a little past two a.m. when Will made his way back to his room. He was still a little shaky coming off the adrenaline high. His thought processes were jumbled, kind of tangled, actually troubled. He kicked off his chukka boots and threw himself into bed.

His first concrete thought was to wonder how the fuck he'd gotten himself into this mess. His second concrete thought? How the fuck would he get himself out of it? He felt trapped. He didn't want to play this game anymore. It was an attraction-repulsion syndrome. Every time something really good happened, it was almost immediately negated by something exceedingly bad. To Will, it always seemed like the bad shit had the upper hand. He thought about the two KGB guys. He came to the conclusion that they weren't really trying to kill Will the case officer. They were natural born killers, just doing what their nature compelled them to do. There was some magnet in Will drawing them in. They were like the others before them that he had hurt with extreme and terrible violence. People who took sadistic joy in hurting others and possessed the compulsion to murder were drawn to Will.

Evil sought him—no, not him, himself. Evil people came to attack the thing with power inside of him. Like a moth seeking the flame, evil found its way to him.

FIFTEEN

When sleep finally came that night, it was fitful and troubled. His dreams took place at the edge of a Catholic church courtyard. There was a small building that appeared to be a school inside the courtyard area. He was watching a group of delightfully cute preschool children all dressed in white, each child with a shiny bright-red sash around their waists running and playing. Some were on swings, others on a merry-go-round and teeter-totters. Several children were playing a game with bright-red oversize bouncy balls. All of the children were moving in very slow motion. He couldn't make out the features of their faces because they were covered by gauzy veils. He was struck by the sweet music of the kids' high voices and how that sound heightened the poignancy of the dream. Then, without warning, a bomb exploded in slow motion in the middle of twenty or thirty children, shredding their tiny bodies into wads of raw flesh and bone.

Somewhere near the crack of dawn, Will awoke, terrified and soaking in his own sweat. After breakfast, Will went to Brad's office to see if he could get a typewriter to write up his report. The only one available was an ancient, beat-up Underwood like the one Will had used back at Fort Holabird. He took the Underwood back to his room and set up at his small desk. He started banging away in his slow-motion two-finger hunt-and-peck system. He continued pecking away at the keys, trying to entertain himself for an hour or so. When he finished, he took the report to Wagner and Lewis's hooch and read it to them. When he stopped reading, Wagner said, "Man, we sound really cool in that report, like we're the characters in a spy novel. I like it."

"Me too," Lewis said.

They signed it, and he left their room. He inserted the report in an envelope, addressed it to Colonel Mahoney, and placed it in the inbox on Brad's desk.

Will spent most of the next two weeks in short bursts of intensive training. It started with Wagner and Lewis introducing him to the Morse code, the single sideband radio, the use of Diana one-time pads for encryption of sensitive or classified information, and "the prick twenty-five" backpack radio. He spent hours attempting to master the keying device, called a bug, for transmitting the dits and dahs of Morse code on the single sideband. At the end of his four days in the commo bunker with Wagner and Lewis, though, it became clear that mastery had not been attained.

"Parish, you suck on single sideband. You may have the piss-poorest fist in the history of radio operators," Wagner told him.

"Ah, give him a break, Jerry," Lewis said. "Nobody can learn to send Morse in four days."

"Yeah, but Parish is supposed to be a fucking genius. I expected him to do way better than the average swinging dick."

"Gee, Wagner, thanks for the vote of confidence," Will said. "Now what do I do when I go into the field? How do I transmit and receive?"

"Like a ten-year-old, Parish, you use your voice and your ears and the phonetic alphabet. You know—what the fuck—whiskey, tango, foxtrot. Got it?"

"Whiskey, tango, foxtrot, cool. Got it," Will said.

After that, his training greatly intensified. The next three days and nights he spent in the jungle outside of Ban Me Thuot, the biggest city in the Central Highlands of South Vietnam. He went with Staff Sergeant Mike Hadley for map-reading exercises and to learn jungle-survival skills. Hadley trained Will in evasion, camouflage, infiltration and exfiltration techniques, how to detect signs of booby traps, especially punji stake pits, and how to become invisible to the enemy in the jungle. The jungle wasn't Will's favorite place to be even for ten minutes, let alone three days. Hadley was a humorless, unforgiving, dogmatic trainer with a jowly bulldog face, bowlegged posture, and a gravelly voice.

At first light on day one they caught a Huey mail run from Tan Son Nhut Air Base to the regional B-Team headquarters, B-23, at Ban Me Thuot. B-23 had operational control of A-team 239 at Duc Lap, Will's next stop after training. From there Hadley had arranged for a jeep ride several miles out of Ban Me Thuot to the edge of the highlands jungle, an area that was theoretically pacified, or not frequented by the Viet Cong. The two of them penetrated the deep jungle canopy and hiked for a few miles and began the training exercise. They were not allowed to carry food with them, so it was a real survival exercise. With a compass and a relief map, Will spent a full day playing pathfinder, trying to discern the hidden topographical features in the jungle and making his way to locations Hadley had marked on the acetate overlay of his USGS quadrant map. Hadley didn't make it easy, and Will got lost a few times. He was amused by his failures, but Hadley ripped into him each time he got lost, telling him he had a bad attitude and little chance of surviving in an A-Team. On the last exercise of the day, Will found his way to Hadley's objective, but rather than congratulate him for finally getting it right, Hadley told him that even a schoolchild could have made it to the goal.

Toward the end of day one, he and Hadley went snake hunting for dinner. Hadley's snake-hunting weapon was a forked branch he had snapped off the crooked trunk of a jambo tree and quickly whittled down with his Bowie-style jungle knife. In the late afternoon there was little light coming through the triple layer of jungle canopy. Hadley was leaning over in a crouch, taking dainty steps that were incongruous with his bulldog frame. Moving very slowly he periodically lifted low-lying leafy ground cover with his jambo stick to search for rat snakes. Will gamely attempted to emulate Hadley's slow, methodical movement in hunting reptilian game, but his heart wasn't in it. Nothing about the exercise seemed real. It was like he was on a movie set playing a role in a low-budget B movie.

After some time had passed, Hadley slipped his forked jambo limb under the broad, jagged leaf of a dark-green jungle plant, lifted slowly, and pointed with his free hand at what was apparently a rat snake. It was brownish with a yellowish cast and had a round head with bulging eyes. It didn't look big enough to provide dinner for two. With a sudden strike of his forked limb,

Hadley pinned the neck of the snake and deftly removed its head with his jungle knife. He held the snake by its tail, smiling as he presented it to Will, writhing and wriggling. Hadley made a slit in the snake's skin, peeled it off, and gutted the snake easily, as if he had done it a hundred times before. The snake was close to four feet long. Its skin removed, the snake's pale, semitranslucent flesh resembled that of a fresh chicken breast. Hadley moved to the edge of a small stream they had forded several times that day and thoroughly rinsed the snake carcass as it continued writhing. When he finished, he stuffed the snake into a lined canvas pouch and put it in the top of his rucksack.

They moved back into a narrow, sparsely canopied section of the jungle, and Hadley approached a magnificent, towering, heavily buttressed tualang tree. "Here's our hooch for the next night or two, Parish," he said as he lifted the strap of his M16 over his head and pulled off his pack, leaning them against the trunk of the tree. The smooth-bark tree looked like it was centuries old. Most of the buttresses were three to four feet high where they came out of the trunk and two and a half to three feet apart, creating a ready-made compartment for a sleeping chamber. "You just string up your poncho, and you have a little tent with rigid side walls," Hadley explained.

Will unslung his carbine and unfolded the metal stock. During the day the jungle had been smeared with color, mostly infinite shades of green; now the sun had just set, and the jungle around the tualang tree clearing was growing darker by the minute. What had been a riot of lush greens from chartreuse to emerald to jade were turning a dull gray and black. As the visual grandeur of the jungle faded, they had come to a stop and fallen silent. Now the cacophony of the jungle soundtrack from buzzing insects to screeching birds, howling monkeys, slithering lizards and snakes, and scurrying rodents erupted in startlingly loud stereophonic dissonance. Through it all, he thought he heard the distant growling of a large cat. The second time he heard it he said, "Did you hear that, Hadley? That sounded a helluva lot like a tiger."

"Yup, that was a tiger all right. They have plenty of them around here and elephants too, not to mention the cobras, kraits, bamboo vipers, and scorpions."

"I guess we're not going to be getting much sleep around here for the next three nights," Will said.

"We'll have to alternate guard duty in five-hour shifts. I'll give you first choice. You want eight to one or one to six," Hadley said.

"I'm so pumped up on adrenaline I might as well take first shift, because I'm sure as shit not going to be able to sleep anytime soon," said Will.

"You'll get used to it in time. You'll learn to sleep with one eye open if you have a strong enough survival instinct," Hadley said. "Now I'm going to cook up dinner. Find me some dry kindling and firewood while I dig out a firepit."

Will was dubious about the prospects of finding anything dry enough to fuel a fire at the edge of the jungle, but he was wrong. There was an abundance of fallen rotting limbs and broken twigs within a hundred-foot radius of the tualang tree. After several rounds of gathering, he made a substantial pile of combustibles next to Hadley's firepit. Snapping out his Zippo, Hadley started a quick, hot fire. He eased his mess kit from his rucksack, followed by the pouch with the snake and a small tin of cooking oil. He pulled a smaller serrated knife from a scabbard on his belt, cut the snake into two-inch chunks, and threw them into the handled pan of his mess kit. He produced a couple of salt and pepper packets and emptied their contents on the snake morsels and poured in an ounce or two of cooking oil. In no time the oil in the pan was popping and sizzling, and Hadley was stir-frying over the open fire. He added some roots and wild taro leaves and tubers he had collected during the day. With a few more minutes of stirring and sizzling, the delectable aroma was making Will drool. His hunger pangs were suddenly acute. He had made up his mind after watching Hadley kill and butcher the snake that he wasn't eating any; now there was no resisting at least a bite. He pulled his mess kit from his rucksack and opened it. Hadley motioned for him to hold out the pan, and he bladed a good-size dollop into it. Hadley forked a piece and blew on it for a few seconds.

"Real men eat the whole chunk of snake, backbone and all, Parish, like this," he said without humor as he started chewing on his first bite. "Let nothing go to waste. The backbone is a good source of calcium. Mmmm, this is fucking delicious, just like crunchy fried chicken."

Will stabbed a piece with his fork, blew on it, put it in his mouth, and started to chew. It was tasty and a lot like chicken. When he chomped into the backbone, he began working it around in his mouth and biting the meat away from the bones. Finally he pulled the spiny material from his mouth and used his front teeth to tear away most of the remaining meat. Hadley started shaking his head from side to side.

"Goddamn it, Parish, you're getting to be a big disappointment."

By the last flickering light of the fire, they made their individual hooches against the base of the massive tree. Will laid out a six-inch-thick wad of elephant grass on the ground of his hooch and spread his poncho liner on top of it. It made a cozy little sleeping chamber, not that Will thought he had any chance of getting any sleep. He lifted his M2 carbine into his hooch and folded the metal stock. He leaned back against the tree and released the thirty-round banana clip into his lap. He cranked the bolt, ejecting the chambered round and catching it in his hand. It brought a trace of a smile to his thin lips.

"Try not to shoot your foot off with your new toy there, Parish," Hadley said snidely. "You got a watch?"

"Yup," Will said.

"OK, you got first shift. I'm going to catch some shut-eye. Wake me at one."

Within seconds a genuinely amazing thing happened. Hadley started snoring like a fucking chainsaw that needed a tune-up. At first, Will thought he was kidding—maybe Hadley had a little bit of a sense of humor after all. He laughed out loud at what he thought was fake snoring.

"All right, very funny, Hadley, so you can imitate a chainsaw. If you keep that up every wild boar in the Central Highlands of Vietnam is going to be on us in a few minutes, or maybe a tiger will be thinking pork chops for dinner. Come on, man, enough."

But Hadley didn't stop. He just kept on chugging and sputtering. Will aimed his flashlight in Hadley's face and realized that the man was indeed out cold.

"Wake up, Hadley, wake the fuck up!" he shouted to no avail. "Come on,

Hadley," he roared at the top of his lungs. Still no response. And the unbelievable snoring went on. Will waited a few more minutes. He was mulling over whether to fire off a round to wake the man up. He cranked a round into the chamber.

The snoring stopped instantly. "What is it? What do you hear?" whispered Hadley.

"I heard some motherfucker snoring like a goddamn locomotive, that's what it is, Hadley. If there's any fucking VC or NVA within ten miles, they are going to be on us like stink on shit. Do you have any idea how loud you snore?"

"Yeah, yeah, I've been told. It comes and goes."

"What the fuck happened to sleeping with one eye open? I was screaming in your face and shining a flashlight from inches away, and you were dead to the world."

"I don't need to sleep with one eye open when both of yours are," said Hadley.

"Shit, what a crock."

Then Hadley pulled out a handkerchief and blew his nose like a foghorn.

"Son of a bitch, Hadley, you're the biggest noisemaker I have ever come across in my life. You should get out of the army and go to Hollywood and start a special-effects sound studio. No one could compete with you," said Will.

"I'm gettin' tired of your constant bullshit, Parish."

He appeared to be asleep in seconds again, but this time he didn't snore. It was just slow deep breathing with a slight chuffing sound.

For the next two or three hours, Will sat bolt upright in the pitch darkness of his tiny sleeping cubicle with eyes and ears wide open, listening to the night noise of the jungle. Insect noises dominated, along with the tree frogs. Every so often something big moved relatively close by. How close? Not sure. He tried to visualize the animals by the noises they made moving through the jungle flora. Some seemed rodent size. Some had to have been as big as dogs or boars. Some sounds came from high in the jungle canopy—had to be monkeys or large birds. Other, louder sounds came from greater distances. Could they be elephants, possibly a tiger? His imagination raced.

Then he heard it, the barely audible low, guttural almost snarl of a big cat. It was close, very close. The prickly feeling began. The static electricity rose, every hair erect. Then the vivid colors came and went. His eyes seemed to be bulging out of his head. He had night vision. He could see the tiger as if it were in full daylight. It was stalking Hadley, moving very, very slowly. He could smell the tiger, its musky, feral scent, its pheromones. It was a female tiger and so very hungry. Will raised his carbine. He was on full auto. He weighed emptying his magazine into the big cat. But he couldn't kill such a magnificent creature—it was merely doing what came naturally for its survival, there was no issue of good versus evil here, only the drive of hunger. He slipped the safety off and fired a short burst to the side of the tiger's head. Real-time movement returned, and the tiger took off like a bat out of hell. Two seconds later Hadley was up, weapon in hand.

"What the hell do we have? What the hell do we have?" Hadley yelled.

"It was a tiger. It's gone. It's gone. It was just about to make a meal out of you."

"How the hell do you know it was a tiger? It's so fucking dark you can't see a damned thing."

"Believe me, Hadley, it was a tiger. It made all of the correct growly tiger noises that only a tiger or a lion can make. I saw its face clearly in the light of my muzzle flash." Will certainly couldn't tell him that he had magical powers that allowed him to see the tiger as if in the full light of the day.

"So you must have hit it. Did you kill it or is it still out there all shot up and pissed off."

"No, it's not all shot up and pissed off. I missed it on purpose. I didn't want to kill it. If it had continued toward you after I fired that burst, it would have been a hard call, you or the tiger—but I guess I would have been forced to grease it to save your sorry ass."

"Don't fuck with me, Parish. I'm not in the mood to be fucked with."

"You might try something like 'Golly, gee, gosh, Parish, thanks for saving my life.'"

"Yeah, well, I don't believe there was any fucking tiger out there. You just started hallucinating and panicked like the pussy that you are. That's what really happened."

"Anybody ever tell you what a prince of a guy you are, Hadley?" Pause. "I thought not."

Neither of them got any sleep for the rest of the night. After sunrise, when it got light enough, Hadley made a big deal out of having Will prove that there really had been a tiger stalking him. It took a while with Hadley closely studying the claw and pad pattern in the loose soil to concede the possibility that a tiger might have been ready to pounce on him. Still, he was incapable of uttering a word of gratitude to Will.

The training sessions continued without incident over the next two days. Hadley went out of his way to confound Will and to try to set him up for failure by sending him into deep triple canopy, which made the topography nearly impossible to read. Yet he continued to improve at map reading and finding his way out of jungle mazes. He didn't do much additional dining on the flora and fauna that Hadley gathered for their daily meal. Will was able to keep his hunger pangs from driving him crazy by periodically gnawing on the chunks of teriyaki beef jerky made from tenderloin strips by the B-57 kitchen staff that he had secretly stashed in his pack. Technically he was cheating, but frankly, he really didn't give a shit. If Hadley hadn't been such an asshole, he might have offered to share some with him. By the time they got back to Cholon, Will's pants were almost loose enough to fall off if he hadn't been wearing a belt. He had been in-country for less than two weeks, and he had already dropped a couple of inches of belly fat.

Will and Hadley didn't say a word to each other on the Huey ride back to Tan Son Nhut or the jeep ride back to team headquarters in Cholon. The sun was just setting when they pulled through the massive reinforced gate and into the parking area. After they got their gear out of the jeep, Hadley blocked Will's path and glared icily at him. Will glared back.

"If you got something to say, get it off your chest, Hadley," he said.

"Yeah, I got something to say, Parish. After three days with you out there in the bush, I'm not impressed. You acted like it was a big fucking joke. The sergeant major told me you were some kind of smart fucker, a quick study, a genius. I didn't see any of that. All I saw was a wiseass punk, a fuckup. No way you should be going to an A-Team with your attitude. You are going to place the members of that team in jeopardy." And for the first time since Will had met him, Hadley actually smiled, a not very friendly, gritted—teeth smile—more like a sneer. Then he walked away.

SIXTEEN

"Mind if I join you gents?" Will asked. "I'm so hungry I could eat snake."
After his three days in the jungle, Will was so hungry he could have eaten ten
rat snakes, bones and all. He had found Wagner, Lewis, and Brad sitting with
Lieutenant Kavanaugh, B-57's intelligence officer, at a large table in the
dining room.

"Hey, we were just talking about you, Will," said Kavanaugh. "But what
we're eating is a hell of a lot tastier than snake. Sit over here next to me."

"God that smells good. French onion soup, right?" Will said as he sat
down next to the lieutenant, trying not to drool.

"That it is," Kavanaugh said.

"I could eat a gallon of that," Will said.

"So the jungle cuisine wasn't to your liking, eh?" Kavanaugh said.

"That would be quite an understatement, sir," said Will. "I must have lost
five pounds in the bush."

Then one of the white-jacketed Nung servers placed a bowl of steaming
soup and a tray with fresh baguettes in front of Will, who dug in with relish.
It was the richest soup he had ever tasted. He savored the brandy in the roux.
He sucked the Gruyère cheese and the caramelized onions off the hard-toasted
sourdough baguette chunks. He struggled to slow down enough to blow on
each oversize soup spoon full to avoid burning the shit out of his tongue.
Tears of joy moistened the corners of his eyes. Then came the Caesar salad.
Once the plate was in front of him, Will had to work hard to restrain himself
from inhaling the salad like a vacuum cleaner. His sense of good table
manners was barely holding on. It was all he could do to keep from licking

the plate when he finished. The main course was a two-inch-thick hunk of perfectly roasted medium-rare prime rib with a baked potato and Yorkshire pudding. A large vessel piled high with sour cream and a smaller one with fresh chives were set in front of him. He dug in while trying to slow down so he could savor every mouthful. As he chewed and swallowed his final bite of beef, he thought he might explode.

"This may be the happiest moment of my life," he said, mostly to his empty plate.

"Are you all right there, Parish?" Kavanaugh asked. "You kind of have that zombie look in your eyes."

"Oh, yeah, lieutenant, I'm just blissed out by that exquisite meal. My last meal was three days ago. This meal made it worth going hungry for three days."

"OK, take an hour to recover and then meet me in my office. We need to discuss your report on the Tudo Street incident with the ICC agents."

"Yes, sir. Will do," Will replied. Wagner and Lewis both gave him an intense knowing look.

An hour later he was in Kavanaugh's office going over the report. He asked Will to go over the story of the incident. He retold it exactly as he had written it, and the lieutenant seemed satisfied.

Then Will listened to him explain what he knew about the International Control Commission. "We have knowledge that these ICC agents are reporting to the KGB station chief at the Russian embassy in Saigon on all armed forces intelligence collection activities in Vietnam."

Will said, "I'm probably a little paranoid about this, but I had a feeling that those two guys following us were looking for an opportunity to visit some violence on Wagner, Lewis, and me the other night. It was one of those if-looks-could-kill moments. From now on every time I leave here, my eyes are going to be wide open."

"It's always a good idea to practice sound defensive surveillance technique whenever you're outside of this compound," Kavanaugh said. "That silly tradecraft stuff they teach at Holabird actually comes in handy around here. It isn't just the ICC agents who are paying a lot of attention to what's going on here. The Viet Cong have plenty of informants who are keeping an eye on the comings and goings through that gate too. It's pretty obvious that something big is being run from inside these walls. Just the number of high-ranking officers passing through tells the spies and informants a lot. But the real tip-off for them is the heavy structural security and the size of our Nung security force. There's never less than twenty Nungs armed to the teeth inside and outside here, twenty-four hours a day," Kavanaugh said.

"I assume that means we're a prominent target for a sapper attack," Will said. "One more thing to be paranoid about."

"If you're in B-57, paranoia is your best friend," Kavanaugh added. "Now we need to talk about what you're going to be doing at Duc Lap. As you know, you will be joining up with a B-57 team member we already have there. He is Lieutenant Aramis Healy, who goes by the name of Ralph. He has no intelligence training, and he can be a bit of a loose cannon. A big part of your role in Duc Lap is going to be trying to keep him from going off half-cocked, like trying to recruit assets without proper vetting, which he has already done twice. Your biggest challenge will be getting him under control and following proper intel procedures. He knows nothing about preparing intel reports, so you will be there to make sure all the proper protocols are followed. We have to run name trace checks on all potential agents in your net. We have to have a lead and development report before any recruitment attempts are authorized. All contacts with agents and potential agents have to be documented by contact reports. All strategic intel data has to be reported in a standard information-report format," Kavanaugh explained.

"I can do all that, sir. I can churn out the reports by the book. I'm assuming we have a specific target to go after?"

"Yes, and it's a high-priority target—what appears to be an NVA division headquarters a few miles from the Duc Lap A-Team location just over the border into Cambodia. The geographical name is Nam Lyr or Lyr Mountain. It's not much of a mountain by American standards—a little over three thousand feet high. We don't have any comprehensive intelligence on the unit. What we do have is conflicting reports. There is some suggestion that the unit is not really NVA but a Chinese Communist division dressed out to appear to be NVA," Kavanaugh said. "You and Ralph will have the operational cover of being the A-Team's Civic Action unit. They have already accepted Ralph's status in the team because of his known history with Special Forces. It will be different for you. They will be suspicious of you. They will wonder what the hell someone with your lack of training is doing among them. They will assume that you are either a spook, possibly CIA, or working undercover for the Criminal Investigation Division. Ralph will be watching your back, but don't get complacent and assume that every member of the team has your best interests at heart, even the ones who start out like they're your long-lost buddy. Like I said before, paranoia can be your best friend."

Will was just sitting there trying to act calm, playing it cool, absorbing the information, nodding from time to time, but inside, a raging storm took hold. Over the past several days he had pretty much come to accept his fate of being sent out to the jungle as a bogus member of an A-Team. But now here was news that the Duc Lap A-Team was squat in the middle of some seriously deep shit. The place was teeming with Viet Cong and NVA, and his odds of survival were shrink, shrink, shrinking away. And the thick brown icing of shit on top was that he might be targeted by members of his own team.

SEVENTEEN

Will walked out of Kavanaugh's office with his head in a really bad place. Then he ran right into Brad, whose head was on the moon.

"Will, baby, just the man I need to see," he said with a happy-go-lucky grin. "Have I got the greatest opportunity of a lifetime for you. You are going to thank me and your lucky stars for the rest of your days."

"Wow, Brad, you do such a perfect imitation of a flim-flam man. I better hold on to my wallet," Will said.

"Don't be so negative. Just hear me out. I have set you up on a blind date with the most drop-dead gorgeous woman in all of Vietnam. Her name is Yvette. She's my girlfriend Brigitte's sister. She's a classic Eurasian beauty, half French, half Vietnamese," Brad said.

"Shit, Brad, I hate blind dates," Will said.

"Come on, Will. Be a good sport. Don't let me down. I have built you up so much, told them what a handsome stud you are, how fucking smart you are. I told Yvette that you graduated from UCLA. For some reason she loves UCLA. And she's a graduate of the Sorbonne in gay Paree. This has got the makings of a match made in heaven. So don't blow this. Besides, you'll make me look like an ass if you don't come along," Brad said.

"Son of a bitch, Brad, you are one hell of a guilt trip artist. Okay, okay, I'll go, but I already have a really bad feeling about this."

"Thanks, buddy, you will not be sorry. I guarantee it," Brad said.

"By the way, Brad, since we are involved in an extremely classified intel mission here, it would be good to have some background on these so-called raving beauties of yours."

"You're right. Their father is Yves Michelin, the head honcho of Michelin Tire in Indochina. He's in charge of the thirty-thousand-acre rubber plantation forty miles from here and the tire plant in Saigon. I think he's the great-grandson of the founder of Michelin," Brad said.

"Oh, shit. Didn't his wife get killed by some screwed-up napalm bombing?"

"Yeah," Brad said. "An F4 Phantom accidentally dropped a bomb near the rubber plantation where she was driving her car."

"I read about that. God, such a tragic way to lose your mother," Will said.

"Brigitte is still traumatized by it, Yvette less so," Brad said.

"I'm amazed that they want to have anything to do with Americans," Will said.

"They seem to be very forgiving people. I think it's their Catholic upbringing," Brad said.

"That is a profound level of forgiveness," Will said. The capacity to forgive is missing from my psyche, Will reflected, and in its place is a deep capacity for vengeance.

The next morning, Will was speed-reading his way through a pile of army manuals describing civic action projects in various Montagnard villages in the Central Highlands. He was able to hang in there and stay awake until past noon. Then he fell fast asleep.

Will was roused from deep slumber by Brad.

"What the fuck, I can't believe you're asleep. It's almost time to go. You have less than an hour to get ready." Brad said.

"Huh, what? Damn, you're torturing me, man."

"A date with the hottest chick in the world and you're fucking sound asleep?" Brad squealed.

"You have to be shitting me, Brad. It'll take me all of five minutes to get ready for this fucking hot date."

"I've checked out one of the jeeps," he said, waving the key at Will. "We'll leave in forty-five minutes. I don't want to be late."

At precisely 1530 hours Brad and Will departed the B-57 compound in the unmarked black Jeep. Brad was attired in his signature civvies, khakis, aloha shirt, huaraches, and panama hat. Will went all out by wearing khakis, his favorite madras shirt, and chukka boots. The traffic was moderate as they worked their way down Tran Hung Dao toward the center of Saigon. Brad wasn't driving like a madman the way he did on the ride from the 525th. He turned on to Le Duan Street, then Nguyen Binh Khiem Street, and pulled into a parking place near the entrance to the zoo.

"We're early, ten minutes to kill," Brad said.

"So, this Brigitte gal, is it true love, Brad?"

"I'd say more like true lust. When you see her, you'll understand. And Yvette is even more voluptuous."

"You are the greatest exaggerator of all time, Brad. There's no way they can be as good-looking as your hyperbolic descriptions."

"Hyper whatever the fuck that means, but you are about to find out if I'm exaggerating."

They got out of the jeep and ambled over to the zoo's main entrance. Will followed Brad to the entrance kiosk, and they bought four tickets. When they turned from the kiosk the two sisters were standing thirty feet away with lovely smiles on their faces. Will was shocked by their beauty. Brad hadn't exaggerated a bit. They were wearing matching white silk ao dai that accentuated their perfect figures. They were indeed drop-dead gorgeous.

Brad made the introductions. "Brigitte, Yvette, this is Will Parish."

"Enchante. Enchante," each sister said in turn.

"Wonderful to meet you," he said to each sister.

Yvette's beauty was more spectacular than Brigitte's but not by much. Brigitte had brown eyes and caramel-colored hair. Yvette had honey-blond hair and striking hazel eyes highlighted by flecks of gold. She was two inches taller than Brigitte with a fuller figure. Her Asian features blended magically with the Caucasian in synergistic perfection. She bore a striking resemblance to Catherine Deneuve. Her beauty was disorienting to Will. He needed to look away from her so he could think straight. This is crazy, he thought, get control of yourself.

They walked into the zoo. "Brad told me you are a graduate of UCLA," Yvette said in flawless British-accented English.

"True, and he told me you are a graduate of the Sorbonne," Will replied.

"Also true. I received my diploma in European history last June," she said

"Very interesting," Will said.

"How so? She asked.

"I, too, got my bachelor's degree in European history the previous June."

"Then we have very much in common. I am also a big fan of American basketball, and especially the UCLA Bruins championship basketball teams. My best friend attended UCLA for three years," Yvette said.

"Wow, quite a coincidence," Will said.

"Yvette," Will said softly as he stopped and turned toward her. "I just want to say how terribly sorry I am for the loss of your mother."

Yvette smiled grimly. "Thank you," she said, then she paused. "But war is hell," she added and continued walking.

As they wandered through the large mammal exhibits, Will kept picking up a strange mixed vibe from both sisters, especially from Yvette. Something wasn't quite right. There was something hidden, mysterious, and perhaps dangerous behind Yvette's lovely eyes.

Will worked to distract himself from Yvette's mesmerizing beauty by focusing on the animals. The gibbons and macaques were entertaining and distracting in the monkey house. Will attempted to lose himself in the botanical gardens to evade Yvette's strange energy. He slipped away twice, but his companions tracked him down each time.

Curiously, Yvette was keen on snakes. She led their group to the reptile house and pointed out her favorite snakes: King cobra, banded krait, green pit viper, reticulated python. She said she almost had decided on getting a degree in herpetology instead of history. Will was purposefully lagging as they started to leave the reptile pavilion. He paused to take a last glance at the King cobra. When he did, the snake moved at astonishing speed to the glass panel separating it from Will. It stood straight up, shockingly, six feet tall, eyeball to eyeball with Will, and he saw the eyes of the cobra slowly transformed into the eyes of Yvette. Will shuddered, and the hallucination was gone. I'm going stark-raving fucking mad, he whispered to himself.

After two hours of seeing nearly every attraction at the zoo, they finally walked back to the black Jeep. It was almost 1800 hours, time for dinner. They all loaded up, and Brad pulled from the curb, took a right turn on Le Duan, left on Hai Ba Trung, right on Nguyen Du to Tudo Street, and down to the edge of the Saigon River. They got out and started walking to the My Canh floating restaurant a few hundred feet away. As they strolled Yvette hooked her arm through Will's. It took all of Will's strength to continue walking smoothly as a vertiginous impulse shot through Yvette's arm to his, nearly knocking him off balance. He recovered quickly and hoped Yvette hadn't noticed his reaction. She slowed down and pulled on his arm. He turned his head toward her. She smiled flirtatiously. He conjured a smile in return.

"I'm having such a delightful time," she said. "I hope you are too."

"Yes, a sensational time," Will said a little too stiffly.

She squeezed his arm and smiled brilliantly at him. Everywhere they had gone in the zoo all of the males over the age of puberty had stared or gawked at the sisters. It was the same on the walk to the restaurant. Men were dropping their jaws and stopping in their tracks to ogle the two sisters, especially Yvette. Then Will started noticing the looks he was getting: they said, you really scored, you lucky dog. He felt like he was on a stage—and he didn't like it at all. Finally they reached the gangplank to the floating restaurant. They were led up the stairs by a young waiter to a table with a panoramic view across the Saigon River. Brad was really feeling the moment.

"I believe this occasion calls for champagne," Brad declared. "What do you say, my ladies?" The sisters giggled their agreement. Brad ordered a magnum of Bollinger. The waiter returned quickly with the magnum and four champagne flutes. He popped the cork and poured the bubbly with enthusiastic flair, showing off to the stunning sisters.

Brad rose from his chair and hoisted his glass, "I propose a toast to the beauty and charms of the Michelin sisters and this magical moment."

Will raised his glass and said, "Here, here, to great inner beauty and charm." They all downed a few sips of the bubbly.

From the moment they arrived at the My Canh, Will couldn't stop thinking about the brutal Viet Cong terrorist attack that had taken place right where they were sitting some sixteen months earlier. VC sappers detonated two powerful bombs a minute apart during the dinner hours on the twenty-fifth of June the previous year. Forty-two people, mostly Vietnamese civilians, including several women and children, were slaughtered, murdered in cold blood, that night. Will was unable to accept that any human being was capable of living with himself knowing that the blood of innocent children was on his hands. In Will's system of right and wrong any person who committed such an act was less than human, the essence of pure evil and deserving of painful annihilation.

When the sisters discovered that Brad and Will had not been introduced to Vietnamese cuisine, they ordered a variety of their traditional favorites: Pho, Banh cuon, Bun cha, Goi cuon, Banh xeo, and Mi vit tiem. Will and Brad agreed to sample them all, but Brad said he had to have an order of frog legs as a backup. For thirty or forty minutes the four of them ground their way through a full spectrum of animal protein including beef, pork, chicken, duck, fish, and prawn. Will liked all of the Viet dishes, but the frog legs, which he had never tasted, were his favorite. Brad was excited to see Will happy, so he ordered two more plates of the tender tempura battered and deep-fried delicacies and a second magnum of Bollinger to wash them down. When the waiter set the plates down on the table in front of them, Will and Brad disappeared them with gusto.

The four of them had imbibed the equivalent of four bottles of champagne in two and a half hours. The ladies were clearly tipsy, but Will and Brad were only slightly buzzed. Brad called for the check and another magnum of Bollinger for the road. Will arched an eyebrow in his direction. Brad ignored him. They placed a plethora of piastres that included a handsome tip for their waiter on the table and took their leave of the floating restaurant.

When they got back to the Jeep Yvette and Brigitte appeared to be having a disagreement over something. They went back and forth in Vietnamese for a minute. Then Yvette forced a smile and said, "Brigitte and I have decided to challenge the two of you to a contest. A game of pool. Our cousin owns a pool hall in Cholon. Brigitte and I are very good pool players. Do you accept this challenge?"

"Hell yes, and we will kick your butts," Brad blurted out boorishly.

"And you, Will, will you accept this challenge?" Yvette asked.

"But of course," he answered as the strange energy vibrated at the nape of his neck.

They climbed into the Jeep and proceeded down Tran Hung Dao with Yvette giving directions. They turned off Cholon's main drag not far from 25 P alley and worked their way through a series of back streets with very little traffic. They pulled up in front of an unkempt concrete-block building that had a small blinking neon sign with two crossed pool cues. It read PHONG BI-A. They went inside. Brad and the girls moved to the bar. Will hesitated. His sixth sense was telling him to get the fuck out of here. All of the clientele were Asian, no round eyes except Will and Brad. A husky, swarthy Vietnamese man came from behind the bar and greeted the girls warmly with hugs. Yvette introduced him as Dung to Will and Brad.

"Xin chao," he said without warmth as he shook hands. He led the four to a pool table at the back of the hall. A set of pool balls were racked on the table and waiting for a game of eight ball. There were more than twenty young Vietnamese men playing pool who gazed at them with lust in their eyes for the sisters and profound hostility toward the two round eyes.

Yvette short-circuited the negative energy by announcing, "Normally, we would lag to see who will break the rack, but I assume true gentlemen like you and Brad will insist on ladies first. Therefore I will start the game by breaking the rack," she said with a surprisingly competitive edge to her voice. She carefully pulled the triangle away from the cluster of fifteen pool balls and selected a cue from the wall. She chalked the tip slowly then leaned over to line up her cue on the white cue ball. There was absolute dead silence as every set of eyeballs in the pool hall watched Yvette. She thrust the cue powerfully, and the triangle of balls exploded across the table. A solid and a stripe dropped into the two side pockets. A round of cheers erupted from the two dozen gawking horny Vietnamese spectators. Son of a bitch, Will thought, she isn't just gorgeous but a fucking pool shark as well. She ran the table and broke a second rack. She was halfway through running the table again when her luck ran out.

Brad was up next. Will was a better than average pool player and a very streaky one at that, but Brad was much, much better. He ran the table in short order amid a continuous chorus of hissing and booing from the hostile Vietnamese men. Brad ran two more racks before he faltered. The angry spectators were pounding their cues in threatening gestures to distract Brad, and they finally succeeded. Will sensed the strange energy powering up within his skeletal system. He visualized having to use the fat end of his pool cue like a baseball bat, launching dozens of young male Vietnamese heads through the pool hall's plate glass windows for tape-measure home runs.

Brigitte's turn. The angry crowd settled down. Brigitte ran the table and finished out the game. She was quite good, better than Will, but not in the same league with Brad and her sister. She almost ran a second table but missed her final shot on the eight ball. Will took over and won the game. He and Brad were up four to two. He broke the next rack and failed to pocket a ball. Yvette again. She ran the table and another. Now they were tied.

Brad slipped out to the Jeep and brought back his magnum of champagne. Before Yvette broke the next rack, he unwound the foil and wire from the top of the bottle, and the cork blew out like a gunshot. Twenty Vietnamese pussies hit the hardwood floor, scared shitless. Brad took a long pull from the bottle then offered it to the girls. Brigitte declined, but Yvette took a hefty sip. She handed it to Will who took a short swill.

The battle raged on for another hour, the advantage seesawing back and forth and the feeling Will got from the crowd getting uglier and uglier. The girls were ahead of the guys now nine to eight. The Bollinger magnum was empty. It was well past twenty-three hundred hours, over an hour past closing. Dung, the proprietor, started moving the spectators through the front door. They didn't want to leave. But Dung was aggressively forceful, and they departed grudgingly in twos and fours until there were only Dung and the four contestants inside the pool hall. Will excused himself to use the pissoir. When he returned, the sisters and Dung were nowhere to be seen. Brad was lying unconscious on the floor. The two KGB thugs from 25 P Alley were standing over him, Makarov pistols in their hands aimed casually at the center of Will's torso.

"So again we meet, Case Officer Parish," said the heavier and uglier of the two through the cruelest of grins and the thickest Russian accent Will had ever heard. "No friend to save you this time. You fall for honey pot with pretty girl? Ha. We have dossier on you with picture." He pulled a photo from his coat pocket and held it out to Will. "You, friend Landau on street, front of Fort Holabird. Baltimore, area studies, spy school." Will was shocked to see a grainy photo of himself and Rob Landau walking down the sidewalk of the main drag, North Dundalk, that ran next to Holabird. The strange energy burgeoned inside Will. The violet-purple rage bloomed. The blackout vertigo moment came and went in a heartbeat.

In a crazy, slow, twisted Slavic accent the thickset, ugly Russian said, "You come with us now for, how you say, hostile interrogation."

The two goons continued to aim their Russian pistols at him. Will raised both of his hands to his waist and formed his index fingers and thumbs into the shape of pistols. He whispered, "Bang, bang, you're dead and gone."

With a deafening roar, lightning bolts shot from Will's fingers, sending the two KGB agents into a swirl of flames. They gyred tightly one into the other until they disappeared into a bright red speck. Will marveled at the way he had actually disappeared them, just like that, without a trace. Then he dropped to the floor to check Brad's condition. He was alive, had a strong pulse. Will gently probed the back of Brad's head, which prompted a groan. Brad had a goose egg but not much blood. Then he groaned again louder.

"What the fuck happened?" Brad said. "Don't tell me I got coldcocked by a goddamn slope in a fucking pool hall."

"I'm afraid that is exactly what I'm going to tell you, Brad."

"Son of a bitch. What the hell did I get hit with?"

"Now that's the fucking irony, Brad. It was that empty Bollinger magnum. One of those horny fuckers nailed you with it," Will dissembled. "But the good news is I fucked him and his friends up much worse. I'm a lethal weapon with a pool cue in my hands."

Will helped Brad get up from the floor and steered him out to the Jeep and into the passenger seat. He got the keys and started the engine.

"Hey, what happened to our beautiful babes?" Brad asked groggily.

"They flew the coop just before you got coldcocked. They set us up, Brad."

EIGHTEEN

During the next week Will was subjected to an academic regimen of lectures and reading. One topic was the organizational history of Special Forces and its early role in Southeast Asia. Another was the history and culture of the Montagnard tribal peoples of the Central Highlands of Vietnam, Cambodia, and Laos. All of the officers and several of the NCOs of B-57 took turns to prepare him for his date with destiny among the Rhade, Jarai, Bahnar, and Mnong tribes sprinkled in and around Duc Lap. Before the segment on Montagnard culture, Will had made the erroneous assumption that the Nungs who provided physical security for B-57 were just another one of the dozens of mountain tribes of the Central Highlands. How wrong he was.

The Nungs were something altogether different from the Montagnards. They had a reputation among Special Forces as being the fiercest warriors in Vietnam. Nungs were descendants of the Zhuang people from Southern China who had been persecuted by various Chinese ruling dynasties over the centuries. This persecution resulted in their eventual migration to the highlands of North Vietnam, where their numbers grew to a few hundred thousand. When the Communists under Ho Chi Minh finally defeated the French in 1954, Nungs who had served as mercenaries for the French migrated into South Vietnam by the tens of thousands. The Green Berets discovered them in the early 1960s and recognized in them a keen sense of loyalty and fierceness in battle. They were avidly recruited by Special Forces for their elite MIKE Forces, for special STRIKE Force teams, and for installation security anywhere the Green Berets set up operations. The Nungs were a little taller and a bit more physically imposing than the typical South

Vietnamese or Montagnard tribesman.

One thing the Montagnards and Nungs had in common was persecution and displacement by neighboring and invading cultures that far outnumbered them. For a thousand years or so the Degar, as they were called before the French dubbed them the Montagnards, consisted of a few dozen tribes who resided peacefully in the lowlands and coastal areas of Vietnam. These tribes were descended from Malay–Polynesian and Mon–Khmer language family cultures. Toward the end of the ninth century, the Cham people of Cambodia invaded the coastal areas of Vietnam and pushed most of the Degar tribes into the Central Highlands of Vietnam. Some pockets of Degar held out into the late seventeenth century in the southern coastal region until they and the Cham were forced out by ethnic Vietnamese. These Degar tribes also fled to the Central Highlands, where they and the earlier Degar refugees remained relatively unmolested by the Vietnamese well into the twentieth century. Their state of sanctuary had a lot to do with the long-held Vietnamese belief that the highlands were inhabited by evil spirits who poisoned the upland streams with the agent that caused malaria.

For more than a thousand years the Degar tribes were relatively insulated and thrived in a culture of animistic belief, slash-and-burn agriculture, and hunting and fishing. In the 1870s the French first began to explore the little-known upland areas of Vietnam, which led to the eventual economic exploitation of the Central Highlands through the establishment of mining operations and rubber, tea, and coffee plantations. Because of these economic pursuits the French unwittingly opened the door to the twentieth-century "Vietnamization" of what was once an exclusively Degar tribal area. Enmity between the two cultures grew quickly. Vietnamese viewed the Montagnards as backward and uncivilized and referred to them derogatorily as *moi,* meaning savage. The more Will read and learned about the antagonistic relationship between the Vietnamese and Montagnards, the more he was struck by the similarity of their history to the American experience with the decimation and displacement of its indigenous tribal people by white European settlement and migratory expansion.

During one of his Montagnard history lessons with Kavanaugh, Will learned that there was a general bias among Special Forces personnel against the Vietnamese and a sympathetic one toward the Yards. This bias had a lot to do with the way the Army of the Republic of Vietnam (ARVN) rank and file persecuted and exploited Yard soldiers and their dependents. Another factor was the tendency for Vietnamese combat units to avoid joint operations with American forces if there was a high probability of combat. Conversely, the Yards never tried to avoid combat when they were joined in force with American units.

"It's important that you know the restrictions that Special Forces have to put up with in our so-called advisory status in the A-Team at Duc Lap, Will," Kavanaugh had told him. "You're going to see some shit out there that is really going to piss you off. You just have to bite your tongue and go along with the program. The A-Team captain isn't really in charge at Duc Lap. The real camp commander is the Vietnamese Special Forces *dai uy*, or captain. He is technically in charge, although he won't make any significant operational decision without the American captain's blessing. Just like the A-Team's twelve Green Berets, there are twelve Red Berets, the Vietnamese Special Forces, or LLDB, that are partnered or counterparted with the Americans.

"You won't see them very much. They keep to themselves in their team house or hooches. They never go out on ambush, search and destroy, or reconnaissance operations. They leave the dangerous work to the Americans and the Yards. Used to be about the only time you would see them was once a month on payday when they performed the ritual of handing out the payroll piastres to the three or four hundred Yard CIDG troops that defend the camp. CIDG stands for civilian irregular defense group. There was a time when the LLDB made a contest out of stealing most of the CIDG payroll that was supplied by the Special Forces by shorting each man's pay envelope. When the Americans discovered this practice, they made the LLDB *dai uy* sit at a table side by side with the Special Forces team captain and count out the piastres as they were handed to each Yard soldier. Finally the LLDB commander refused to participate and left handing out pay to the American team," Kavanaugh said.

"If all the Vietnamese are like that it makes the odds against winning the war awful steep, doesn't it?" Will said in response.

"Yes, it would if all of the Vietnamese were like that. But there are some good Viet officers and soldiers here and there, although they're definitely in the minority. And there just might be enough of them around to make a difference. I'll tell you a story about an incident a couple of years back near Duc Lap that will give you a deeper understanding of Montagnard–Vietnamese animosity. Back in the late 1950s, the Montagnard tribes in the highlands area of Vietnam, Cambodia, and Laos created an organization to fight for an independent nation, the United Front for the Liberation of the Oppressed Races, FULRO. The leaders of FULRO had encouraged their supporters to join Special Forces CIDG groups to receive combat training and get arms and ammunition. After many years of mistreatment at the hands of the Vietnamese Special Forces, the CIDG members, with coordination from FULRO, started a rebellion in five A-Team detachments in the highlands. The Yards disarmed all of the American team members and locked them in their team houses. Then they took the LLDB team members prisoner.

In the A-Team camp at Buon Sar Pa, about two and a half miles from the Duc Lap camp where you'll be going, the Yards went rogue. Their rage was uncontrollable, and they slaughtered nine members of the LLDB team, cut them up in little chunks, and tossed them in the garbage pit. The uprising got the Yards a lot of attention and a directive from the brass in Saigon to the local-level Vietnamese command structure to treat them with respect for their unique customs. There were some improvements in their treatment, but not enough to make a lasting difference. The Buon Sar Pa camp was closed down quickly after the insurrection, and it was replaced by Duc Lap A-239, your next port of call. The point I'm making here, Parish, is that there is some serious, nasty, deep-shit hatred between the Yards and the Viets. So don't get caught up in the middle of it—keep your distance and watch your back. Stay paranoid," cautioned the lieutenant.

Will didn't say anything. Kavanaugh seemed to be expecting a response. Will just wanted to internalize his response. He thought, Yeah, I'll do that, stay paranoid, as if there were some new quantum level of paranoia he could climb to. His paranoia and anxiety were already explosive enough that with the right ignition, he could be launched to the moon.

"Are you OK, Will? Are you going to be able to handle this?"

"Yes, I'm OK," he lied.

Will's next block of instruction gave him everything he'd ever hoped to know about the history of the Green Berets and their role in Vietnam. Among many arcane and forgettable chunks of data, he learned how the Special Forces had its origin in the same place as the Central Intelligence Agency— namely, the Office of Strategic Services (OSS) during World War II. Basically, the OSS wrote the book on unconventional warfare, which became the cornerstone of Special Forces operations. The Tenth Special Forces Group was established in 1952 as part of the Psychological Warfare Group under a former OSS officer, Colonel Aaron Bank.

The early focus of Special Forces training was on all phases of unconventional warfare. The reason for the unit's existence, in Bank's own words, was "to infiltrate by land, sea, or air, deep into enemy-occupied territory, and organize the resistance/guerrilla potential to conduct Special Forces operations, with emphasis on guerrilla warfare." By 1958 the basic operational unit of Special Forces had evolved into today's twelve-man team of two officers, an operations sergeant, an intelligence sergeant, two weapons sergeants, two communications sergeants, two medics, and two engineers, all cross-trained in one another's specialties.

When John F. Kennedy became president in January 1961, the Special Forces were actively engaged in missions around the globe. JFK was an ardent admirer of the Special Forces and lionized them for what he envisioned as their future role in antiguerrilla counterinsurgency. At the beginning of JFK's brief presidency, there were three Special Forces Groups: First, Seventh, and Tenth. Under his direction, the Pentagon expanded the total to seven with the creation of the Fifth, Eighth, Sixth, and Third, in that order. The assassination of JFK in 1963 played a pivotal role in elevating Green Berets to near mythological warrior status. JFK had ordered the army to restore the previously banned Green Beret for the exclusive use of Special Forces as "a symbol of one of the highest levels of courage and achievement of the United States Military."

By the time Will was transferred to B-57 at the end of October 1966, there were more than 250 Special Forces outposts, mostly A-Teams, all over the remotest areas of Vietnam conducting counterinsurgency operations with some sixty thousand CIDG forces made up of Yards, Nungs, and Cao Dai warriors. Thousands more were involved in civic-action projects such as building schools, hospitals, and government offices and digging wells.

Will endured sixty or so mostly tedious hours of instruction and had to read dozens of pamphlets, journals, and binders about the indigenous peoples of the Central Highlands and Special Forces history and organization. Then, the time had drawn near to dispatch Will to Duc Lap. All of his training was complete with one notable exception. He wasn't airborne-qualified. It was the one part of the training program that he had dreaded the most: every time the idea of jump school came into his mind his guts started clenching and churning, and it was all he could do to hold off the panic attack. Toward the end of his training Colonel Mahoney told Will he had decided against sending him to jump school because of the urgent need to get him to Duc Lap to produce reliable intel on the NVA division on Lyr Mountain.

Just when it seemed to be settled that Will was going to dodge the jump-school bullet, Captain Michaels made an impassioned effort to persuade the colonel otherwise. The captain argued that it was a travesty to send Will into the A-Team as a so-called "leg"—the airborne soldiers' dismissive term for anyone who hadn't gone through jump school.

"We can't send Parish out to Duc Lap and expect him to overcome the stigma that goes with being a leg," Captain Michaels said. "Any self-respecting Green Beret can sniff out a leg from a mile away. I'm in contact with an old friend who's the American jumpmaster assigned to the Dong Ba Thin jump school. He is willing to put Will through a three-day training cycle that will get him his wings. I think it's the right thing to do. What do you say, Colonel?"

"Well, I have my doubts about the importance of his airborne status, Bert, but if you feel that strongly, I'll go along with it. Still, I'm having a hard time picturing that young man jumping out of an airplane in three days when it's a challenge for most men to deal with it in three weeks," said Colonel Mahoney.

"Thank you, sir. I believe it's for the best. That lad is made of a lot grittier stuff than meets the eye. He'll come out of Dong Ba Thin a lot tougher, and it will make his reception in the A-Team a whole lot more hospitable. I'll get him to Nha Trang bright and early tomorrow and have him back here the day before Thanksgiving. We have him scheduled to head out to Duc Lap the day after Turkey Day so he'll still be on schedule," Captain Michaels said.

"Well, then, there it is," said the colonel.

When Captain Michaels replayed for Will his conversation with the colonel later that day, Will came close to experiencing liftoff from planet Earth. The fight-or-flight adrenaline surge almost shut him down. He fought back the panic attack.

"You don't seem very excited about this incredible opportunity, Will," the captain said.

"Believe me, captain, you could say that this may be the most excited I've ever been in my life, more exciting than when I enlisted in the army, more exciting than when I got my orders for Vietnam," Will said.

"Are you fucking with me, soldier?" he asked.

"Not at all, sir, it's the absolute truth."

"All right then, get your gear packed after dinner and go to bed early. I'm going to take you to Nha Trang and Dong Ba Thin myself to introduce you to your private jumpmaster. We leave at zero four thirty to catch a Huey out of Tan Son Nhut," the captain said.

NINETEEN

Will said very few words on the jeep drive to Tan Son Nhut and even fewer on the chopper ride to Nha Trang. Captain Michaels carried the conversation, while Will mostly nodded and repeated, "Yes, sir." They dined at the Fifth Special Forces C Team headquarters mess before catching their ride to Dong Ba Thin. The captain cleaned his plate of SOS, scrambled eggs, and sausage. Will struggled to force down a couple of bites of egg with his black coffee.

"What the hell happened to your appetite, Will? You didn't have dinner last night, and now you're eating next to nothing for breakfast. You better chow down while you have the chance. I hear the food sucks at the Viet airborne school—lots of dog and monkey," Michaels said, laughing.

"I've decided to slip into my mean and lean persona, captain. I won't be eating much for the next three days. It will help me focus my energy and discipline for leaping out of a plane," he lied.

"Suit yourself, Parish. I hope that works for you."

The captain arranged transport by jeep south to Dong Ba Thin. The driver was a reed-thin speedy four who was even less talkative than Will. After they passed through the garrison security gate, Will saw dozens of tiger-striped soldiers in red berets, the Vietnamese Special Forces official headgear. The driver stopped his jeep in front of the Quonset-style HQ building. The captain told Will to wait while he went inside to get the jumpmaster. A few minutes passed, and the captain came out of the building with a tall, handsome, muscular black master sergeant who bore a striking resemblance to the actor Woody Strode. Gladiatorial images of Kirk Douglas as Spartacus battling Draba in the Roman Coliseum danced across Will's mind.

"Sergeant Will Parish, meet your jumpmaster, Master Sergeant Wilbur Jones," Captain Michaels said. The two sergeants looked each other in the eye, took each other's measure, and shook hands. The jumpmaster's hand was half again the size of Will's, and he shook his hand with the force of a vise grip. Will was prepared and squeezed back with all his strength.

"Good grip for a fuckinleg, Parish. And when you spell *fuckinleg*, it's all one word," he said, laughing out loud as he released Will's hand. "What we will do for the next three days, if you're man enough, if your balls are big enough, is turn you into an airborne studley-do-right, a real fuckin' paratrooper, and no longer will you be a lowly fuckinleg. It ain't gonna be easy. I'm gonna ride you like a fuckin' donkey and bust your lily-white ass sixteen ways from Sunday. You're gonna hurt like you've never hurt before. What do you say about that, fuckinleg?" he said with the biggest shit-eating grin Will had ever seen.

Will couldn't help himself. He laughed cathartically, explosively, and said, "Bring it on jumpmaster, bring it on." Will instantly loved this guy. He was pure magic, bigger than life.

"That's the spirit, white boy. That's what I need to hear you say, fuckinleg." He turned to Captain Michaels, winked, and said, "You know, you know this just might work . . . this fuckin' craziness just might work."

Will pulled his gear from the jeep. Captain Michaels grabbed Will by the shoulders and said, "This is a once in a lifetime opportunity, Parish. You jump through every hoop he gives you without thinking. Don't let me down. I'm counting on you."

He turned to the jumpmaster. "I really appreciate you doing this for me, Wilbur. I owe you big."

"Not at all, Bert, not at all. What goes around, comes around, you know." They shook hands and did a kind of half-assed, hope-no-one-is-looking hug. When the captain got halfway into the jeep he turned to Jones and said, "I'll be back in three days unless I hear from you sooner."

"You got it."

It was a few days later that Will learned that Bert and Wilbur had grown up in the same household and were both raised by Wilbur's mother. Bert's father was seventeen years older than his young bride. He was forty-five when his wife died giving birth to Bert. Wilbur's mother, Ramona, was the full-time cook and housekeeper in the Michaels home in the old-money Houston neighborhood of River Oaks. When Bert's mother died, Wilbur was four months old and living with his mother in the caretaker house behind the sprawling Tudor mansion of the Michaels estate. Ramona was raised as a strict Southern Baptist, and she raised Wilbur and Bert accordingly. She was a loving mother to both of them, but a strict adherent to the school of tough love. The boys rarely stepped out of line.

Will and the jumpmaster watched as the jeep pulled away.

"What're you gawking at, fuckinleg? Follow me," he barked and took off running at a near sprint. Will chased after him as fast as he was capable and barely kept up. The jumpmaster stopped at a metal-roofed, sandbag-bunkered hooch and threw open the door. He pointed to a bunk and told Will to toss his gear there. He rushed back outside with Will in tow.

"All right, a little PT time for you, fuckinleg—get down and give me a quick fifty push-ups. Count 'em out loud."

Will obliged him with a smile.

"OK, white boy, so you can do a few push-ups. Now give me twenty burpees."

Will obliged him again, minus the smile.

"Now we're going to get you warmed up before the shit hits the proverbial fan. We're going to run a little five-miler. I'll set the pace. And fuckinleg, you better keep up with me, or we'll know this is a lost cause."

He took off with Will at his side, running at a pace that Will knew he couldn't sustain for five miles. But after a few minutes, the jumpmaster's breathing got ragged, and he slowed down to an almost manageable seven-and-a-half-minute-mile pace. A couple of miles farther and he picked up the pace again, and Will was challenged to match it. After a few minutes, it became apparent to Will that the jumpmaster was struggling as much as he was to maintain the faster pace, and he backed it off again. Will figured out that Jones was trying to break him early and send him back to B-57 still a leg. About a mile later they came to a gradual rise leading to a small hill that ascended for a quarter of a mile or so. Jones started pushing the pace again. Will began to fall behind.

"Don't you be fallin' behind, fuckinleg white boy, or there'll be hell to pay!"

Will dug deep and stayed within a few yards. Near the top of the hill, Jones was gasping, and Will caught up. As they descended, both gradually recovered their wind.

"OK, white boy, half a mile to go. Let's see what you're made of." He headed off at a full sprint. Will stayed at his own pace and let the jumpmaster take off like a jackrabbit. No way he can maintain that, Will thought hopefully. He's going to hit the wall in a minute or so and then I'll reel him back in like a great black whale. After a minute Will started to worry, as Jones increased his lead to thirty yards. Then, finally, the jumpmaster hit his wall and started to stagger. Will began gaining on him, twenty, fifteen, ten, five yards. When they were a hundred yards from the gate, Will realized he had enough in the tank to break into a sprint. He went flying by his spent tormentor like in a scene from the tortoise and the hare.

"See ya, jumpmaster," Will spat out laughing as he powered by him.

"You better run, fuckinleg, you better run," Jones gasped after him.

Will stopped at the gate to wait for him. Then they were both leaning over with their hands on their knees, gasping for air. When he got his wind back, the jumpmaster stood up with that big grin and said, "You're way too cocky for a white boy, fuckinleg. Now you go back and run the course the other way" as he pointed Will in the direction they had just come from.

"Oh, shit!" Will cried.

"Yeah, 'Oh, shit' sounds about right. Let's see how cocky you are when your fuckinwhiteleg ass comes draggin' back in here."

Will started to jog in that direction. "I said run not jog, boy. Now you get your white ass runnin'."

Will tried to speed up, but there was nothing left in his tank. Jones kept shouting, "Faster, faster, fuckinleg," as he burst out in laughter. Will could not keep from grinning through his pain as he jogged away. When he finally made it back to where he'd started from over an hour later, he saw the jumpmaster sitting in a chair in the shade of a tree near the camp's entrance. He was holding an oversize glass of what appeared to be lemonade. There was plenty more in a glass pitcher on a small table next to him. He slurped noisily from his full glass with dramatic flair.

"Mmm, mmm, mmm, this lemonade sure is delicious. You must be almost dying of thirst after your ten-miler, fuckinleg. And forgetful ol' inconsiderate me, I forgot to bring a glass for you. Oh, well, what the hell, if you don't mind drinkin' out of a black man's glass, I guess I can share mine with you. But you best understand how hard it is for me to share my glass with a fuckinleg and a white one at that."

He finished off his glass, refilled it, and handed it over to Will, studying him closely. Will took the glass in his hands without hesitation and said, "Thank you, jumpmaster. I'll try real hard not to get any of my fuckinleg white boy cooties on your pristine, immaculate glass." Then he chugged it down.

From that moment on, Jones's edge seemed to lose its sharpness. Will had the feeling that the man was actually pulling for him to succeed; that he, like Will, couldn't help but like the other guy, no matter how adversarial and antagonistic their roles were supposed to be. But none of that prevented Jones from opening up one after another of his good-natured cans of whoop-ass on Will over the next three days.

Will had arrived at jump school without a sense of how he would become airborne-qualified and get his wings. If he had given it any rational thought—something other than his cowering, scared-shitless thought processes about being forced to jump out of a plane—he would have expected to learn how to put on a parachute and how to land without becoming an invalid. If he had thought it through, he would have expected his instructor to demonstrate how it's done several times and then have Will do it until he got it right. Day one had already started out to be a horror story. He had never run farther than five miles in his life; ten miles was insane. His ass was seriously dragging. It was ten in the morning, and he had yet to see a parachute.

"OK, fuckinleg, listen up. The real torture process is about to begin. Running ten miles this morning was just a little taste of what is to come. The powers that be at your undercover spy outfit somehow pulled strings and got you orders from on high in MACV, from General Westmoreland himself, in fact, to put you through jump school in three days time. I've seen a whole lot of stupid shit in this man's army, but this sets a new record for dumbfuckery. Getting your ass jump-ready in less than forty-eight hours is going to take an act of God. And throwing your leg ass out the back of the plane five times in one day is going take five more acts of God. Now it's time for a reality check. Jump school is a three-week course. Week one is groundwork week. We've got about seven hours left of daylight today to cram in forty hours of groundwork training. The biggest problem I have is deciding whether it's better to strap a parachute on your back and just kick your sorry fuckin' whiteleg ass out the back of the plane with no training. I'm thinking that training you is just going to confuse you, leg. Training, no training, I'm thinking that the odds of you surviving are about fifty-fifty either way," he said, with that ever-expanding shit-eating grin of his.

As scared shitless as he was, Will couldn't help but return the grin. "OK, then, do we kill me off with training or without training? That seems to be the big question. I vote for no training. Let's end it quickly."

"That's the spirit, leg, that's the spirit. That shows me you got some fight in your ass after all!" He roared with laughter. "Much as we agree on no training, I'm afraid I have no choice. If we killed your worthless leg ass off without training, my ass would be grass. We're going to have to do the training. That way we kill you by US Army regulations, meaning the scheduled third day of training," he said through that infectious grin.

"That's good, master sergeant, because the last thing in the world I'd want to do is get your ass in trouble with the US Army," Will said in mock seriousness while returning the grin.

"You need to know, whiteleg, just how much of a silver lining you're getting in this shortened training, because there's not enough time for me to give you all the bad shit and harassment you deserve. Don't get me wrong. You're gonna catch the fullest ration of shit possible from me until you get out of here. But it's clear to me you've got no problem with physical fitness other than you being a fuckinleg. Now it's time to test your manhood."

For the next seven hours, with just a ten-minute break to consume a lunch of army C rations that oddly tasted pretty damned good right then, Jones made Will jump off everything but the kitchen sink. He jumped from chairs, benches, trash cans, barstools, stacks of pallets, loading docks, barracks porches, railings, and finally, toward the end of the day, the school's jump platform. Jones demonstrated the techniques of the drop, the fall, and the landing, and Will repeated them over and over until he mastered them. When they finally moved to the two-foot platform, Will jumped so many dozens of times executing various parachute landing falls (PLFs) that his leg muscles turned into rubber. Every one of his five precious bodily points of contact was calling out in agony.

They took a ten-minute "smoke 'em if you got 'em" break. Then they moved to the lateral drift apparatus. Jones enlisted the assistance of two young LLDB NCOs to assist with rope pulling and PLFs with this device. They yanked him and jerked him every which way but loose for an hour and finally gave it up when Will couldn't lift himself off the ground. This was cause for another ten-minute break. When there was about an hour of light remaining before sundown, they were joined by two more red-bereted jump school cadres. Then Jones introduced Will to the swing-landing trainer and gave him his first taste of a parachute harness. He outfitted him with the harness and a reserve parachute on his chest. One of the Vietnamese cadres demonstrated the proper technique of lift up and jump off from the edge of the platform. Then he walked Will out to the edge of the twelve-foot platform and directed him drop off the edge with Jones controlling his rate of descent with a rope. He did this over and over executing front, side, and rear PLFs until the last light of dusk expired and forced them to give it up for the day. Thank God, Will said to himself because his body was toast.

"Time to grab some chow, fuckinleg," Jones said. He motioned Will to follow him to the airborne school mess hall. Will followed him stiffly, moving like an old man with full body pain. When they got to the mess hall, the place was empty. Jones told Will to sit at a nearby table while he proceeded through the swinging doors to the kitchen. He came back shortly carrying two foil-covered trays. He set them on the table and sat down across from Will. He yanked the foils off the trays. The aromas wafting off the food made him salivate. There was a generous size bowl of steamed rice on each tray and a plate of stir-fried meat and veggies. Will was ravenously hungry. He was salivating so heavily that he actually had drool running from the corners of his mouth like some Charles Dickens character. He waited for the jumpmaster to dig in. Jones grabbed his chopsticks and dug in voraciously.

"Pork or chicken?" Will asked hopefully.

Jones paused and studied him for several seconds, narrowing his eyes. "No, no, I'm thinking it tastes more like dog, maybe monkey or rat."

The look on Will's face must have been something to behold because the jumpmaster exploded with laughter spitting a partial mouthful of food across the table. "Goddammit, you fuckin' finicky eatin' fuckinleg. You think I'd be eating this if it was dog, or monkey, or rat? Shit, white boy, get over yourself and eat the fucking food before you starve to death."

Will attacked the bowl of rice. He didn't even take the paper off his chopsticks. He used them as a dozer blade pushing rice into his mouth from the edge of the bowl as fast as he could swallow it. He poured the stir-fry over the rice and dozered that into his mouth as well. From what little he could actually taste, he was pretty sure it was pork.

By the time Will got back to his hooch, it was pitch dark. His exhaustion was so extreme that he had barely enough energy to get his boots, socks, and fatigues off. He was asleep before his head hit the pillow.

Early the next morning before the sun began to shine, Will was roused from sleep by Jones's booming baritone. "Fuckinleg, get your sorry white ass out of bed! You've got five minutes to get out the door. We're taking a little run, loosen your ass up before the shit hits the fan."

Every cell in Will's body cried out in agony as he attempted to sit up on the edge of his bunk. Jones was standing in the open doorway. There was no sign of dawn behind him. Will pulled on his jungle fatigue pants and socks. He winced in pain with the effort of getting his lightweight jungle boots on and tied. As soon as he made it through the door, Jones took off running. Will took off in pursuit, but each stride made him want to shriek at the top of his lungs to offset the pain in his legs and glutes. He couldn't keep up with Jones until well after the first mile. Then the adrenaline-endorphin cocktail started to kick in, allowing him to catch up slowly with his tormentor. Jones remained uncharacteristically silent for the duration of the run. He made no attempt to take off in a sprint. Their pace was mercifully slower than the day before. They were both sweating profusely when they reached the steps of the mess hall. Their breakfast consisted of several cups of weak coffee followed by a couple of generous bowls of pork-fried rice laced with scrambled eggs. Will was granted fifteen minutes to shit, shave, shower, brush teeth, and, in the words of the jumpmaster, "to pray for the mercy of the almighty to get your white ass through this day in the valley of the shadow of death," before his second day of torture began.

When Will stepped through the door of his hooch fifteen minutes later, he could see the edge of the sun rising out of the South China Sea over the jumpmaster's shoulder. "Well, fuckinleg, it's time to put you through a day that'll make yesterday seem like you were playing patty-cakes. We're going to repeat everything we did yesterday, except in half the time," Jones said with the usual toothy grin.

Will managed a smile and said without much conviction, "Bring it on, jumpmaster. Bring it on."

For the next four hours, Jones had Will jumping off everything that he could access. He ran him mercilessly through the full spectrum of the day before at breakneck speed including the same chairs, benches, trash cans, barstools, stacked pallets, loading docks, porches, and railings and then added fence posts, boulders, and a shed roof. The pace was frenetic, and Jones never stopped critiquing his technique.

"You're fuckin' up. You're fuckin' up, leg. Too much anticipatin'. Too much anticipatin', leg. Keep your fuckin' knees together. Feet too fuckin' far apart. Too much hesitatin'. Too much hesitatin', leg. Stop leanin' forward," Jones barked incessantly.

Then it was on to the two-foot platform. Will's calves and quads were burning. The lactic acid was building up and had a tight grip on him. Jones never stopped pushing him. Just when he was tapped out with his legs turning to rubber and he was ready to take a header, Jones finally gave him a ten-minute break.

Next was the lateral drift apparatus with several dozen repetitions until Will's legs rubberized again. After a five-minute break, they moved to the twelve-foot tower with the swing landing trainer where they were joined by five Vietnamese red berets who served as the holdmen, the two ropemen, and the unhookman. Jones had one of the holdmen demonstrate the pull-up and jump from the edge of the platform. Then Jones helped Will strap on a harness and a reserve parachute with one of the ropemen's assistance. One ropeman attached the risers to the D rings on Will's harness and handed the rope to the other ropeman while maintaining tension on Will's risers. Jones took the rope from the ropeman in the pit and called "Clear the platform" then gave the rope a firm tug. Will landed and rolled ad infinitum for nearly an hour and absorbed extreme verbal abuse from the jumpmaster on his technique and his status as a complete spastic basket case in the world of parachute skills. After a while, Will couldn't hear the abuse. He became an automaton. Unhooking and running up the steps of the platform and rehooking and landing and rolling on command from Jones. After what seemed like fifty repetitions Will's legs finally gave out ascending the steps of the platform and, losing his balance, he tumbled head over heels backward down the steps. His parachute pack and helmet saving him from a broken neck or fractured skull.

Will was lying at the bottom of the steps, and Jones was standing over him with an expression on his face that had a hint of sympathy.

"You OK, leg?"

"Yeah, nothing broken," Will said.

Then Jones burst out in laughter and said, "If you ain't the sorriest sack-of-shit excuse for a soldier I have ever seen in this man's army."

Will struggled to gain his feet. Jones, still laughing his ass off, reached a hand down to help him up. The jumpmaster's mirth was infectious, and Will started laughing himself. Jones's laughter turned uproarious, and he started staggering around, losing control like a drunkard. Then something broke loose in Will, and he started laughing almost hysterically and so hard that he lost his balance and collapsed to the ground. Then Jones saw Will on the ground exploding with laughter, and he too went down for the count, gasping in paroxysms of laughter. Neither one could stop laughing and, try though they did, neither one could stand up. Just when it seemed that they were starting to gain control, they looked at each other and started shrieking in laughter all over again. Another thing that fueled their laughter was the Vietnamese Special Forces cadres, each one just staring at the two of them stone-faced, disdainful, and not amused. Every time they saw the Vietnamese in their red berets looking down at them in confusion, it prompted a new round of uncontrolled laughter.

When the Vietnamese finally walked away shaking their heads, the two men were able to lift themselves off the ground and, by avoiding eye contact with each other, gain some small degree of control. They sat down on the platform stairs. It was lunchtime. Jones pulled C rations out of his rucksack and handed one to Will without looking at him. Then he produced two canteens of lemonade and set one of them on the stairs next to Will, who opened his immediately and started chugging.

Jones reached over with his massive hand to angle Will's canteen down and said, "Slow down, leg. You don't want that coming back up when you start runnin' the gauntlet again."

But they both wolfed down their C rations faster than they should have. Canned beans and wieners never tasted so good. Hardtack biscuits, cheddar cheese, and pound cake followed, all down the hatch in two minutes flat. Will could have easily eaten two or three more, but it would have been a big mistake. When they had finished eating, they proceeded to the thirty-four-foot tower for Will's final phase of training before jumping out of a plane.

"If we were back at Fort Benning in the land of the big PX you might have gotten to jump off the 250-foot tower. Don't have a 250 here at slope jump school," Jones said as they approached the thirty-four-foot tower. "We've got about three or four hours to teach you how to jump out of a plane without killing yourself."

They climbed the steps of the five-story tower. Seven or eight red-bereted LLDB were spread out between the base and the top of the tower. Jones greeted them in Vietnamese. When they got to the top of the stairs, Jones led him to an opening that looked like the open back hatch of an airplane. An

LLDB sergeant was standing near the opening. He was wearing a full jump harness assembly attached to four straps hanging from a metal bar five or six feet above his head.

"All right, leg, Sergeant Trung here is going to show you how it's done."

Jones directed Trung to demonstrate the body posture and movement to prepare to leap from the mock door of the simulated aircraft. Trung did so over and over and over. Jones called out "stand by" and then "go," and Trung finally leapt from the door and glided down the cable trolley assembly to the ground thirty-four feet below.

"Your turn, leg," said Jones as he waited for the ropeman to return the cable assembly to the tower. He hooked Will up to the straps and moved him into position. Will mimicked the motions that Trung had executed. Again, Jones called out "stand by" and "go," and Will jumped from the edge. Will felt a massive surge of energy flow through him. Full invigoration. Better than a Disneyland E ticket ride. He pulled high on his risers, kicking his legs forward and preparing for impact. He executed a perfect landing and roll. At least he thought so. A red-bereted Vietnamese sergeant yelled at him with scorn, and Jones shouted expletives from the tower about his form on landing. And so it went for the next three hours solid, with just one five-minute break.

TWENTY

Dark and early the next morning, Will was jarred from sleep. He heard a fist pounding on the door of his hooch followed by Jones's booming voice: "Rise and shine, leg. Change of schedule. Earlier flight time."

Will checked his alarm clock, which he had set for four forty-five. It read four twenty. "I am risen, jumpmaster, but not shinin'," he managed to shout back at Jones. It was his D-Day, the day of his moment of truth, or as Jones put it, "the day you reach down between your legs and get ahold of balls and cock or a hairy old pussy."

Will's body was still in extreme agony even after overdosing on aspirin. He struggled in pain to get dressed. Once he woke up enough to think about what awaited him, his heart started pounding against his rib cage. The panic made him feel like puking—he was glad they had agreed he would make his first jump on an empty stomach. When they started marching toward the airfield a half mile away, he could see the light of the hangar. The sky was stark black except for a billion wildly kinetic stars. There was no trace of dawn on the eastern horizon. As they neared the hangar, Will's legs felt like they were slogging through a pool of blackstrap molasses. The jumpmaster noticed Will slowing down and jerked his chin in the direction of the light. It took all of his will to force his legs forward. As they reached the open doors of the hangar, the lights of the landing strip turned on. In the distance, there was a faint whine of an approaching aircraft. They both turned to watch the blinking lights on the horizon as a plane descended toward the runway.

"Hey, that's not a C-130, it's got two engines instead of four," Will said.

"No shit, Sherlock, what gave you your first clue? That's a Caribou,"

Wilbur said. "It's more than enough to lift your leg ass up for a jump."

Will followed the jumpmaster into the hangar and through a door to a storage room. Piled on the floor were a main and a reserve parachute pack with a combat helmet on top of them. Will pulled the main onto his back and fumbled with the straps and fasteners, which prompted the jumpmaster to go off on him.

"Son of a bitch, you ignorant fuckinleg! I showed you how to do it two, three times, and you can't get it right? Bert, er, your Captain Michaels told me you are some kind of fucking genius. Now you've got your shit all fuckin' tangled up," Jones said as he started readjusting Will's mess.

"You know, jumpmaster, I don't know why anyone would think I'm some kind of fuckin' genius. I got a high score on some stupid-shit army test that any third grader could have aced, and now I'm fucking Albert Einstein. It's total bullshit," Will said. "If you showed me how to harness up a dozen times, I would still fuck it up."

"Oh, that's not good news, leg. Failing to pay attention, that's how people get killed jumping out of planes. You've got to do better than that."

"When I jump out of that Caribou I'm going to be paying a whole lot of fucking attention."

"*Now* you're talking right."

They walked back into the central section of the hangar as the Caribou made its turn at the entrance. The prop blast swirled up a shitload of dust and grit that burst onto the side of Will's face. A few seconds later the pilot shut down the two turboprops, and there was perfect silence. Will's gut was silent too. He tried to convince himself that nothing could go wrong. Wasn't he mostly, sort of invincible? But that was then; this is now. What about this time, he thought? What if the risers get tangled and I turn into a streamer? What if the strange energy doesn't manifest? There's no guarantee. He shuddered. His asshole felt like it was turning into a suction cup looking for an immovable object to grab ahold of. No way out. He had to fight for control. He couldn't embarrass himself, couldn't stand the shame. Grow a fucking backbone. Grow a fucking backbone. Grow a fucking backbone. His new mantra.

"Come on, leg, time to pop your cherry, turn you into a he-man," Wilbur said. Grabbing the straps of Will's main parachute, he pulled him toward the Caribou, and they both started walking toward the dropped cargo bay door that had become a loading ramp.

"Kind of reminds me of the giant sperm whale that swallows Pinocchio and Jiminy Cricket in that old Disney movie," Will said.

"What the fuck are you talking about, leg?"

"I'm saying that dropped door looks like the lower jaw of a big sperm whale."

"Shit, Parish, your imagination is running way out of control. I thought you were talking about jackin' off and shootin' sperm all over," Wilbur said as he mounted the loading ramp.

Will followed him up the ramp, and when they got inside, Wilbur did an about-face. He grabbed ahold of Will's shoulders with his massive hands and stared powerfully into his eyes. Neither spoke for several seconds. There was a transformation, a softening in Wilbur's face and eyes. Kindness radiated from him. His eyes moistened.

"Listen, kid. This is where the bullshit ends. This is deadly serious business. Having you jump out of this plane after only two days of training is absurd and asinine. I am going to go on record here and now saying that I am officially not OK with this. The US Army has a history of doing some epically insane things. In my personal experience, this tops the list. I am forced to stop and consider that, yes, this is war and people do incredibly stupid things in war. I have an urge to call you Yossarian. And if I did, then it would all make a lot of sense. You and I, we would just be zany characters in a book of fiction about the craziness of war. And we would play out our roles accordingly. But we are not fictional characters. You are Sergeant Will Parish, and I am Master Sergeant Wilbur Jones. We are real people, and we want to go on being real, living, breathing people. So from this point forward, no more clowning around, no more comic relief."

"Excuse me, master sergeant, but why is it you suddenly remind me of a college professor? What happened to the constant whoop-ass?"

"That was all for effect, Will. It's hard to be taken seriously at a jump school using the voice and demeanor of a college professor. Starting now, we do not kid around. I am going to take you through everything that can go wrong, every malfunction that can occur in this, your first jump. I need you to pay close attention to every detail."

Then Wilbur took Will through a description of every known parachute failure and a solution to correct each failure and to save his life. Needless to say, this particular bit of training and instruction only brought Will into a more profound level of anxiety. He tried with everything he could muster to pay close attention to what Wilbur was telling him. Panic was not a useful catalyst in learning. It wasn't going in one ear and out the other, but it was not far from that. He really did try. Really.

Dawn was well along. The Caribou pilots started the engines. High anxiety. High adrenaline. Shit. Fuck. Damn. The ramp began to rise. The plane started pulling away from the hangar. Can I do this? Will asked himself. He thought of a book his mother had read to him when he was a kid. *The Little Engine That Could.* He started repeating in a whisper, "I think I can, I think I can, I think I can," over and over. It helped. It comforted.

Will's main parachute was tethered to the anchor-line cable. He was standing in a state of paralysis, watching the tailgate, saying to himself, "You can do this, you can do this." The Caribou was nearing the drop zone. The ramp started descending slowly. The noise was deafening. The jumpmaster, who was also wearing two parachutes, was right behind him. The ramp was fully open.

"Hit it, Will!" Jones roared.

Will froze.

"Hit it now, or my boot is going up your lily-white asshole!" he screamed.

Will could not force his body to move. Total paralysis. Terminal embarrassment. Then every hair on his body stood straight out, instant shutdown, darkness. Then another dazzling light show at a thousand times the speed of light. All stopped. No movement. No sound. Everything around him a fixed frame. Jones's size sixteen combat boot was millimeters from his behind. As if with a mind of its own, Will's left hand wrapped itself around the jumpmaster's ankle as Will sprang from the ramp, taking Jones, light as a feather, with him.

In slow motion Will felt the tug of his parachute starting to open. Jones was dangling upside down below him, weightless. Then everything returned to real-time speed. Jones yelled at Will to let him go. Jones became too heavy to hold, and he slipped from Will's grasp, dropping away in free fall. A few seconds later Jones's chute opened. Will felt sudden exhilaration and relief. Gliding down in the parachute was a fantastical experience. But his reverie was short-lived when he thought about what Jones might do to him when he landed. He decided to play dumb. When he hit the ground with legs bent and executed a perfect side roll onto his shoulder, Jones was standing in front of him with a hard frown on his face.

"What the fuck was that? How the fuck did you do that? You dragged me out of that plane upside down like I was a fucking rag doll. I want to know how the hell you did that. That's some seriously weird shit."

"I don't know what you're talking about, jumpmaster. All I remember is I froze, and you kicked me in the ass, and I went flying off the ramp. I didn't drag you."

"Bullshit, bullshit, bullshit, Parish! I'm not imagining this shit! I know what happened, and I know there's no natural explanation. Somehow you overcame the law of gravity for a few seconds. It's just not possible, yet I know it happened."

"What you're saying doesn't make any sense to me. Something happened to you up there that did not happen to me," Will lied.

"Oh, I think you know exactly what happened up there, Parish. You are the world's worst liar. It's written all over your fucking face. Now, are you going to come clean and tell me how you did that?"

Will extended his open palms as he shrugged his shoulders. From his facial contortions, it seemed to Will that Jones was considering punching him out. There was a split second of hesitation, indecision, and then Jones decided not to swing.

"OK, Parish. That's it. Your first jump was your last jump. I'm giving you your wings. I'll falsify the paperwork and say you did your five jumps. In return I want you to promise me that you will never, ever, for the rest of your life tell anyone, not even your fucking grandchildren, what took place up there this morning."

"I still don't know what we are talking about, master sergeant. Nothing happened up there except me getting an ass-kicking."

"Suit yourself, wiseass. Now I need you to shake on it," he said, extending his massive outstretched palm. Will reached his hand out a little too timidly, and Jones seized it violently.

"You know I think I could crush every bone in your hand if you were a normal human being. But you aren't a normal human being, are you? There is something very weird about you, Sergeant Will Parish. I can feel a kind of electrical resistance building in your hand the harder I squeeze. How much harder would I have to squeeze to get turned into a rag doll again?"

Before Will could respond, Jones released his viselike grip. Will's hand hurt like hell, and he had been squeezing back as hard as he could. He wondered whether Jones could have broken every bone in his hand or if there would have been an intervention. Good question. He'd never know the answer.

They gathered their chutes together and wadded them into their respective packs. An open LLDB-marked jeep with a red-bereted driver pulled up next to them. They threw their packs in the back and drove back to Dong Ba Thin. No words were spoken between them. When they got back to the jump school compound, Jones sent him to his hooch to gather the little gear he had and to wait for a driver to take him back to Fifth Special Forces headquarters at Nha Trang. Jones said he would contact Captain Michaels to arrange for a flight back to Tan Son Nhut. An hour later the driver, the same Special Forces speedy four who dropped him off two days earlier, came to the open door of his hooch. The jumpmaster was standing a few feet behind him with an unkind smirk on his face. He handed Will a sealed envelope addressed to Captain Michaels and told him it was his jump school certification, for what it was worth. They walked back to the jeep, and Jones kept shaking his head. Will opened the passenger door and looked back at Jones, who was still shaking his head.

"Watch your back, freak," Jones called out, with a trace of a smile on his face.

Will nodded a smile and got into the jeep. He and the driver headed for Nha Trang.

TWENTY-ONE

Will wasn't happy with the way it ended with Wilbur. He had a very high opinion of Wilbur, but he knew it wasn't mutual. He wished he could have just let the jumpmaster's boot kick his ass out of the Caribou, then everything would have been fine. He guessed it was a friendship that wasn't meant to be.

Later in the afternoon, Will got very lucky and caught a ride from Nha Trang back to Tan Son Nhut on a De Havilland U-1A Otter. He and the pilot were the only occupants of the ten-seat aircraft. The pilot was a wild and crazy redneck chief warrant officer by the name of Bobby Ray Leeds from Louisiana. For the entire two-hour flight back to Saigon he never stopped yacking.

After a few minutes Will succeeded in tuning him out. He started to think about what came next, and the butterflies of anxiety fluttered in his guts. What was to come next, the day after tomorrow, was his rendezvous with destiny, his day at Duc Lap. Tomorrow would be Thanksgiving. There would be a feast, his last supper?

The plane landed and taxied to a group of low-lying Quonset huts, and Will saw Brad sitting on the hood of one of the black B-57 unmarked jeeps. He had a prodigious shit-eating grin. Will climbed out of the Otter with his rucksack in hand.

"You're just in time for dinner. I hope you're hungry, because Cookie is making his famous paella tonight in your honor, Parish. Pretty fucking impressive getting your jump wings in three days. Congratulations!" Brad said as he pumped Will's hand.

They jumped into the jeep. The B-57 company clerk took off like a wild banshee with his signature peel-out. It was yet another epic episode of Brad's death-defying renditions of Mr. Toad's wild ride through the streets of Saigon all the way back to Cholon and the B-57 villa fortress. Unlike the first wild ride, Will took this one in stride. After the stoic Nungs opened the security gate and waved them in, Brad cruised slowly into the courtyard, where a group of fifteen or so B-57 members stood clapping. He got a lot of handshakes and backslaps before they sang their apparent ritual song "For He's a Jolly Good Fellow" followed by the raised middle-finger salute and a hearty "fuck him."

Will loved it. He felt like he really belonged. He was one of the guys, no longer a lowly leg. But he couldn't keep from thinking, God, if they only knew, they wouldn't be celebrating me and singing my praises. They would be thinking what a fucking pussy and, probably, like jumpmaster Jones, what a fucking freak he was.

The commanding officer and Captain Michaels were waiting for him at the bar. The colonel shook Will's hand and placed his other hand on Will's shoulder.

"Quite an accomplishment, young man, you really amaze me. I had serious reservations about authorizing Captain Michaels to send you to Dong Ba Thin, but it had an excellent outcome. Being jump-qualified will take the edge off your reception by the A-Team members. You know, Will, it's not just an old soldier's tale that airborne troops can smell a leg a mile away," said Colonel Mahoney with a wink and a chuckle. "We really can."

The colonel directed Will to his table and pointed to the chair next to his. Captain Michaels took the chair on the other side of Will. In honor of Will, it was paella night in the dining room. Will, of course, had no idea what paella was.

Several Nung servers in starched whites marched to the colonel's table and placed the grandest plates Will had ever seen in front of the six diners at their table. Each plate held a small mountain of rice. What captured Will's attention most powerfully was the number—and size— of the chunks of lobster tail in the mix. It was sublime in texture and succulent richness. His fork had managed to find a small, tender chunk of chicken, a few green peas, chorizo, and a scallop imbedded with crusty saffron-infused-rice *socarrat*. This combination made tears well in the corners of his eyes. Once again he had died and gone to gustatory heaven. He attacked his mountain of paella with gusto, quickly reducing it to a small hill.

Then he found the large crystal glass half filled with wine that cast a brooding, dark-garnet hue. He took the glass in hand, swirled, and sniffed the bouquet. It was something he had never smelled before, yet it seemed vaguely familiar. He sipped fully. It was a beautiful beast of a wine. It played off the richness of the lobster and the robust spice and game of the sausage. It was the best glass of wine he had ever tasted, but that wasn't saying much. He asked to see the bottle. The colonel waved over a Nung, who produced the bottle from a sideboard behind him. The label read Penfolds Grange Hermitage, Bin 95. The vintage was 1955. It was an Australian Shiraz. He had never heard of Shiraz, but now he knew it was glorious in his mouth, especially as the taste lingered at the tail end of a sip.

"What do you think of the wine?" Captain Michaels asked.

"I know very little about wine, captain, but if you told me that there is a better-tasting wine in the world, I would say that was impossible."

"You're a fortunate young man, Will, because our commanding officer here happens to be a gourmet, a true epicure. I should say more correctly that you are in luck for a brief period of time but unlucky in the long term, because you are unlikely to dine this well ever again in your life," the captain said.

"Now come on, Bert, that's a discouraging thing to say," the colonel said. "Maybe after Vietnam he will become a wealthy man and retain a private chef and eat like this every day. Then again, these meals could inspire him to become a great chef himself or a celebrated winemaker someday. You have to have a fairly refined palate and nose to react to the Aussie Shiraz the way you did, Will. That wine is considered one of the great wines of the world. For a twenty-four-year-old you have a very discriminating nose and palate."

"Thank you, sir. I don't have much to go on. I've been exposed mostly to cheap jug wine and until now, I've had to spit out nearly everything I tasted," Will said, as he poured himself a third glass of the ethereal Grange.

When the slower diners had finished their paella, the table was cleared to make room for the elegant antique bone-china cups and saucers and the customary individual French presses with fresh-ground Kona coffee beans. Another Nung server followed with small cut-crystal dessert-wine glasses. Next came the dessert in dramatic fashion, the pièce de résistance, an oversize tray full of flaming bananas Foster. A Nung server set one in front of Will, who waited for the flames to die, then took his first bite. It was rich and delicious in the extreme. He thought, How the hell will I ever be able to go back to army-mess-hall dining after eating like this? Yet another starched Nung made the rounds filling the dessert wineglasses with a golden elixir. Will was the last to be served and asked to see the bottle after his tiny glass had been filled. The label read Chateau d'Yquem, Sauternes, France 1949. He had never heard of it, just like all of the other great wines of the world of which he was ignorant. He concentrated on the dessert with a smile on his face. The melding together of hot ripe bananas, butter, brown sugar, cinnamon, dark rum, banana liqueur, and vanilla ice cream was beyond delicious.

He was in a state of euphoria. As much as he wanted to lick his plate, he resisted. He reached for the tiny wineglass filled with the amber liquid and raised it to his nose. The bouquet was lovely and mysterious, and again vaguely familiar. He had to work at it to figure out what aromas he was sensing. Honeysuckle maybe? Caramel, apricot, and pineapple came to mind. How could these delicious scents be coming from this glass? He took a small sip. The dense, honeyed mouthfeel astonished him. It flowed in very slow motion to the back of his palate. It was so sweet and thick yet not cloying. He could feel the high acidity rise on the finish, which demanded that he take another sip at once and another and another. Then, sadly, it was gone.

The colonel was smiling broadly at him. "Looks like someone else has fallen victim to the seductive charms of Yquem," he said. He shoved back his chair and came quickly to his feet holding his dessert wineglass in the air. "Gentlemen, I propose a toast," the colonel said. Everyone in the room jumped to their feet, including Will.

"I would like to take a brief moment to honor a young man in our midst who achieved something quite spectacular over the last three days. I'm not going to wax poetic here but suffice it to say, job well done, Sergeant Will

Parish." Turning to Will, he lifted his glass higher, as did the rest of his men. "To Will," he said. It was followed by a series of echoes and the sounds of the men slurping down what remained in their glasses.

Will was standing and turning a slow crimson. This generous, kind man was making such a big deal over what Will knew was not really worthy of celebration. Will just stood there and absorbed it with an appreciative smile as the officers and the NCOs of B-57 slapped him on the back and shook his hand.

The dining room emptied, and several celebrants repaired to the bar for a nightcap or two.

"Good work, Will. Dong Ba Thin couldn't have been easy. You apparently passed with flying colors. Your airborne certification papers had a sort of cryptic message from brother Wilbur, though. He enclosed a note that said 'Best of luck with the freak.' I'm curious what he meant by that. I'm guessing that he called you a freak because you were able to pull it off."

"I think so, captain. I don't think he gave me a snowball's chance in hell of getting through it. And I don't blame him, because I doubted that I could do it myself. And there was a slightly freaky incident that happened on our first jump when we got tangled up exiting the airplane," Will said.

"What was that?"

"It kind of felt like we overcame gravity for a second or two. We were sort of hanging there briefly going out of the plane, and he got upside down somehow. But it all corrected itself."

"Sounds pretty weird."

"Yes, sir, very weird."

Will went back to his room a little after ten. He felt oddly mellow for a change. He thought it probably had to do with those two exquisite wines that he had imbibed during dinner. There was something—more than alcohol—pure beauty in the Grange and the Yquem that put him into what felt like an exalted state of consciousness. He really wanted to say thank you to . . . Then, he asked, Who can I say thank you to? Do I say thank you to You, God? Are You really there looking out for me? Do I have guardian angels? It's obvious that I would be dead many times over by now if someone or some higher power were not looking out for me. So please, please identify yourself. Tell me who or what You are. It would mean a lot to be able to understand what keeps happening to me. Just a small hint would be appreciated. Really. Am I too ignorant to understand what's going on here? Am I a puppet dangling on Your strings? I do want to take out the bad guys—always have. But why does it have to be so full of drama, so complicated, so conflicting? Why can't I just go out there with this power and annihilate them all? Why does there have to be so much angst? This could be so easy if You would just unleash me, let me run amok. I could clean up this world so fast. Will waited in vain for an answer. Then he fell into a deep, deep sleep.

TWENTY-TWO

Will slept in late on Thanksgiving morning. It was almost zero eight hundred. Upon awakening, he had an unusual sense of well-being that momentarily made him forget where he was. When he got back in sync with the present, that sense of well-being quickly dissipated. One last day in the luxury appointments of the B-57 villa, he thought, and then off to his very own *Jungle Book* adventure and the vagaries of Duc Lap. Who and what would he be when—and if—he returned from that place, he wondered? A voice in his head told him to stop being so melodramatic. So he stopped talking to himself. He showered, shaved, and dressed as fast he could, barely making it to the dining room for one last gourmet breakfast. The Nung servers suggested that he stuff himself and then some because there would be no lunch. The Thanksgiving feast was scheduled for sixteen hundred. He was quite happy to oblige the Nungs in their kind suggestion.

With a belly swollen beyond capacity, he returned to his room to start packing. He made a pile of a dozen lightweight socks, a week's worth of boxer shorts, T-shirts, and kerchiefs all in olive drab, and three sets of lightweight jungle fatigues. He added two sets of jungle tiger-stripe fatigues and two pairs of Viet Cong–style black pajamas to the pile. He pulled his second set of jungle boots from the wardrobe and put them near the pile. His Dopp kit was ready to go. He would have no need for civilian clothes in Duc Lap, so he left his Levi's, khakis and two madras shirts in the wardrobe. Next was his hardware. Tom Pritchard had set Will up with a fine complement of weaponry. He had asked for permission to take his three favorite rifles to Duc Lap: the M2 folding-stock carbine, the compact CAR-15, and the CAR's big brother, the M16. Also, he requested two pistols, the Colt forty-five with a holster for his right hip and a .357 Magnum with a four-inch barrel and a chest/shoulder holster. Permission was granted to take all five. He had three full thirty-round clips for each rifle, two magazines for the forty-five, and several boxes of Magnum cartridges for the .357. Pritchard had told him to lighten his load by taking less of the ammo that was plentiful in the A-Team and to bring extra rounds for the .357 because those would be scarce at Duc Lap.

He sat on his bunk thinking about what else he needed to take on this next strange trip of his. Reading material came to mind, and more specifically, escapist novels. He knew that he still had three books in the bottom of his duffel bag, all favorites that he had read before. One of them was his personal bible, *Stranger in a Strange Land.* Another was *Catch-22.* He had read it once, but it was way past due for a second reading. Heller's benchmark World War II novel was Will's favorite non–science-fiction novel. His number-one all-time piece of fiction was, of course, *Stranger.* The third book was James Jones's brilliant milestone *From Here to Eternity.* The book had been a challenge for him as a fifteen-year-old; he had always intended to take a second run at it when he got older. Perhaps now was the time. He dug up the paperbacks and placed them on his pile of clothing.

Colonel Mahoney and Captain Michaels had scheduled a final briefing and pep talk with Will at fourteen hundred. The commanding officer's door was wide open when Will reported for the meeting. He was waved in by the captain and offered a chair.

"Captain Michaels and I have been going back and forth on what your status should be at Duc Lap, Will. After a lot of thought and discussion, I have decided you will go there with the rank of chief warrant officer two or CWO2. Under normal circumstances sending you in your true rank of sergeant E5 would be fine, but the circumstances at Duc Lap and A-Team 239 are not normal. I believe you will have a higher likelihood of succeeding in your mission by going in as an officer. It will make it easier for Lieutenant Healy to take directions from you in the area of intelligence protocols, and it will make your life a lot easier gaining the respect of the regular A-Team members, too. They will not be as likely to mess with a warrant officer as they would with a sergeant," the colonel said.

"Is that a rank that will fit my cover as a Civic Action specialist?" Will asked.

"Yes, it's not uncommon," said the CO.

"In Special Forces as well, sir?"

"Yes, Will, even in Special Forces. I know of a handful of warrant officers who wear the Green Beret. Don't worry; we have done our homework, but I like your concern for congruity. You think like a spy. That is a good thing," he added.

"Do you have a problem with succeeding in your assignment at Duc Lap in the capacity of warrant officer, Will? Would you be more comfortable as an NCO?" the captain asked.

"No, sir, I'm comfortable in either capacity. And I say this with all the respect in the world for both of you. I would be willing to go to Duc Lap as an organ grinder's monkey if you told me to."

The two officers burst into laughter. Will hadn't seen this side of them. They laughed for a really long time—in fact, Will would call it cracking up.

"Please forgive my zaniness, sir. I'm just going through a period of extreme adjustment. Less than a month ago I was a lowly private, down on my luck and looking at the possibility of a court-martial. Then you rescued me and so generously promoted me to sergeant, and now it looks like I'll be playing the role of a chief warrant officer. It's pretty heady stuff, sir. But I can do it, and I will give it everything I've got."

"That is all we ask, Will, that is all we ask," the colonel said. "And I want you to keep this in mind: we would not be sending you out there in this capacity if it were not commensurate with your intelligence, your education, and the way you comport yourself. We have a lot of confidence in you, young man."

While the CO was talking to Will, the captain went to the map wall. He pulled a rod hanging from a curtain and slid it over to reveal the top secret map of the B-57 operations in several A-Teams on the Cambodian border. The heading on the map read "PROJECT GAMMA." Will had viewed this map before. Duc Lap was somewhere near the middle at the bottom of the II Corps Tactical Zone Boundary. Directly across the border from Duc Lap on the map an irregular red line encompassed an area with what looked like a flag with a red star in the center. Nam Lyr was printed in bold red letters above it. The CO lifted his pointer and thrusted it at the red star.

"There's your intel target, young man: Nam Lyr, a.k.a., Lyr Mountain, headquarters of the Twenty-Fourth Division of the North Vietnamese Army, the NVA. Or is it a Chinese Communist division masquerading as the Twenty-Fourth NVA? That is the question you will go to Duc Lap to answer. You will exploit indigenous Montagnards coming from Cambodia to the A-Team refugee center as your assets to go back into the Lyr Mountain area to determine who is actually there. You will need to recruit and train them using the protocols you learned at Fort Holabird. You will have to be very careful because a few of these Montagnards may well be Viet Cong sympathizers. You will need to keep your wits about you at all times," said the colonel, nodding to Michaels.

The captain took it from there. "As you are already aware, you will be working with Aramis as a two-man team. Lieutenant Healy is a great guy and an excellent soldier. I am sure you will develop an immediate rapport. That said, he can be a bit of a loose cannon and go off half-cocked in the intelligence arena. Strategic planning for collecting the intelligence will be in your able hands, Will."

Will involuntarily glanced at his hands and had doubts about their able status. The operations officer continued the briefing with Will, giving him some background on the A-Team's intelligence NCO, Nicolai Chekov. Theoretically he and the A-Team commanding officer were the only members of the team who were aware of the B-57 mission. Captain Michaels stressed the importance of not divulging the nature of the mission to any other member of the A-Team. He used the phrase "Loose lips sink ships and sensitive intel ops as well."

"The A-Team members who don't already know what you're doing there are going to work hard to find out. They will guess that you're either a spook or an undercover CID agent trying to bust their black-market operations. Just keep stressing the nature of your civic actions duties while carefully watching your back. Fragging isn't a myth—it really does happen," the captain said.

The briefing went on for a while with more minutia about case-officer collection procedures. When the captain was finished, he handed Will a top-secret packet with background files on existing Lyr Mountain intel and a wad of tactical USGS topographic maps covering the areas between the A-Team and Lyr Mountain.

Will returned to his room in a state of high anxiety. The loose lips and fragging stuff had gotten to him. He tried to read the intel reports but couldn't focus. He distracted himself by thinking about what Cookie would be serving for the Thanksgiving feast. Soon, he bounded up the stairs to the club level and into the elegant bar.

Nearly every member of the unit was there already, thirty minutes before the dinner. The Nung bartender arched an eyebrow at him. Will grabbed a handful of pretzels from a bowl, ordered a Manhattan, then placed an elbow on the bar. He was joined immediately by Wagner and Lewis, who were holding martini glasses and appeared to be well on their way to inebriation. Will thought it would be nice to join them.

"Son of a fucking bitch, Will, where the fuck have you been hiding?" Wagner said, with a little slur.

Lewis nodded. "You haven't gone uptown on us now, have you, Will? You haven't been avoiding your old lowlife Tudo Street drinking buddies, have you?" he said, laughing.

"Hell, no," he said. "I've just been jumping through everybody's hoops and got turned into the invisible man for the last couple of weeks. Geez, you guys didn't go thinkin' I didn't love you no more, did you? Because that would be all wrong. Why the way we bonded over yonder in 25 P Alley, how could you . . ."

Wagner quickly put his hand over Will's mouth with a hissing "Sshhhh, don't fucking mention that place, Parish. Are you crazy? You'll get us in a load of shit."

Wagner removed his hand, and Will started laughing a loud, therapeutic laugh as he remembered the Princess bar scene and Wagner with his lady love sitting on the bar, his head locked between her thighs. Wagner and Lewis erupted in laughter too.

"Hey, what the hell is so funny over there, you three?" Brad asked from the other end of the bar. "Let the rest of us in on it if it's so damn funny."

"You had to be there, Brad," Will replied, laughing. "It was just a bunch of barroom silliness."

"Tell us about your crazy three-day jump school, Parish," Lewis said.

"It was beyond fucking crazy. That jumpmaster made every effort to kill me off before I even got close to jumping out of an airplane. Getting my wings like that was bogus. I am not really airborne-qualified the way you guys are. It just can't be done in three days. So, I'm a bullshit paratrooper, a fake, a phony, a fucking dilettante—but please don't tell anyone I told you," Will said, laughing.

"A dilla-fucking what?" Wagner said.

"A pretender, a phony."

"That's bullshit, Parish. If you jumped out of a plane on day three, you're no phony. You've got iron cojones. You're a motherfucking stud. So don't go around bad-mouthing yourself," Wagner said, "because there're plenty of us around to bad-mouth you already."

"Fucking A, Parish, you've got something to be proud of. You shouldn't be making light of it. It was a shit-kicker accomplishment," Lewis said holding his empty martini glass up in a toast.

"All right, you guys, have it your way. I'm a shit-kicker studley-do-right and drop-dead good-lookin' son of a bitch to boot."

"Now you've gone too fucking far . . ." Wagner said.

Then the three of them started laughing again, like they were schoolkids without a care in the world. God, how Will loved to laugh like that. It was the best drug in the world. They kept laughing until it was time to eat.

The Cordon Bleu–trained half-Nung, half-Vietnamese chef and his staff had outdone themselves. There were three ten-foot tables laden with an astonishing array of food. At each end of the run of tables were two carving stations. At one end there was a prime rib carver and a leg of lamb carver; at the opposite end, a turkey carver and a ham carver.

Will fought for self-control: he really wanted to taste everything, not just pig out on the traditional favorites. He went for the turkey first and could choose from three different preparations. One was a variation on duck à l'orange; it had been marinated in orange-zest-and-chili-pepper brine. The second one was deep-fried, Southern style. The third was a traditional butter-basted bird. Will took a modest serving of each. Then he found the mashed potatoes and served himself a healthy mound. Next up was a tureen of stuffing made with cornbread, porcini mushrooms, chestnuts, sausage, and sage. He heaped a mound of that on his plate too. As he sat at a table a Nung server held up two bottles of wine, a red and a white: the red was a Châteauneuf-du-Pape Chapoutier 1961; the white was a Domaine de la Romanée-Conti La Tache 1959. He was in a decidedly big-red mood and pointed to the Chapoutier. He took a quick sniff and a sip and was dazzled by the sexiness of the wine.

He turned all of his attention to the task at hand. He sampled the mashed potatoes—they were the richest he'd ever had, loaded with butter, cream cheese, and sour cream. It was hard to stop at two bites. He tried the dressing, and again, it was the best he'd ever tasted—the melding of texture and flavor was spectacular. Next he went after the traditional butter-basted roast turkey. Then he took a taste of the deep-fried turkey. Both were equally delicious in their own right, but the deep-fried version was the juiciest. He slathered the remaining turkey with rich brown gravy, mixing in random dollops of mashed potatoes and dressing. It was all so sublime, then gone from his plate. Next he focused on the orange-chili-brine-basted turkey. There was a small pitcher with a card indicating its use with the spicy turkey. It was a chili plum concoction. He poured it over his two slices of orange chili turkey and took a bite. Another delicious flavor profile, it was stunning with just the right amount of exotic, spicy heat. Then his plate was clean. He went back to the buffet for a second helping of what he had just finished. When his plate was clean again, he still had plenty of room. For the next two hours, Will spiraled into gluttony.

The colonel broke Will out of his near stupor with the feast's grand finale. Extending a box of Cohibas, he said, "How about it, Will? One last touch of decadence before you head out to the jungle? And the vintage port is on the way."

Will snipped and lit the black-market Cuban cigar while a Nung server poured Graham's 1948 Vintage Port into a small crystal glass. After a couple of draws on his Cohiba, he took a sniff and a sip of port. Astounding, an epiphany moment, violins playing, the flavor was from a different galaxy. It was mystifying. He could lose himself in this tiny glass. The stuff defied description. It was opulent, concentrated, and complex. It was elegant and ethereal. The finish was pure joy and lasted almost forever. He took a few puffs from his cigar and revisited the port. A match made in epicurean heaven, he mused. My God, what am I turning into? He had two more tiny glasses of the divine ambrosia.

He stayed another twenty or thirty minutes, working his cigar and losing himself in the heavenly elixir called port. He had become oblivious to anyone else in the dining room or bar. He was in a trancelike state and finally noticed that everyone had departed and he was alone. The sun had set without his awareness. It was dark. He could hear the mixed whine of traffic on the main drag of Tran Hung Dao. He returned to his room and lay down on his bed, crowding against the piles of clothes. He was still ridiculously full. It felt good to lie down. He had that mellow feeling again. Ah, port!

He had no intention of falling asleep, but he did.

TWENTY-THREE

Will awakened abruptly and sat up at the edge of his bed. The light was still on in his room. His bedside clock read zero three hundred, so he had been asleep for seven hours. In three hours he would be on his way to Tan Son Nhut airport to catch a private flight to Duc Lap. There would be no more sleeping tonight. His adrenaline pump was starting to work, tension in his body rising. He put the last of his stacks of clothes into his duffel bag. He put on a set of lightweight jungle fatigues and his jungle boots. He was ready to go, but it was way too early. He pulled a cigarette from the pack on his nightstand and put his Zippo in his pocket.

He walked out into the courtyard and looked up at the mostly cloudy night sky. The temperature and relative humidity were both above eighty, and a light sweat collected on his forehead. He listened to the sounds of the night—there was the background music of crickets in the courtyard garden. The daytime din of Cholon's teeming humanity was gone, replaced by the intermittent flow of a cyclo here and a taxi cab there. He lit his cigarette. Within seconds a Nung security guard leading with his M16 came around the corner of the villa in search of the source of the tobacco scent. He spotted Will, nodded, and continued on his patrol.

Will sat on a bench under the courtyard pergola and took a long, slow drag from his cigarette and exhaled slowly. In that instant something was wrong, strangely tilting out of balance. The cigarette slipped from his fingers. It fell in very, very slow motion. Night sounds ceased. Will dropped into the energy field. His follicles went electric. He was enfolded within the stroboscopic purple lights and swept away. It hit him faster and harder than ever before, the blackout, then back to the here and now. Time had either stopped or barely crept by. Then he saw what had created the anomaly. A massive satchel charge hung in mid-air, stopped mid-motion five feet above the stone wall that surrounded the villa. The burning fuse was short. The sapper's bomb had cleared the dense array of razor wire atop the wall in front of him. Will darted to the wall as the satchel charge slowly descended. He leaped high in the air, grabbed the end of the belt that held it together, and slung it back over the wall to its point of origin. He heard a group of freakishly drawn-out screams from the other side, followed by a massive explosion. The ground moved sharply beneath his feet.

Hell broke loose inside the compound. Bursts of distorted, prolonged reports of automatic weapons came from all directions. He strained to hear whether it was inside or outside the villa. He moved to the corner of the building and peered around the corner. Two black-pajama-clad Viet Cong sappers with AK-47s were stepping in slow motion over the body of the Nung guard Will had seen a minute before. His inner beast raged. He flew at them. By the time he hit them, they were barely aware of his presence. He watched dispassionately, almost as if from a distance, as the evil sappers erupted in a red-pink cloud inside a radiant field that shrank slowly before his eyes until it and they were gone. The two AK-47s lying on the courtyard tiles were all that remained of the VC. They had vaporized.

He picked up one of the Kalashnikovs and strode toward the sound of gunfire. He released the banana clip from the rifle and ejected the round in the chamber. Sensing that the clip was full, he quickly rammed it back into the housing. Cranking a fresh round into the chamber, he came to the courtyard wall and chanced a peek over. He saw two more dead or badly wounded Nung security team members on the ground. More Nungs were firing toward the breached street entry of the villa from the wall at the far wing. Had to be an inside job, he thought. Two or three VC sappers were firing from near the gateway. At their next movement, Will emptied the AK-47 clip into them on full auto without aiming. He heard the thud of bodies dropping and knew they were dead.

The energy field retreated from Will. Sound and motion returned to normal. One of the Nungs raised his head above the wall and ducked back as fast as he could. He repeated the movement twice. Then he raised his head, looked at Will, and motioned that he was going to proceed to the entrance. He crawled out from behind the wall. Two other Nungs emerged above the wall to cover him. When he got to the breach in the entry gate, he waited several moments before he rose and gave the all-clear sign.

It was difficult for Will to measure the passage of time when the energy field overtook him. What seemed like it could have taken ten or fifteen minutes to unfold was actually less than a few minutes. Two more Nungs came from around the far wing and were joined by more than a dozen B-57 team members who were armed to the teeth. About half of them spread out carefully across the compound to assure that all of the sappers were dead and accounted for. The other half of the team filed slowly out of the entry to do an aggressive perimeter check. Will followed them out and noted three dead VC in a pile near the entrance. All three had taken head shots, and they weren't looking too pretty. Will puzzled over how the bullets he fired had reached them—the burst he fired would have had to make a ninety-degree turn to nail them. He decided not to overanalyze it and accepted it cheerfully.

He walked around to where the satchel bomb had exploded outside the wall. Wagner and Lewis were standing about fifteen feet away from the center of the blast holding M16s and powerful flashlights aimed at the carnage. It was grisly. Chunks of legs, arms, hands, skull fragments, and intestines littered the side of Tran Hung Dao Street.

"Fuck me, this is what's left of three or four sappers," Wagner said.

"They must have been amateurs, real dumb fucks," Lewis said. "They couldn't figure out how to delay the detonator, and it blew them to kingdom come. What a way to go," he added almost admiringly.

"Oh, you think that's what happened to them?" Will smiled inwardly as he asked.

"Hell, yes, there's no other explanation," Wagner said.

"Yeah, I guess you guys are right." Will was happy to go with that theory.

The three of them reconnoitered for ten or fifteen minutes with the rest of the team.

"Something's not right about this. No sign of anything left behind. Someone had to open that gate from the inside, unless one of the sappers figured out a way to get inside," Wagner said.

As they turned to go back inside the compound a deuce-and-a-half truck full of Vietnamese National Police, the White Mice, in full riot gear pulled up in front of the villa. The policemen unloaded and formed a cordon around the field of body parts and the perimeter of the villa. Several of their number prepared for a forensic crime scene investigation, which frankly wasn't going to amount to much. When Will, Wagner, and Lewis reentered the compound, the colonel and Captain Michaels were talking to the chief of the Nung security team. The CO saw Will and waved him over.

"Will, we were just talking with Security Chief Nong Van here about his casualties," Colonel Mahoney said. "He lost two of his men, and one was badly wounded. A member of his team said you came to their rescue and killed the three VC sappers at the gate who had them pinned down. His man said you shot them through the wall with an AK-47. Tell us what really happened, Will."

"Yes, sir, I woke up around three and couldn't sleep. I came out in the courtyard for a smoke. I heard an explosion and auto gunfire. I went across the courtyard and found an AK-47 with a full clip on the ground. I went to the firefight at the gate to help out. I could see the sappers at the gate firing at the Nungs behind the wall. I waited. When I saw movement, I unloaded the clip. None of my shots went through the wall. It was probably beginner's luck and maybe the gift of ricochet that nailed those VC at the gate."

"Now that makes a lot of sense, Will. Nong Van is also trying to figure out where your AK-47 came from and a second AK-47 he found in the courtyard," the CO said.

"I saw that one too. It was lying next to the one I found. I have no idea where they came from, sir," Will fibbed.

The CO turned to Captain Michaels. "Take charge of this, Bert, and keep me posted on any developments," he said.

"Yes, sir, will do," the captain answered.

"Well, young man, your time is drawing near," the colonel said, turning to Will. "I don't expect you will be getting any more sleep. I hope you realize that you saved a lot of lives here tonight."

"I guess I did what needed to be done. It was all about survival instinct," Will said.

"You are going to do great things out there in the field, Will. General Westmoreland and I are counting on you."

The colonel patted him on the back and walked toward his office. He watched him walk away. Will went back to his room and sat down on his bed. He noticed that his pulse was still elevated. He could feel his heart pounding against his rib cage. He took a long deep breath and exhaled slowly. His anxiety about going to the jungle had decreased dramatically.

Will reflected on the violence of the night. He was bothered by the coincidence of the sapper choosing to throw the satchel charge precisely where he was standing. He came to the conclusion that it wasn't a coincidence at all. He believed that the sapper's aim had been triggered by a beacon effect, a magnetic attraction that induced evil entities to target Will. They were trying to kill him. Why? It had to be the mysterious, powerful energy field.

Will thought about the young men he had killed. He felt no remorse, no guilt—they had tried to kill him and every man in his unit. Thou shalt not kill? Will asked himself. Except . . . Unless . . . Will was a creature of the Judeo-Christian culture: he didn't take the Ten Commandments lightly. But he did not consider himself a murderer. Were these VC sappers evil? Of course they were, Will reasoned. Here in Vietnam his commandments were "Do unto evil as evil would do unto you" and "Kill or be killed." Easy to think. Easy to say. Hard to do.

Two hours later Brad knocked at his door. Will was ready. "Ah, the hour of my rendezvous with destiny has arrived," he said.

"It's your moment of truth, eh, Will," said Brad.

"You know, Brad, I've had a whole bunch of those moments ever since I boarded that ship for Vietnam."

"You're right about that, man. You really have seen some shit. Tonight was a test of everyone's manhood, but mostly yours. They are telling stories about you, Will. Mythical accounts are being created as we speak. The Nungs think you aren't human. They're saying you are a spirit creature. One of those Nung idiots is telling a story of how you blew up two VC sappers with your hands, and they disappeared in a cloud of red light. Another one claims you killed the three VC at the gate with head shots that went through the wall without leaving a mark. I'm not making this up!"

Will threw one of his duffels at Brad, who dodged it.

"Tell anyone who buys those stories that I have a bridge in Brooklyn that I can sell to them cheap," he said.

"It's just the way of the Nungs. They want to believe that every event in their lives was caused by some mystical spirit entity. No round eye here believes a fucking word of it," said Brad.

"Good, now enough of that shit," Will said, strapping his Colt forty-five to his hip and cinching the web belt. He picked up his heaviest duffel bag—the one with his weapons and ammo—and heaved it to his shoulder. Brad grabbed the lighter duffel.

They walked to the jeep and put their loads in the back. The sun was starting to rise over the city. There was still a beehive of activity, with the Nungs buzzing around inside the compound and the White Mice scurrying. Brad got in the driver's seat. As Will started to get in the passenger side, he noticed three Nungs bow toward him with their heads almost on the ground. Brad didn't see them.

"Let's get the fuck out of here fast as you can, Brad," Will said as he slammed his door closed.

"Yes, your fucking highness." Brad laid rubber on his way through the now wide-open gate, almost mowing down a handful of slow-moving White Mice, who raised their batons and pistols shouting at the crazy driver who nearly ran them over.

Brad and Will howled with delight at the close call. The two of them didn't stop laughing until they got to Tan Son Nhut.

Once inside the airbase, Brad drove to the Quonset hut area where he had picked Will up upon his return from jump school two days earlier. The same De Havilland Otter was warming up before them. Brad helped Will load his gear into the Otter, then they laughed an uneasy laugh and shook hands.

"Go kick some ass and take some names in Duc Lap for this speedy four desk jockey, will ya, Will?"

"I'll do that, Brad."

Brad spun around quickly and went back to the jeep. Will could have sworn for a second that Brad was starting to tear up, but nah, no way, not Brad.

Will climbed into the plane. It was the same pilot who flew him back from Nha Trang, good ol' Bobby Ray Leeds.

"How y'all doin', pa'tnah?" Leeds greeted him. "Hey, what the fuck, two days ago y'all were a buck sergeant. Now yer a CWO just like me? Son of a bitch, you spooks, y'all get to play dress-up any ol' way y'all like."

Will had a momentary doubt about the new rank on his collar. "Oh, yeah, Bobby Ray, about that. The colonel gave me a field promotion to chief warrant officer two when he found out I was a genius with an IQ over two hundred. He said if he could have, he would have promoted me to *his* rank, but that the army brass frowned on that kind of shit."

"Yer so full of shit them eyes turnin' brown on ya. You fuckin' spooks," the pilot said, shaking his head.

The pilot taxied the Otter to the takeoff point. Bobby Ray gunned it, and they were airborne in a matter of a few heartbeats. Will was amazed how quickly the Otter got into the air. Bobby Ray told him the flight would take less than two hours. He explained that the flight plan wasn't taking them directly to Duc Lap because the A-Team landing strip was still under construction. He had been directed to take Will to the old A-Team site of Buon Sar Pa, which had a decent landing strip.

"Did you say Buon Sar Pa?" Will asked.

"Yup, Buon Sar Pa," he replied.

With a shudder, Will remembered the story of the Montagnard uprising Kavanaugh had told him.

"Have you landed there before?" Will asked.

"Sure have. Dropped off a lieutenant couple times from y'all's unit, maybe six, eight weeks back. Landing strip's in fair condition."

"I guess that's reassuring."

"No reason for worry. Just leave the flyin' and the landin' to ol' Bobby Ray."

Will settled back in his seat and closed his eyes. He hoped that closing his eyes would keep Bobby Ray from talking his head off. He really didn't think he had a chance of falling asleep—he was way too worked up for that. Surprisingly, he did nod off, a forty-minute-or-so catnap. But he awoke with a start. He had been in the middle of a bad dream; not surprisingly, it was about an intense firefight. Even with the dream, though, he felt refreshed, a little more alert. He looked out and down through the fuselage windows at the infinitely hued greens of Vietnam. The jungle's color was interrupted only by vast expanses of rice paddies and rubber, coffee, and tea plantations, many of which appeared to be abandoned.

The Otter flew over areas of denser jungle canopy interspersed with stands of bamboo and napier grass, what the GIs called "elephant grass." The topography turned more irregular. More and more hillocks were intermingled with sparser jungle growth. In the middle of it all, Will spotted a skinny, naked rectangle—their landing strip. Next to it was a rubber plantation that appeared to be healthy and in operation. Bobby Ray did a flyover, and Will spotted a deuce-and-a-half truck and two jeeps parked at the edge of the runway. There appeared to be a security force of about twenty to twenty-five soldiers spread out around the landing area to create a secure perimeter. Bobby Ray was talking into his headset to someone on the ground. He banked the Otter steeply to the left, turning back to make his landing approach. As the Otter started to descend toward the strip, two bright-purple-violet smoke grenades ignited, giving the all-clear sign. The perimeter was secure.

When they were a hundred feet above the edge of the landing field, Will's skin started to crawl, and his hair follicles went wild. He was engulfed by a different purple. The blackout came and went in an instant. The Otter had come to a stop, hanging in midair. The first few .50-caliber rounds tore through the cockpit at agonizingly slow speed and ripped off the top half of Bobby Ray's skull, splattering his brains across the cockpit.

Another twenty or thirty .50-caliber rounds lazily followed a head-height path from the cockpit toward where Will was seated. He watched as they shredded the fuselage in slow motion, then he lowered his head below the line of their trajectory. Just as he ducked, the plane made a sudden and violent flip to the right—Bobby Ray's nervous system was still reacting to the head shots. Will continued to experience time at a creeping crawl, so he felt the plane's wrenching as a gentle roll, but the violence of the fuselage splitting and centrifugal motion forcing him through the jagged gash that had opened was undeniable. He began, slowly, to fly through the air a hundred feet above the rubber plantation. The lighter and softer of his two duffels had exited the plane with him and rested against the side of his head, rib cage, and hip. He landed in the top of a very forgiving twenty-foot rubber tree. The upper branches snapped against the duffel bag that cushioned him one after another and brought him to a nearly gentle stop in the low crotch of the trunk. Almost simultaneously the bag with his weapons landed a few feet away. Time returned to its normal pace and brought with it the sounds of automatic weapons fire. Will shouted out, "Ah, come on now, you have to be shitting me!"

Will gathered his bags quickly and threw himself flat on his back next to the trunk of the mangled rubber tree that saved his life. He opened the top of his duffel and yanked out the CAR-15 with its thirty-round magazine. He racked a round into the chamber and flipped off the safety. He breathed very deeply to try to overcome his sense of panic. Then he waited to be thrust back into the purple zone. A brief moment later he heard a long burst from a .50-caliber machine gun followed by the loud explosion of a fragmentation grenade. Then came the blessed sound of silence. He waited a moment. He heard voices. They were speaking in English.

"Hey, over here!" he called out as he stood up.

"My God, you survived that fall?" said a voice with a heavy German accent.

Moving toward him through the overgrown rubber tree canopy was a tall, muscular, ruggedly handsome young man. He wore tiger-stripe camouflage fatigues with a matching floppy hat and held an M16 across his chest.

"I cannot believe you are alive and in one piece. This is very much the miracle, is it not? I saw you fly out of the plane and fall in the trees," he said as he inspected the shattered tree where Will had landed. "Are you not injured?" he asked.

"A little bruised and beat-up, but no broken bones, nothing serious," Will answered. "I'm Will Parish," he said as he extended his hand.

"I am Lieutenant Uwe Barnhardt," he said, shaking Will's hand. "I am the new XO of A-Team 239. I am pleased to meet you, Will."

"Good to meet you too, lieutenant."

"Call me Uwe, please."

"Hell of a dramatic arrival, partner," said a voice from behind Uwe.

A fellow came through the branches of the rubber trees. He was outfitted identically to Uwe. He grinned and held out his hand. He reminded Will of a young James Arness from *Gunsmoke* only he wasn't six-seven like the fictional Matt Dillon—more like Will's height of six-one.

"Howdy, sidekick! You gotta be Will," he said with a hint of an Appalachian drawl. He shook Will's hand vigorously. "I'm Ralph, your teammate. If you were a cat, I'd say you used up all nine lives on that one. Maybe someone up there is lookin' out for you. That's the good news. The bad news is the Otter blew up when it crashed, and it's still on fire. We had no chance to rescue the pilot. Please tell me that wasn't wild Bobby Ray flyin' that plane."

"I'm afraid it was Bobby Ray. Was he a friend?"

"More like an acquaintance. He flew me back and forth a couple times, and we got to know each other a little. I feel terrible about this. Shouldn't have happened. Our Yards did a shitty job of establishing a secure perimeter. I can't see how we could have missed that fuckin' VC with the .50 caliber. He was dug in deep and well hidden, but we should have found him. He and his fucking bunker mate are dead now. Uwe got 'em with a grenade. What an arm—the Yankees could use an arm like yours."

"*Ja, danke,*" Uwe replied, reverting to German.

"It's time to get the flock out of here and back to the hill," Ralph said.

"*Ja,* let's get going," Uwe agreed.

Will picked up his heavy duffel and Ralph grabbed the other. A light drizzle was falling, and the ground was wet. They walked to one of the jeeps and put the bags in the back.

"Will, this is Jonny," Ralph said, introducing him to the Montagnard in the driver's seat. "He's our interpreter-translator."

Jonny turned around to face Will. Will studied his face. He thought that Jonny didn't look like a typical Yard. In fact, he looked like a dark-complexioned teenage version of Jack Palance.

They shook hands. "I'm happy to meet you, Jonny."

"I hoppy meet you, sir."

Will turned toward Ralph and said, "I'm curious about Uwe and his German accent."

"He enlisted in the army over in Munich so he could become a US citizen," Ralph explained.

With his CAR in hand, Will got into the cramped back seat. Ralph took the shotgun seat. Jonny started the jeep, and they waited while Uwe and his driver mounted up. They watched the twenty-plus CIDG Yards climb into the deuce and a half. Will saw that most of them carried M1 or M2 carbines. Two members of their unit carried Browning Automatic Rifles, and another two were equipped with M79 grenade launchers. One had a sixty-millimeter mortar strapped to his back, and the radioman had a PRC 25. When they had finished loading, the deuce and a half lumbered down the failing macadam road, the jeeps following.

TWENTY-FOUR

The road was rutted, and the jeep's ride was rough. Will was forced to weave his legs sideways across the back seat through his duffel bags because the jeep's floor was thick with sandbags. The terrain was mostly flat with occasional hillocks rising up fifty to a hundred or more feet above the highlands plain. The flora was erratic as well. Scruffy thickets of bamboo were interspersed with broad swaths of sharp-edged elephant grass as tall as eight feet. The patches of vegetation were interrupted by equally broad zones of naked soil. Dioxin—Agent Orange? Will wondered. There were mixed clusters of trees: hopea, Indian chestnut, Moluccan ironwood, bang lang, bon-bon, lychee, and the ubiquitous, colorful crape myrtle. Some of these clusters close to the road were too-convenient ambush sites. Each time they approached a shady grove Will gathered himself up on high alert.

But, to Will's relief, the fifteen-minute drive turned out to be uneventful. Their little convoy approached the outer gate of the A-239 compound. The deep dark-red of the naked laterite soil of the hill that commanded the landscape here was striking. It looked as if it had been dyed by the blood of a million soldiers. Will was impressed and reassured by the configuration of what the team called Hill 722. It was kidney-shaped, a kind of double hillock, one section about forty feet higher than the other. There was a natural saddle area between the two summits that gave a sense of defensibility. Multiple barbed-wire perimeters advanced up the entrance. There were heavy metal pickets every few feet on which massive coils of concertina razor wire were mounted. Below the concertina stacks were wads of tangle-foot barbed wire covering every inch of the ground below. Just in back of the wire perimeters, a foot above the ground, there were a veritable shitload— hundreds, at least— of deadly rectangular green claymore mines. Will spotted three separate sets of these assemblies every thirty to forty feet rising up the hill. Inside the last set of claymores was a network of sandbag-parapeted bunkers with corrugated-metal roofs. He could see several M60 machine gun barrels sticking out from among the sandbags. The bunkers appeared to ring the entire hill. Dozens of Montagnard men, women, and children were milling about around them.

The deuce and a half stopped near the bunkers, and the CIDG force unloaded. The two jeeps continued up the hill to a second security gate, behind which the headquarters was located. Security was remarkably heavy at this point. The uniformed guards bearing M16s at the inner gate seemed to be from the same cut of Nung guards that secured B-57's Cholon headquarters. Waiting outside the entrance of the team house were three Americans in olive-drab T-shirts and jungle-fatigue pants. They wore no headgear and had no indication of rank.

"Here we are, Will," said Ralph—who Will knew was First Lieutenant Aramis Healy—"this is our commanding officer, Captain Jack Cassidy."

"Great to meet you, captain," Will said as he shook hands with the A-Team CO.

"Holy horseshit, Will Parish, news of your feat of derring-do precedes you. I just heard a very hairy story over the radio about you. Is there any truth to this tall tale of a flying man? And, by the way, call me Jack."

"Total exaggeration, Captain Jack, not a shred of truth to it," Will said.

"Ha, ha, ha, well said, Parish, but methinks he doth protest too much, eh, me merry band?" Cassidy said, mixing his metaphors, as he glanced at the others and laughed a hearty belly laugh. The CO bore no resemblance to Hopalong, or to Hamlet's mother, or to Robin Hood. He had a narrow forehead over intense sapphire-blue eyes, an aquiline nose, and razor-thin lips that gave him a highly dramatic look. Will liked him and his zany sense of humor at once. "So be it then, flying Will, meet a couple of the members of our merry band. This is our team sergeant, Master Sergeant Roland Masters," Cassidy continued.

"Welcome to Duc Lap, Chief Parish. It's great to have you on our team. Just call me Rolly," said Masters.

"Great to meet you too, Rolly," Will replied, shaking his hand and asking himself if he had heard correctly—Did that guy really just call me chief?

With his natural tonsure, Rolly could have been a ready-made Friar Tuck in a Robin Hood movie. He was rotund, as well, packing at least two hundred and fifty pounds on his five-ten frame. He was the first overweight Green Beret Will had met.

"And last but not least," the captain said, turning toward a shorter, wiry man with dark hair and intense, brooding, coal-dark eyes, "meet Sergeant First Class Nicolai Chekov, the team's intel NCO, also known as Nick the Cossack. I'm sure you two will have loads to talk about."

Will was stunned by Nick's facial features. The guy was an absolute dead ringer for Eli Wallach, the actor who played Calvera, the evil bandido leader who terrorized the Mexican village in *The Magnificent Seven*.

"Good to meet you, Nick," said Will as they shook hands.

"Yeah, likewise," Nick said.

"OK, that's it for now," Cassidy said. "I'm sure Ralph is going to give you the red-carpet tour and show you how things work here at two thirty-nine, Will."

"Yeah, that's exactly what I'm going to do, Jack," Ralph said. "Come on, Will, I'll show you our hooch."

Ralph led the way back to their jeep. They each grabbed a duffel bag and their rifles, and Will followed Ralph to their hooch about fifty feet from the team house. It was a twelve-by-fifteen-foot shelter with a tin roof dug into the gently sloping top of the hill about three to four feet below grade. The walls looked like shiplap pine and were laid out horizontally. Sandbags three rows thick lined the exterior. The floor was half-inch plywood over perforated steel plate (PSP) sheeting.

Ralph pointed to the cot at the opposite corner of the room. "That's your bunk over there."

Will walked over, leaned his rifle and duffels against the wall, and sat on the edge of the cot. Ralph's cot was at the opposite end from his. Against the wall across from the entrance there was a beat up two-by-three-foot table with a single sideband radio like the one Will trained on at B-57. A battered metal folding chair was centered in front of the table, and at the edge of the desk there was a steel file cabinet with three locking drawers. A kerosene lantern sat on top, and a second lantern hung in the corner, near the entrance. There were two four-foot-wide by foot-and-a-half-high screened window openings on the side of the hooch. They had no glass. The windows looked out over the defensive perimeter of the hill to the panorama of the highlands plain and the thick, undulating jungle canopy beyond. Hinged below the windows were plywood shutters to cover the windows at night.

"Do the VC ever probe your perimeter to test the camp's readiness?" Will asked as he gazed through the screened window.

"At least four or five times since I've been here a squad of Charlie has opened up with AK-47s on full auto. By now I think they've probed all four points of the compass to check our reaction time. All the probes have come around midnight to zero-one-hundred, I guess. They're firing from a couple hundred meters outside our perimeter. Our Yards have always returned fire with BARs and M60s within seconds, and we launch mortar-flare illumination in less than thirty seconds. We figure the VC vamoose before our Yards return fire. Never seen a trace of them in the light of the flares," Ralph said.

"So they keep testing, and the team keeps passing the test," Will said.

"So far, yeah, but we know that some night it won't be a probe or a test because they'll be comin' with everything they got. And I'm not talkin' about the local Viet Cong—I'm talkin' about that NVA division dug in over there on Nam Lyr," Ralph said excitedly.

Ralph's words sent a chill down Will's spine. The follicles on his scalp and skin on the back of his neck puckered for a few seconds.

"All right, Will, are you ready for a tour of Hill 722?" Ralph asked.

"I'm ready. So it's 722 as in elevation in meters, a little over twenty-four hundred feet?" Will said.

"Yeah, it's right there on our USGS quadrant map," Ralph said, pointing to an acetate-covered map on the wall of the hooch above the radio table.

Will followed Ralph out of the door of the hooch and into the drizzly gray light of a late November Duc Lap morning. Ralph oozed confidence from every pore as if he were the master of this hill. Will felt safer just being around the guy. They walked to the highest point of the hill, the southernmost of the two knolls of the encampment, which was thirty or forty feet higher than the northern summit. Three hundred feet away, the northern knoll was pocked with crudely bunkered shelters, machine gun bunkers, and mortar-firing pits.

Small groups of Yard soldiers and their families were huddled around cooking fires in clusters that gave the place the air of a small aboriginal hamlet. The defensive perimeter with its concertina wire array was shaped like a long triangle with rounded corners. Will estimated the camp was about two thousand feet from north to south, with an average width of a thousand feet—forty or so acres inside the outer defensive perimeter.

Standing near the A-Team team house, Ralph pointed to the Vietnamese Special Forces team house about a hundred feet away. It was a lot bigger than the American team house because it served as the billet for the twelve-man LLDB team of Red Berets as well. Between the two team houses there was a heavily fortified command-post bunker dug into the top of the hill. Ralph pointed out the sandbagged stairwells of the two entry/exit locations.

"The CP is set up to be impregnable during a full-scale VC or NVA artillery, mortar, and rocket barrage. It serves as a radio communications center and ammunition bunker too," said Ralph.

On the other side of the team house away from Ralph and Will's hooch was the A-Team bunkhouse, and about thirty feet below that was an elevated sandbagged structure housing a .50-caliber machine gun that commanded a view of at least two-thirds of the camp's perimeter. Walking back around the team house to the entry side, Ralph led Will to an impressively reinforced mortar pit a stone's throw from the team house. It was about twenty feet long and ten feet across. Two large mortars—one eighty-one millimeters and another four-point-two inches—were positioned in the center of the pit about eight feet apart.

"We have at least another dozen sixty-millimeter mortar pits sprinkled around the edge of the hill down by the Yard hooches. They're all manned by the CIDG fire teams," Ralph said.

"So how many Yards are there here in the CIDG force?"

"Close to four hundred. About half of them live here with their families; the rest live in the hamlets within a klick of our perimeter," Ralph said.

"Are the Yards on this hill mostly Rhade?"

"The CIDG is about half Rhade and half Mnong, and we have an all-Nung security force inside the Special Forces perimeter," Ralph said.

"Why only Nungs inside the fence?"

"Of all the mountain tribes the Nungs are the most consistently loyal to us round eyes. They are the fiercest fighters. They hate the North Vietnamese and the Viet Cong. Almost all of the Yards around here love us and are loyal, but we know that there are VC and NVA sympathizers among the Rhade and Mnong in this area. Most of the sympathizers aren't really sympathizers at all—they're just a lot more scared of the VC than they are of us. If they cross the VC, they and their families could get their heads lopped off by the terror squads that go around executing villagers who help Americans. So with few exceptions, we allow them access to our compound," Ralph said.

"Is our translator a Nung?"

"Jonny is half Nung and half Rhade. He speaks both of those tongues plus Mnong, Vietnamese, French, and English."

"No shit?"

"No shit."

"That's pretty fucking impressive. Does he have access to this compound?"

"Yeah, full access. He's the most trusted and the most valuable man on this hill. He's on our payroll. He works for you and me. But the A-Team relies on him to hold the hill together. Without him here their job would be a hell of a lot harder," Ralph said.

Pointing to a row of narrow shacks, Ralph said, "There's the most important structure on the hill, Will, the shit-house latrines. Thank God the wind blows from here to there ninety-nine percent of the time. The garbage pit is right next to them. I think that covers the compound tour pretty well. If I think of anything I left out, I'll show you later, because now it's almost time for lunch."

Will followed Ralph into the team house. It had the same design as their hooch, but it was six or seven times bigger. It was a wide-open space with partitions in one corner that created a kitchen area with a serving counter pass-through. On the kitchen side was a grouping of four three-by-eight-foot tables that created an oversize dining table large enough to seat the twelve-man A-Team and a few more diners. Will's attention was drawn to the poorly lighted area of the room adjacent to the kitchen. He could make out what looked like stacks of cartons partially covered by canvas. He walked over to take a closer look. "You have to be shitting me!" he blurted out. Beneath the canvas were cases of beer stacked six feet high. There must have been close to a couple of hundred cases: Schlitz, Budweiser, Carling Black Label, Pabst Blue Ribbon, Blatz, Hamm's, Stroh's, Falstaff, and Ballantine. The only disappointment was the absence of his favorite, Coors.

"Hey, Will, come over here and meet Cookie and his loyal assistant, Bugfucker," Ralph said, standing at the entrance to the kitchen.

Will walked over as Ralph waved the two cooks out of the kitchen to introduce them.

"Cookie, this is Will, our new team member."

"Good to meet you, Cookie."

"*Enchanté*," said Cookie, as he shook Will's hand.

"Huh?" said Will.

"Cookie speaks Nung and French and a little English. I think he said he was pleased to meet you in French."

"Ah," Will said.

"And here's our noble savage and kitchen assistant, Bugfucker," Ralph said.

"Yes, I numbah-one big-time Bugfuckah," he said, holding his hand out to Will.

Bugfucker looked like he was ten years old. He was tiny but carried himself with a defiant swagger, a fierce expression, and fire in his eyes.

"Bugfucker is Mnong, and his name is unpronounceable. But it sounds kinda like Bugfucker, so that's what we call him and what he calls himself now. Mother and father were killed by the Viet Cong. We took him in and made him our kitchen boy. A few of the team members have been teaching him every profanity in the English language. He has no idea what he's saying, so don't be surprised if he calls you a motherfucking cocksucking piece of shit with a smile on his face. He's a good kid but kind of feisty," Ralph said.

The two kitchen workers went back into their work space.

"Cookie is a good cook, but don't be expecting any of those Cordon Bleu meals you were eating at the B-57 penthouse," Ralph said. "We eat well here, but nothing like that fancy grub in Cholon."

"What's with the giant beer stash? Did you guys hold up a beer truck?" Will asked.

"Beverage of choice around here, mainly because it's free."

"How can it be free?"

"This A-Team has the best scrounger-dog robber in Two Corps, that's how. His name is Captain B. J. Sims. He's the supply officer for B-Team Twenty-Three in Ban Me Thuot, which is in charge of this A-Team. B. J. is the king of barter. He has been known to turn a fake Viet Cong flag with a few bullet holes and a little chicken blood and a captured Viet Cong AK-47 into a pallet or two of beer, compliments of a supply sergeant at Tan Son Nhut. He traded one of those flags and a Yard crossbow for a couple of twenty-five-pound cases of filet mignon from an officers' mess at MACV headquarters in Saigon," Ralph said as he turned toward the door to greet a group of team members arriving for lunch.

TWENTY-FIVE

"Hey, come over here and meet my partner in crime," Ralph called out, waving his arm. "This is Will Parish, my new Civic Action team member. Meet Lieutenant John Prior, our outgoing executive officer. John's DEROS is the end of the week, so you won't be seeing much of him as he gets ready to flee back to the real world."

"Good to meet you, lieutenant," Will said as he reached for Prior's hand.

"Good to meet you too, Will. Call me John," he said.

"Here're my two old teammates, Will. We served together back in sixty-four. Jake Pasquale, medic, and Fred Jones, radio sergeant."

"Jake, Fred, good to meet you," Will said, as he shook hands with each man.

The door to the team house opened again and Captain Jack, Uwe, Rolly, and Nick the Cossack filed in. They greeted one another and made their way to the dining table. Bugfucker placed a long platter of filet mignon, a large bowl of stir-fried vegetables, and a massive casserole of fried rice on the table. Loaves of Wonder Bread and plates of butter were scattered around the table.

"Son of a bitch, not filet mignon and fried rice again. Goddammit, Cookie, you're in a fucking rut," Chekov shouted toward the kitchen.

"What are you complainin' about, Nick? I love this stuff," Jake said. "I could eat this for every meal."

"Yeah, well, I can't," Nick said, tossing his fork on his plastic plate.

"Take it easy, Nick," said Captain Jack. "We don't want Will to think we're a bunch of prima donnas who can't appreciate a wholesome meal. Maybe Cookie has something more to your liking, say some delicious C rations or a peanut butter and jelly sandwich. How about it, Nick?"

Nick rose from the table dramatically, as if he really were Eli Wallach, and walked out the door without saying a word. Will watched him go and thought that Nick was really upset about something, but it likely had nothing to do with what was for lunch.

Will dug in with gusto, just like the rest of the team members. Unlike Nick the Cossack, he had no quarrel with this meal. The delectable tenderloin was overcooked by his standard—more medium than his preferred medium rare—but it was still delicious. During the meal, he learned from Rolly that the other six members of the A-Team were in the field on either training exercises or recon missions with the CIDG forces. They were all expected to be back in time for dinner that night. After lunch, Will and Ralph made their way back to their hooch.

"Ol' Nick seems to be stressed out of his gourd, Ralph. Either that or his hemorrhoids are acting up. What's going on with him? It can't be too much fucking filet mignon," Will said.

"You're right, he's very stressed out. For the last two weeks his local intel net has been reporting that the NVA division over the border on Nam Lyr is fixin' to wipe us off this hill. He's been getting feedback about company-size troop movements crossing the border. Nick is sure they are headed in this direction. I have a principal agent who runs a net of five Cambodian Yards. His guys report the same troop movements. Based on where the information is coming from, we seem to be the most likely target," Ralph said.

"Man, do I ever have immaculate fucking timing. Looks like I arrived just in the nick of time to walk into a serious shit storm here."

"Now don't go overreacting. You have to keep one thing in mind. The VC are masters of deception and misinformation. They go out of their way to keep us off balance. It's well known that Victor Charlie has a strategy of constantly chattering to indicate an imminent threat at all times. It's just like the boy who keeps crying wolf—eventually nobody believes there's a wolf. With the VC, eventually the intel stops being credible, and the danger is that we aren't as alert as we should be," Ralph said.

"What's your best guess about the probability of a siege?"

"My hunch is that it's going to happen sometime, but not anytime soon. All the intel we're getting is secondhand. The info isn't reliable. Nick the Cossack thinks an all-out attack is imminent. His sources are different from ours, but he hasn't convinced me that his info is any more reliable."

Ralph reached into his pocket, pulled out a key, and unlocked the three-drawer file cabinet. He opened the top drawer and removed a folder. Handing the file to Will, he said, "Here's a bunch of my raw debriefing notes from our two principal agents and from Jonny's sources over the last month. You should be able to read my chicken scratch. Jonny's hand is more legible than mine. Read what's in the file and tell me what you think is happening out there."

"Thanks, I'll do that. I have some background and situation report files that Captain Michaels gave me. I haven't had a chance to look at them yet. I guess I need to spend the afternoon catching up on what's been happening here in my new neighborhood," Will said.

"Good idea. Jonny and I have a meeting with one of his agents in an hour or so. We meet him at a refugee camp about a klick outside the camp's gate."

Will devoted the remainder of the day to grinding through what to him was mostly gobbledygook provided by Ralph's and Jonny's sources. From what he could gather, none of the so-called field agents had observed any troop or heavy-weapons movements. It was all second-and third-hand reporting at best. One of Jonny's agents, who was native to the Lyr Mountain area, had been equipped with a spy camera. The tiny Minox was concealed in the base of a tall woven-bamboo backpack made to carry firewood. There were several grainy photos of what was supposed to be the perimeter of the Nam Lyr NVA divisional base camp, but the prints were of such poor quality that Will could make nothing of them.

When he had finished with Ralph's file, he turned to the background material provided by Captain Michaels. These files were mostly order-of-battle information for the suspected NVA division on Nam Lyr. Halfway through reading the soporific documents, he decided to head to the team house in hopes of finding a strong cup of coffee. Cookie was happy to make him a fresh pot. Will returned to the hooch with a mugful of caffeine and struggled to speed read his way through the rest of the boring files.

Ralph and Jonny returned to the hill at dusk, just in time for dinner. They collected Will and walked over to the team house together. The entire team was present, and the joint was rocking. It was Green Beret happy hour. Buddy Holly's "Peggy Sue" was blasting out of the giant Akai speakers. Every man had a can of beer in his hand. At least half of the team members were smoking cigarettes. They were scattered around the room in small groups of two and three, with a couple of loners here and there. Ralph introduced Will to the remaining members of the A-Team.

Rolly came over and handed Will a beer. "I'm guessing you're a Budweiser man, Will. We're getting ahead of you. You got some catching up to do."

"Thanks, Top, good guess. Budweiser's one of my favorites. I pretty much love all beers except that foul panther piss called Ba Muoi Ba they serve down on Tudo Street."

Rolly laughed. "Now what you got against formaldehyde?"

"Must be an acquired taste," Will said.

The tape deck switched from Buddy Holly to "Blue Suede Shoes." About halfway through Elvis's rendition of Carl Perkins's groundbreaking rock-and-roll standard, Cookie and Bugfucker started placing platters of Southern fried chicken and biscuits and bowls of mashed potatoes, gravy, and corn on the table. An A-Team member turned the music off, and every man in the room took a seat. Will's wasn't the only ravenous appetite at the table; he had a lot of competition. The food was simple and delicious. It disappeared quickly. Cookie and Bugfucker resupplied just as quickly.

By the time the meal was finished and the dining table was cleared and wiped clean, Will was on his fourth Budweiser. He was actually starting to feel relaxed. Ralph told him that he was going back to the hooch to write some letters. Will watched one of the team members change the massive twelve-inch reels on the tape deck and start a new set of music. The dulcet operatic crooning of Roy Orbison began to fill the room with "Blue Bayou." Everyone slowly fell under Orbison's magic spell and migrated into their own solemn, contemplative moods. When "In Dreams" started playing, Will's heart and mind slipped down a wistful, nostalgic pathway. He was drifting, transported far away to a different time and place. Then a hard-edged voice yanked him from his reverie.

"You and me, we need to talk," Nick the Cossack said. Will had been leaning back on one of the worn-out sofas with his hands laced behind his neck and his feet stretched out in front of him.

"Huh? What? OK, yeah, let's talk." Will said.

Nick seated himself on the sofa next to Will. Will looked around the house, concerned about the privacy of their talk. Half of the team had departed the room after dinner. The remainder were starting a poker game in the far corner.

"Don't worry," Nick said. "No one can eavesdrop on us with the music blaring."

"All right, Nick, what's on your mind?"

"I got a shitload on my mind. Did Ralph brief you on the barrage of intel coming in during the last week? Has he told you that we are under imminent threat of having our asses overrun by that fucking NVA division you guys are supposed to be spying on?"

"Yes, he has. He gave me his and Jonny's source files to review. He added his take on what he thinks is happening out there," Will said.

"Oh, he did, did he? Well, forget what he told you. Ralph can't see the jungle for the trees. He doesn't know his ass from a hole in the ground. I know Ralph told you he's not buying all the warnings. He thinks it's VC misinformation, trying to lull us to sleep. Well, let me tell you something. He's wrong, wrong, wrong, wrong as the day is long. My sources are better trained and more reliable than his. I'm figuring the NVA has moved at least one and possibly two battalions across the border from your Lyr Mountain division. They are going to throw everything they got at us, maybe as early as tonight."

Will did not like what he was hearing, didn't like it one bit.

"What makes you so sure about this imminent attack? Ralph said the info was all second- and thirdhand reports. None of his or Jonny's assets saw anything with their own eyes. He said none of yours had eyes on either," Will said.

"That's right. But my agents' sources are far more credible than his. In the world of intel, Ralph is blind and I'm the one-eyed man who's king. He hasn't been doing this as long as I have, you see. His instincts are all wrong for this business," Nick said.

"OK, so you're the guy calling the intel shots around here. It's not Ralph, and it's certainly not me. So what do you want from me?"

"The real shot-caller is the captain, your new best buddy Jack Cassidy. He listens to me, but Ralph also has his ear. Big fucking mistake. I need you to be the voice of reason. I figure you did the Area Studies Agent Handler course at Holabird. That makes you the only professional on your team. So I need you to compensate for Ralph. Tell the captain that Ralph doesn't know what he's talking about."

"You know I can't do that."

"Why not? You never met the guy until today."

"Because we're teammates, and there are these things called loyalty and trust. You're asking me to commit an act of betrayal. I won't do that. I've been on this hill for less than ten hours. I don't know shit from Shinola. I'm struggling to understand how it is you give a shit about Ralph's intel input. What possible difference could it make? Are you suggesting that this A-Team isn't prepared for an attack because of Ralph's point of view?" Will asked.

"There's prepared, and then there's really fucking prepared. We're prepared, but the captain isn't taking the threat as seriously as he should. I blame that on Ralph. We should be on the highest-level alert here. We need to have at least three or four early-warning ambush teams out there every night," Nick said, waving his arm over his head in a circular motion. "But we don't. We have only one Yard team with not one fucking American out on ambush."

"OK, I'll take a harder look at the data and have a talk with Ralph," said Will.

"Yeah, a fat fuck of a lot of good that will do," Nick said. He leaped from the sofa, face screwed up in anger, and stomped out of the team house in high dudgeon.

Now that guy has a seriously bad attitude, Will thought. He almost laughed out loud.

He leaned back on the sofa, trying to get back into that mellow space. Orbison's "Dream Baby" beckoned, but Nick's tirade had poisoned the magic well of dreams. Will left the team house. He took a step outside and marveled at the pitch darkness of the night. He stood there waiting for his fully dilated eyes to adapt to the extreme dark. Roy Orbison continued to croon behind him. Will stood in dead stillness for five minutes. No moon, no stars, the cloud cover was low, a promise of rain in the air. He started to see vague outlines of the Yard structures below on the hillside. He could make out subtle variances between dense jungle and plantation scrub. How many Victor Charlie and NVA are out there in the jungle at this moment preparing to launch a killing strike at Hill 722, he wondered? He tried to conjure the night vision that had come to him a time or two from the strange energy. He pictured the tiger stalking him and the asshole Hadley in the middle of darkest night outside Ban Me Thuot. He had seen the big cat as if it had been broad daylight. Right now he wanted to be able to see the enemy beyond the perimeter, if any were out there, in that same light. But he couldn't make it happen.

He found his way back to the hooch. A faint light bled out of an edge of the door; the lantern on the file cabinet was alight. Ralph was sitting in front of the sideband radio signaling on a side key in Morse code. He was sending an encrypted report to B-57 HQ in Cholon using a Diana one-time pad. Ralph nodded at him and continued to play the key. Will loved that sound, the *dit-dah, dit-dah, dit-dah-dit* making its own unique music. He had some obscure, muddled memory relating the dots and dashes to a mid-1950s TV documentary from when he was twelve or thirteen years old. It was called *Victory at Sea,* and he thought he remembered it opening with a Morse code signal *dit-dit-dit-dah,* the letter *v,* followed by the opening four notes of Beethoven's Fifth, representing V is for victory. He wasn't sure that he remembered it quite right.

When Ralph had finished transmitting his report Will briefed him on his encounter with Nick the Cossack.

"What an asshole," Ralph said.

"My sentiments precisely," said Will.

"He wasn't always such a prick. He used to be pretty much a normal guy in a kind of intense way. I think he's freaked out over the possibility that we're going to get wiped out by the NVA. He's been obsessing over the NVA division on Nam Lyr. Ever since he learned that B-57 was in his A-Team to gather intel on that unit, he hasn't been the same," Ralph said.

"So, bottom line, Ralph, are we going to get hit tonight?"

"I don't believe so, no. Not tonight—maybe in a week, a month, a year, but not tonight. Nick may think I'm a dumbfuck in the world of intel, but no, not tonight."

"OK, that's good enough for me. I'm ready to crash and burn. I can be asleep in less than a minute flat," Will said.

"I'm right there with ya, partner."

Will quickly lined up his M16, CAR-15, and M2 carbine in a row against the wall at the head of his bunk. Each had a full thirty-round magazine, a round in the chamber, and the safety locked. He placed his Colt forty-five under his pillow and the Smith & Wesson .357 at the edge of the bed. He wasn't paranoid, just a little extra careful. He lay down on the bare mattress and pulled his poncho liner up to his waist. He reached for the powerful revolver and fingered the trigger guard gently. He closed his eyes and was asleep in seconds, dreaming of things past.

TWENTY-SIX

Will awoke at the first thin line of dawn slicing through the edge of the hooch's door. The .357 still rested reassuringly in his hand. The first sound of the day was the soft note of Ralph's snoring. Will knew exactly where he was. There was no disorientation. He had slept a deep, restorative sleep for maybe ten hours, which was unprecedented since he had joined the army. It must have been Ralph's promise that the A-Team wouldn't come under attack that allowed for such a sound sleep. He sat on the edge of his cot and sniffed his armpits. Nothing malodorous. Another day could pass before he needed to bathe. Ralph snapped awake. He looked at Will with surprise.

"Huh? Oh, yeah, right, got a new roommate. Forgot for a second. Good morning, Will. How was your first night in Duc Lap?"

"I got a great night's sleep. We didn't get overrun by an NVA regiment. All in all, I'd have to say it was a helluva good first night."

They got dressed and joined the rest of the team for breakfast. Afterward Captain Cassidy suggested that Will and Jonny should accompany Lieutenant Prior with a Yard security team to Duc Lap District HQ to meet Captain Nguyen Van Phuc, the district commander. Nguyen had invited the soon-to-depart Prior so he could present him with a going-away present.

"That's a great idea, Jack," said Ralph. "Will needs to get a feel for the lay of the land in the direction of the district headquarters. He needs to see what we're up against in the form of our treacherous Vietnamese ally Phuc."

"Now, now, Ralph, we don't want to poison Will's mind prematurely. We'll let him draw his own conclusions about our district chief," Cassidy said.

"Did I hear *Win Van Fuck* correctly? Is that his real name?" Will asked.

"He pronounces it *phoop;* we pronounce it *fuck,*" Ralph said.

About an hour later Will was ready to load up in the jeep. Jonny was already sitting at the wheel. Will wore tiger-stripe fatigues and floppy jungle hat. He had packed a light load of gear on his web belt and harness. He carried his M2 carbine with three thirty-round mags in his ammo pouches. His .357 was holstered on his left shoulder, his forty-five on his right hip. He had fastened a couple of M26 grenades to his web to add some versatility to his firepower. Meeting him at the jeep was team medic Tom Berwick, who had decided to do a village sick call. While waiting for Lieutenant Prior Will chatted with Jonny. The kid appeared to be fifteen or so, but Will knew that the translator was older than him, probably thirty. Jonny was at least three or four inches taller than the average Yard, maybe five nine or five ten.

"So Jonny, Ralph tells me you are half Nung and half Rhade. I'm curious to know if your father is Nung or Rhade?"

"My father Nung, mother Rhade," he said.

"Were you born and raised near here?"

"Born near Pleiku. Move here after French lose Dien Bien Phu 1954."

"Are you married?"

"Yes, have wife, three kid, two boy, one girl."

"How old are you?"

"I thirty-five year."

"You look a lot younger than thirty-five."

"Yes, we Yard age well," he said with a wry grin.

Will cracked up laughing. "Well said, Jonny, you have aged quite well. I didn't know you were a comedian as well as a translator."

"Yes," Jonny said, laughing. "Yard can be very funny sometime."

"I'm doing some quick math here. You must have been about twenty-three years old when the French were defeated at the battle of Dien Bien Phu. Did you work for the French?"

"Yes, first I soldier, then interpreter, work with my father for French. No like Ho Chi Minh. No want communist."

"Is your father still alive?"

"No, he killed with French in Dien Bien Phu."

"Oh, I'm very sorry for your loss, Jonny," Will said.

Jonny bowed his head and said, "Thank you."

Prior appeared and loaded up in the driver's seat of the jeep. The A-team's interpreter, Pham, was riding shotgun. Two young Yard soldiers, who looked not a day over fourteen, carried carbines and sat on the back of the jeep, their legs dangling over the rear end.

About twenty minutes before their small contingent left Hill 722, a twenty-four-man squad of Yards had preceded them to provide security for the two jeeps on the mile-and-a-half drive to the district HQ. The security team had spread out at roughly two-hundred-yard intervals on both sides of the road nearly two-thirds of the way to the district compound. The A-Team jeep took the lead. Jonny, Will, and Berwick followed about a hundred feet behind.

The road was in terrible condition. Less than half of the macadam remained, and large potholes full of water from the overnight squalls impeded their progress. It was a slow slog at maybe ten or twelve miles an hour. A leaden sky hung over them, threatening an eventual downpour. Along the way Will sighted several aging tualang trees with their imposing buttresses. The massive sentinels stood at the edge of an abandoned coffee plantation. Just like on the road from Buon Sar Pa, there were many worrisome points for possible ambush. He spotted a member of the Yard security force about a hundred feet off the road shuffling along, lackadaisically rocking a Browning Automatic Rifle back and forth on his shoulder. That guy isn't making me feel all that secure, Will thought.

First came the tingling at the nape of his neck, then the accelerating burst of energy up his scalp and down his spine, every follicle pulsing, and the inevitable oh-shit-not-again feeling. The swirl of color and fade to black, the sense of going somewhere out of this world at blinding speed, the instantaneous return, then the eerie super-slow motion in his field of vision. A powerful explosion erupted under Prior's jeep and launched the vehicle five, ten, fifteen, twenty feet into the air. The supersonic blast wave struck Will's face. He watched four legs tear loose from the hip joints of the two young Yard soldiers who were sitting on the back of the now ascending jeep, their faces morphing from playful grins into grimaces of horror, all in excruciatingly slow speed.

The terrible sound of the detonation of the massive mine rolled over him. The inevitable fusillade of AK-47 bullets floated slowly and harmlessly over the heads of Will and the other occupants of his jeep. The sound of the rounds bursting from the Russian assault rifles followed shortly, more terrifying because of their transformation into distended, elongated chuffing noises in Will's perception. Will was in instant motion, levitating out of the jeep. He had already circled behind his jeep and deep into the jungle scrub before Prior's jeep had started its descent back to the ground. He spotted muzzle flashes—static star-shaped flares to him—from at least seven locations at two hundred feet from the road. He saw the hapless Yard with the Browning take multiple hits and begin to fall so very slowly to the ground. Will flipped the safety on his carbine and set it to single-shot mode. He jogged to the flank of the enemy's firing position. He fired seven rounds from the hip without aiming. In his mind's eye, he saw the path of each bullet as it found the middle of each ambusher's forehead. He sensed that the rounds he had fired became enhanced by the energy within him as if they were tiny guided missiles. He heard the slow, soft thump of the crash of Prior's jeep as it came back to earth. Then silence.

Time returned to its normal pace, and Will ran back to his jeep as Jonny and Berwick were lifting themselves from the ground at the edge of the road. They were splattered with the blood of the unfortunate young Yards. Berwick reached quickly into the jeep and grabbed his medical bag. He raced to the lead jeep to attend to Prior, who was slumped against the steering wheel. Will and Jonny ran to the two Yards, who were lying legless in a grisly pile in the middle of the road. The backs of their skulls had been sheared off by a chunk of metal from the rear of the jeep. They were obviously dead. Jonny moved quickly to the other side of the jeep to check Pham's condition. The interpreter was conscious and, miraculously, appeared to have suffered no serious injuries or wounds except profound shell shock. Jonny grabbed the handset from the PRC 25 mounted at the base of the jeep's dashboard.

"Mayday, mayday," he said forcefully and without panic into the handset. "Ambush two klick from camp. Mine blow up *Trung uy* Prior jeep. Prior hurt bad. Need medevac. Two CIDG dead. No other wounded. Shooting stop.

Ambush over. No need reinforce. Need medevac chopper now."

Will asked Berwick if Prior was alive.

"Yeah, he's breathing and has a strong pulse. Both of his legs are broken. He must have hit his forehead hard against the steering wheel. He has a major contusion and major swelling here above his supraorbital ridge. I'm sure he's got a concussion. I'm worried about internal bleeding, possible ruptured spleen. His ribs seem to be intact," Berwick said.

"Can we get him out of the jeep?"

"Not yet—I'm afraid we might make his injuries worse," said Berwick.

The jeep's radio emitted a stream of static, then Captain Cassidy's voice.

"Medevac ETA twenty minutes out. What's Prior's status?"

Berwick picked up the handset. "He's unconscious, possible concussion, broken legs, and possible internal bleeding."

"Uwe is on the way with the cavalry, a platoon of CIDG. ETA ten minutes. I'm a minute behind them. Are you under fire? Is the area hot?"

"Negative. No fire. No heat. They unloaded on us with AK-47s full auto. There was return fire from behind us, then . . . strangely . . . all quiet. They backed off quick," Berwick replied.

"What about Parish, Jonny, Pham?" Cassidy asked.

"They're fine."

"Roger that. We'll be there shortly."

By the time Uwe and the cavalry—which consisted of a jeep sandwiched by two deuce and a halfs—arrived, the remainder of the force had established a perimeter around the two jeeps. Uwe directed his platoon into a double-flanking formation to surround the area where the attack had been initiated and to flush out any sapper stragglers. Captain Cassidy drove his jeep up to the bumper of Will's and jumped out with the vehicle still rolling. He hurried to Prior.

"John, John, it's me, Jack. Hold on, buddy," he said as he gently rubbed Prior's shoulder. "The medevac's almost here. We're going to get you out of here and get you home to Clare and the kids. You're going to be fine, buddy. Just hang in there." His eyes were tearing up as he spoke soothingly to his executive officer. Prior seemed to respond to the captain. He turned his head slightly and opened his eyes for a few seconds. A smile nearly formed on his face.

"That's it, John. You're going to make it. You're going to be fine, buddy. Just keep hanging in there."

Will heard the sound of the chopper's blades before anyone else. He hesitated several seconds then said, "Incoming, we've got incoming. The medevac is almost here."

Everyone looked at him and listened, straining their ears to hear it. Finally they all heard the Huey's unmistakable signature chop. The medevac was over them in seconds, following the trail of a bright-yellow smoke grenade ignited by Berwick. It landed quickly within fifty feet of the pod of jeeps. Two medics jumped from the helicopter before it touched down. One carried a stretcher. They ran to Prior. One of the medics was a doctor from the field hospital in Ban Me Thuot. He did a quick exam and started an intravenous plasma transfusion in seconds. The doctor supervised the careful removal and placement of Prior, groaning in great pain, on the stretcher. Will, Cassidy, Berwick, and the dust-off medic lifted Prior's gurney while the doctor held the plasma bottle high, and the five of them loaded him on the Huey. The doctor and the medic leaped aboard, and the helicopter lifted off immediately. The doctor gave the anxious foursome a reassuring smile and thumbs-up as the Huey turned away toward Ban Me Thuot.

"He's going to make it. He's going to be OK. I'm sure of it," Cassidy said.

Will, Berwick, and Jonny nodded in agreement.

Will's nervous system was discombobulated. He was in a state of high anxiety, stressed out of his skull. As he grappled with his sanity, he watched Uwe and the CIDG platoon return from their quick search-and-destroy maneuver. Uwe's body language signaled disappointment.

"So, they all skedaddled?" Will asked.

"What are you saying?" Uwe asked.

"The Viet Cong, did they do the *di di mau,* disappear-into-the-jungle-quick trick?"

"*Nein,* no, they did not *di di mau.* They went nowhere. We found seven dead NVA. One round in middle of forehead, all seven the same. It is very unusual, no? Our Yard soldiers are all the expert marksmen, no? This is hard for me to believe."

"Very strange," Will said. "So how do you know they're NVA?"

"They are NVA because they are wearing NVA uniforms, not black pajamas like VC."

Uwe walked over to the crater created by the mine that had launched Prior's jeep into near orbit. One of the team's demolition specialists, Sergeant Gabe Pickens, was removing the remnants of a large shell casing from the center of the blast hole.

"Looks like they used a one-fifty-five howitzer round. That makes for a shit-kicker powerful mine. I'm amazed the jeep is in one piece," Pickens said. He walked to the side of the road and reached down, pulling out two strands of wire that had been buried under the loose soil.

"It wasn't pressure detonated, it was command detonated," he said as he continued to lift the wire and walk into the jungle scrub. He followed the wires to a thicket of bamboo a hundred and fifty feet from the road. He held up the frayed ends of the wires to show where they were torn away from the battery pack used by the NVA sapper who'd set off the mine.

"This is where the fucking NVA asshole triggered it," Pickens said.

Eventually the small task force got back in their vehicles and returned to Hill 722 on high alert. When they made it through the last gate and into the Special Forces compound, Ralph was waiting for Will. His characteristic grin was missing, and lines of tension marked his face.

"You're startin' to worry me, partner. You're turning out to be a real shit magnet," Ralph said.

"Tell me about it. I'm worrying myself. I got a bull's-eye on my back, but it's the people around me who are catching the shit," Will said.

They went into the team house.

"Uwe says seven confirmed kills, all in NVA uniforms. That's something new. All of our kills have been VC in black pajamas until now," said Ralph.

Cassidy and Uwe came into the team house, with Nick the Cossack strutting in right behind them like a puffed-up banty rooster.

"*Now* do you get what I've been saying?" asked Nick. "Are we going to start taking the threat from across the border more seriously? It's time you people started paying attention when I tell you what has to be done here," he said almost imperiously, shifting his intense, accusing gaze back and forth from Cassidy to Ralph to Will and back.

"All right, enough with the attitude, Nick. Your point is well taken, but not the dripping indignation you're wrapping it in," Cassidy said.

"OK, OK, captain, I'll back off," he said with an edge to his voice, "but—"

"No fucking buts, Chekov," Cassidy snapped. "I'll listen to what you have to say when you can say it with a civil tongue in your mouth."

Nick took several deep breaths that allowed his face to unscrew. "I just want to talk about the consequences of being ambushed by an NVA unit. This is a game changer. Where there are seven NVA KIA, there's bound to be a shitload more of them close behind. I would like to see a lot more nighttime patrols setting up ambushes—maybe three or four a night."

"All right, Nick, we will have more patrols. I don't know how many. I'll sit down with Uwe and Top, and we'll come up with the right number."

"Thank you, captain," Nick said. As he walked out of the team house, he looked pointedly and smugly at Ralph as if he were dying to say "I told you so."

After the team enjoyed lunch, the captain asked Will and Ralph to join him, Uwe, and Top in the command bunker to review the encounter with the NVA. The five of them sat around a table with a grouping of USGS quadrant maps that included the road between the A-Team and the district HQ. Cassidy asked Will to take him through the ambush sequence from the moment of the mine detonation until the firefight ended. Will summarized the skirmish. When he got to the part where he had to decide how to describe his role in killing the seven NVA sappers, he realized he had no choice. He had to come clean, sort of. There was no other way to explain it.

"So, I rolled out of the jeep with my M2 in hand before Prior's jeep hit the ground and ran into the jungle scrub. I spotted the NVA firing at us a couple of hundred feet from the road. Amazingly they couldn't see me as I flanked them, and I got close enough to make it like shooting monkeys in a barrel. At least two or three of them were in the process of changing magazines. I was on single fire, and I just shot them one at a time. They were so shocked when I started firing that they froze. The last one standing, number seven, should have nailed me but he had a misfire and a jam. It was unbelievable how it happened," Will said.

"Well, yeah, Will, that's the word that works for me too," Cassidy said. "What you just described strikes me as impossible. Shooting seven NVA dead center in the forehead is the stuff of myths and legends. Maybe a hundred years from now folks can spin this yarn and it will sound believable. You're a spooky guy, Will. First you fall from the sky, a fall that would kill us mere mortals. I can give you that one. You landed in a forgiving rubber tree on top of your duffel bag. It's a long shot, maybe a billion to one, but within the realm of possibility. Next you sneak up on the flank of these seven NVA regulars and snuff all of them in identical fashion like there's a bull's-eye in the middle of their foreheads. The real world just doesn't work that way." Cassidy paused, vexation written across his face. He looked hard at Will. "Convince us you're not a goddamned alien from some distant galaxy."

Will paused for an uncomfortably long moment. "OK, captain, you got me. It's true. I am a God-blessed alien from a distant galaxy. My people sent me here to help all of you pathetically fucked-up earthlings."

Will waited, didn't say a single word. Cassidy was the first to start laughing and Ralph a very close second. Then Will cracked up and the dam burst. Uwe and Top began to laugh. The laughter fed on itself in full catharsis. Ralph fell out of his chair. Everyone lost control, not a dry eye in the bunker. It took a few minutes for them to get a grip, then everyone tried not to look at the others to avoid losing the grip all over again.

The first to speak was Captain Cassidy, as he wiped his cheeks dry with his sleeves. "Thanks, Will. I needed a laugh."

"You're welcome, Jack. We all needed it, me more than anyone," Will said.

There was a loud squawk of static from the radio system.

"Fandango jitterbug, fandango jitterbug, this is bushwhacker bravo. Do you copy?" asked a gruff voice over the radio.

Cassidy grabbed the handset and responded, "Bushwhacker bravo, fandango jitterbug copies you loud and clear, over."

"Good news for you and your team, your medevaced X-man is out of danger. Two broken legs set, mild concussion, and removal of ruptured spleen. He is stable and resting comfortably, over," said the gravelly voice against the cheers of joy coming from the men in the bunker.

"That's fantastic news. Thank you for the update, bravo, over and out," Cassidy said.

"Beautiful," Will said. Thank you God, he said to himself. Now I can shed the guilt and stop feeling like a freaking Joe Btfsplk spreading bad luck wherever I go.

Ralph and Top celebrated by jumping in the air and belly-slamming, shouting "Yeah, yeah, yeah" over and over.

Uwe's response was more restrained: he thrust his fist in the air and said, *"Ja, ja!"*

Cassidy beamed a broad, bright shit-eating grin then fell to his knees, bowed his head, and clasped his hands in a silent prayer of thanks.

TWENTY-SEVEN

After Will's wild first twenty-four hours as a member of A-Team 239, the violence and drama subsided. In the next ten days he, Ralph, and Jonny made the rounds of the Montagnard refugee villages and hamlets within a mile or two of the A-Team. There were four in all: two Mnong, one Rhade, and one Jarai. The Rhade and one of the Mnong villages were actually big enough to be worthy of being called villages. Each had between a hundred and fifty and two hundred residents and several well-made, traditional longhouses. There were also dozens of temporary huts made of bamboo and thatch. The other two Montagnard settlements, Jarai and Mnong, were tiny, with at most fifty to sixty residents living in temporary huts. At best, they were hamlets.

The larger Mnong and Rhade villages were nearly a mile apart and had apparently been there for a while. The Jarai and Mnong hamlets, on the other hand, looked as if they had been there for a few weeks or months at most. Ralph and Jonny had been doing most of their Civic Action work during the previous seven or eight weeks in the two villages. They distributed rice, bulgur, cooking oil, evaporated and powdered milk, aluminum cooking utensils, farm tools, and blankets. They also assisted in digging community wells and organizing medical sick calls and immunizations, or MEDCAPs, with the A-Team medics. Using their Civic Action calling card as a cover for intelligence gathering, they had recruited five Yard agents who had fled their hamlets in Cambodia. These indigenous hunter-gatherer inhabitants of Nam Lyr had fled their historic homeland after the NVA established its divisional headquarters in their backyard.

From Will's point of view, the hamlets were the more fertile gardens for harvesting agents, since most of Yard refugees from Cambodia seemed to be concentrated there. The majority of the new arrivals in the established villages were in-country refugees escaping Viet Cong atrocities and conscription. Most of these Yards had no familiarity with the target area. The Mnong hamlet had more recent arrivals from the Lyr Mountain area than the Jarai hamlet, where most of the refugees came from an area far north of Lyr.

After several days of trawling the four refugee destinations for potential agents, Will decided to focus his energy on the Mnong hamlet. The hamlet's chief, if he could be called such, was an affable and surprisingly sophisticated young man. His name was Y Srun. It was challenging for Will to determine his age, but he put it at thirty-something. Y Srun had an alluring wife, K Jrun, who wore a traditional black-silk sarong that fell to the middle of her calves and failed to cover her lovely breasts. It became a struggle for Will to keep his eyes from wandering to this distraction. When speaking to Y Srun, if his wife was near, he turned his back toward her or positioned Jonny to screen her from his view.

During a four-day period in the first week of December, Will and Jonny made daily visits to the hamlet to meet with Y Srun to assess his value as a principal agent. Will never arrived empty-handed, always bearing gifts of food, cooking utensils, blankets, tools, and candy—especially candy. That was because Y Srun had the cutest, most irresistibly charming twin daughters that Will had ever laid eyes on. He estimated their age at three or so. The angelic pair had their mother's beauty and their father's easy, infectious smile. Their spectacular and compelling eyes seemed to take up half of their faces. At first they played peekaboo with Will from the behind the safety of their mother and father's legs. Next came a game of chase: he ran after them through the maze of thatched huts, then they tried to catch him. Will was smitten. Each day he came with bags of M&Ms and handed them to the toddlers. By the third day, in anticipation of his arrival, they were waiting for him and came running over when he was a couple of hundred feet from the edge of their hamlet. They grabbed his legs and wrapped themselves around his ankles and held on as he completed the walk to their parents' hut. Then he handed them the M&Ms as their parents smiled in appreciation.

When he and Jonny made their first visits to the hamlet, they were accompanied by a Yard security contingent of twelve or so CIDG. The squad leader was a grizzled, wiry Rhade who seemed ancient to Will. Before Jonny introduced Y Grok to Will, he explained that the old man had gained a legendary reputation as a fierce warrior fighting Ho Chi Minh's communists in the service of the French during the Indochina war of the late 1940s and 1950s. When Will met Y Grok, they shook hands in the customary tribal manner: Each man wrapped his left hand around the wrist of his own right hand as they gripped each other, and each made a respectful bow of his head to the other. Y Grok's grip was remarkably firm. When Will started to release his grip, Y Grok tightened his and enclosed Will's hand with both of his hands. He raised his head slowly from its bowed position. He stared into Will's eyes. In that instant, something strange passed between them. Y Grok's eyes opened wider and wider like he was seeing a ghost. He shuddered and fell to his knees trembling, still gripping Will's hand tightly. Will thought he was having a heart attack or a fit. Finally Y Grok released his hold on Will's hand, stood, and bowed deeply to Will. Y Grok began to speak to him softly in French. Will looked at Jonny, who started translating Y Grok's words.

"Y Grok say he see a great power inside you. He say you have powerful magic, powerful medicine. He call you magic man. He apologize for touch you. He very, very sorry, no want to offend."

Will addressed him directly. "Y Grok, you have nothing to apologize or be sorry for. I'm not a magic man. I'm just a man, the same as you," he said, and Jonny translated.

Will reached out and took both of Y Grok's hands in his. Y Grok's body shook as if a jolt of electricity had pulsed through him. Will smiled at him and bowed his head. "I am not an untouchable. That only happens in India," he said, laughing. The frightened expression on Y Grok's face turned into a smile, and he bowed.

Jonny placed his hand on Will's forearm. "Y Grok my uncle. He your bodyguard," he said.

Will smiled. He could see the resemblance now. "Tell your uncle that I am very honored to meet him and to have him be my bodyguard," Will said bowing deeply to Y Grok.

The little Mnong hamlet was three-quarters of a mile from the A-Team. It was so close that they always traveled there on foot with Y Grok's squad of Yards—or the Grok squad, as Will started calling them—providing security against ambush. During the fourth of their visits to Y Srun's hamlet, Will was confident that he would be a high-quality asset as a principal agent. In fact, Will had already initiated a name-trace check on Y Srun and his wife through B-57 headquarters and the CIA station in the US embassy in Saigon. Each time they ventured to Y Srun's hamlet they approached from a different direction to avoid ambush. The hamlet sat in a brushy meadow clearing with a small creek at its edge. It was bordered on two sides by moderately dense jungle and scrub. Y Srun's modest thatch hut was shaded by two medium-size strangler fig or banyan trees. The two elegantly intertwined trees created an idyllic setting for his two daughters to play under.

This day Will and Jonny spent an hour debriefing Y Srun on his observations of the NVA's Nam Lyr installation. Will scribbled notes on a small tablet. The chief had not been inside the facility, but he had gathered wood within a few hundred feet of its perimeter. He described the security precautions as minimal and the guards lacking a high state of alertness. It wasn't easy for Will to understand Jonny's translations, due to the latter's limited vocabulary. Will was doing a lot of extrapolating and interpolating, which had been part of the intelligence debriefing training he'd gotten. Y Srun said there were a handful of armed and uniformed soldiers in and around the area of the installation. He had noticed large troop movements coming and going three or four times during the previous year. His description led Will to believe that these were at least company-size or larger troop movements, perhaps battalion size. Y Srun described an almost daily flow of porters and donkeys packing goods and supplies to the post.

When the debriefing had concluded, the loquacious Yard asked Will and Jonny if they would return the next day with more rice, cooking oil, and blankets. Y Srun explained that two more families had moved into his hamlet from Nam Lyr during the previous night and that their supplies were running low. Will agreed to return the following morning for a resupply. Before leaving, Will requested that his de facto agent ask the new arrivals about NVA troop movements they may have noticed in recent days. Y Srun assured Will and Jonny that he would be happy to do so.

Back on Hill 722 that night, right after a splendid dinner of wild boar roasted on a spit, Will and Ralph returned to their hooch. Will briefed Ralph on his progress with Y Srun and his intention to recruit him as a principal agent. He shared the limited intel he had gathered from the hamlet's chief as well. Ralph was excited about the possibility that Y Srun might be a breakthrough asset in their mission.

When Will awoke the next morning, he was in a troubled state. He hadn't slept well. He had awakened two or three times from disturbing dreams, dreams he couldn't remember—or didn't want to remember. As his mind became more focused, he realized what day it was. That was the trouble. It was his birthday, December 7. He was twenty-five today. He hoped he was the only person on Hill 722 who knew—he didn't want to hear any happy fucking birthday sentiments. When he was a little kid trying to blow out the candles on his birthday cake like any other little kid, he was blissfully unaware of the stigma of the date of his birth. As time went by he became less and less blissful on his happy fucking birthday. Eventually he was able to keep almost everyone he knew from knowing his birth date. When pressed, he claimed November 27 as his day of birth.

When Will's mother had told him the story of the circumstances of his birth, he could tell that she struggled with it. She became more and more emotional as her memories unfolded. He had eventually felt a need to put his arms around her to comfort her. He realized that his birthday had been a black mark in his life since the day his mother had told him her experience. Somehow he felt responsible and guilty for her suffering, both physically and psychologically, giving birth to him.

Will and Ralph went to the team house for a breakfast of fresh tropical fruit and what his partner called porridge and he called oatmeal. After they ate, he and Ralph had a meeting in their hooch with Jonny to discuss recruitment strategy and how to better identify potential assets with knowledge of and legitimate access to the target area. Will stressed that the small Mnong hamlet led by Y Srun appeared to hold the highest potential for spotting refugees from Nam Lyr. The others agreed with him but made the case that it was unwise to overlook the potential of the other communities. Ralph and Jonny brought up two Rhade tribesmen who were recent refugees from an abandoned hamlet near Lyr Mountain. They had discovered them in the Rhade village. Jonny said he thought they had good potential to get near the NVA HQ.

When the meeting was finished, Will asked Jonny to muster his security squad for a quick visit to Y Srun's hamlet to deliver the supplies he had promised for the hamlet's new arrivals. Before he replied, Jonny's body language announced to Will that he wasn't in favor of this request.

"Y Grok say he worry about go to Y Srun today. He hear many VC in area of Mnong hamlet. Have informers see us go too many day. He think bad medicine go back today. Much danger. Better wait two, three day, then can go," said Jonny.

"I appreciate Y Grok's concern, Jonny. Normally I would heed his warning. But I made a promise to Y Srun that I would bring supplies for his newest refugees. I don't want to let him down. And I don't want him to lose face with his newest arrivals. We really need to go today. Can we increase the size of our task force, add more good soldiers to our security team, and practice a higher level of readiness and safety?"

"Y Grok and I follow order of Chief Parish. You say go, we go," Jonny said with a strained smile.

"I'm glad to hear that, Jonny. I'll meet you at the gate in thirty minutes. Here's the supply list."

When Will arrived at the gate, Y Grok and Jonny were waiting with a twenty-four-man security team. They were an impressive group of seasoned fighters. Will was reassured that none of them looked like fifteen-year-olds. Two of the team carried a supply sling tied to a rail that rested on their shoulders. Blankets, soap, rice, and cooking oil, Will assumed. The group moved out at a brisk pace. A pair of formidable-looking Nungs were leading the security detail and trading point position every two or three hundred feet. When they were within a thousand feet of the hamlet, Y Grok sent a squad of ten soldiers into the jungle making a lot of noise as a diversionary tactic.

The main column moved slowly along the densely overgrown, nearly invisible trail to the settlement. As they arrived about five hundred feet from their destination, they were silently rejoined by the other ten soldiers. The two Nungs on point started moving very slowly and stealthily, then stopped and motioned everyone to the ground. Will was carrying his folding stock M2 carbine. He was locked and loaded. He waited for the spinal tap of energy to come. Nothing came. A minute passed. The two Nungs finally rose from the ground and motioned the formation ahead. Healthy paranoia, Will surmised.

They started moving at a more normal speed. When they were close to the hamlet Will knew that something wasn't right. Usually they were greeted by the sounds of children playing and making noise as they approached. Not this time. The place appeared abandoned. As the formation came to the back of the banyan trees, Y Grok motioned the two Nungs on point to take the rest of their force and circle around in the cover of the brushy area beyond the meadow. He held Will and Jonny behind the banyans for a moment. Then the three of them, Y Grok and Jonny on point, crouched and moved slowly forward at high alert. As they rounded the trees, Will felt a fluttering of energy at the base of his spine. He saw Jonny and his uncle looking up at the nearest banyan tree, a look of horror spreading across their faces. Will turned and followed their gaze. He was paralyzed with horror and refusal to accept what he saw. Tied up in one banyan tree were a naked and emasculated Y Srun and his family. The decapitated head of his wife was entangled in his disemboweled viscera. His genitalia were stuffed into her mouth. Most heartbreaking was the two tiny heads of his twin daughters on each of his shoulders mounted on bamboo pikes shoved through his armpits and out the top of the little girls' heads.

What form of evil could do such an act? Will started to lose it, to break down and cry, but the savage raging beast inside him broke loose, all sadness, all sanity swept away. The white-hot rage engulfed him. The purple lights swirled, surged. The blackout came and went. He became untethered from time, moving at his own pace while the world around him slowed.

In what felt like ages to him, he watched a dozen or more black-pajama-clad Viet Cong and a single green-uniformed soldier emerge from behind the hamlet's thatch huts. The terrorists' carbines and Kalashnikovs spouted fire and brimstone. The bullets barely moved. Will pushed Jonny and Y Grok to the ground forcefully. A terrible and brutal power arose from deep within him. He opened his lips as if to scream, but what erupted from his mouth was beyond all imagining. The beam of energy that emerged from his mouth was the most horrific sound he had ever heard in his life. His hands shot to his ears to block out the terrible noise, but without success. He turned to direct the beam of avenging sound at each of the assailants. One by one they burst into flames. Their screams were the most agonizing notes of suffering he had ever heard. The savagery inside him celebrated their unbearable pain.

Will came back to his almost normal state. By force of will, he pushed the beast back down into its cage deep inside him and locked it in. The entire hamlet was rising in flames now. He cast a last glance into the banyan tree to make sure he saw what he thought he had seen, and his heart broke all over again. He fell to his knees with his face in his hands and started to cry. Jonny and Y Grok got up from the ground and stood on either side of him. A minute or two passed, then each placed a gentle, consoling hand on his shoulders. Will finally got control of his emotions and wiped his tears away. He got to his feet. He was surrounded by the twenty-four-man security team. They were all on their knees with their heads bowed low and their arms outstretched with open palms toward him in a pose of worship. Y Grok and Jonny had joined them.

"Jonny, what are you doing? Get up. Get off the ground. Tell everybody to stand up, now."

Jonny stood up, his head still lowered, and told them to get up. They didn't move.

"Come on, Jonny. Tell them to get up. I don't like this. Tell them I'm getting angry."

Jonny translated. They all sprung from the ground in unison, their heads still bowed. Abject fear, the great motivator, Will said to himself silently.

"Y Grok, Y Grok," Will said. The wizened Yard would not look at him.

"Jonny, please ask your uncle to look at me." Jonny translated, and Y Grok slowly raised his eyes to Will's. The man was clearly terrified. Will stepped to him slowly and placed his hands on his shoulders. Y Grok closed his eyes. He was trembling. Will spoke directly to him in the softest, gentlest voice he could muster.

"Y Grok, I need your help. Will you please take Y Srun and what is left of his family down from this tree and bury them or burn them in the custom of the Degar people?"

When Jonny finished his translation, a warmth came to Y Grok's eyes and spread over his face. He nodded twice to Will and took action. He ordered a handful of his men to climb into the Banyan and begin cutting the vines that bound the family to the tree.

TWENTY-EIGHT

As the Yards started their grisly task, Will bowed to Y Grok and walked back alone to Hill 722. He passed through the main gate and went up the hill to the inner compound gate. It was mid-morning, and the sky was overcast. He went on to his hooch without encountering any team members. He sat on his cot.

He spoke to himself, "This is your birthday, Will. Happy fucking birthday to you. You are responsible for the slaughter of something that was truly beautiful, a family of four innocent souls. They did not deserve to die. They did not deserve to be killed in that brutal way. It's all on you. You have innocent blood on your hands. You were indiscreet. You played it way too loose. You were careless, cavalier. You were not covert. You paid no heed to tradecraft. You were stupid, and those sweet innocent babies paid for it with their lives. You fucking piece of shit, you killed them. You killed them. You don't deserve to be alive."

He pulled the .357 Magnum from his holster. He cocked the hammer. He put the barrel to his temple. He squeezed the trigger. It wouldn't yield. He kept squeezing. It wouldn't give. He took the revolver in his left hand and placed it against his other temple and pulled as hard as he could. An outside force was blocking him. "Stop it! Stop it!" he shouted.

A powerful voice from somewhere inside of him commanded, "This is not your path. This is not your time. You will continue on."

"Why did you allow those innocents to die that way? You could have interceded."

"In time you will come to know the answer."

"No, no, I don't want to know the answer," Will shouted out, as he continued to pull harder on the trigger.

"What the fuck are you doing?" Ralph yelled as he sprinted across the room and grabbed the pistol from Will's hand. "Are you fucking insane? Are you really trying to blow your brains out?"

Will hung his head. Fuck me, he thought, I can't do anything right. I can't even kill myself.

"Listen, Will, I know why you're so upset. I was there. I saw them take what was left of that family out of the tree. It was the most horrible, gruesome, inhuman fucking thing I have ever seen the VC do in this war. But don't go blowin' your fuckin' brains out. I understand that you feel some responsibility, but you gotta get a grip. This is war, man. Bad shit happens. You're in a state of shock because you've never seen anything like that. You need to grow a thicker skin, and fast. But right now you have to pull yourself together," Ralph implored him.

"And what's this crazy story the Yards are spreading that you set a bunch of VC on fire with a big noise?" he continued. "What the hell is that all about? Jonny says the Yards and even the Nungs are spooked by you."

Will raised his head and looked at Ralph. He turned his head slowly from side to side. He held out his hands, palms up, questioningly.

"I haven't a clue," he said. He wasn't lying. He—the real, human Will—didn't have the faintest idea where the killing power came from.

"I'm very concerned about the state you're in, Will. I thought you were made of sterner stuff when we first met. Now I gotta worry about doing a suicide watch. Hand over your forty-five. I'm going to have to take your assault rifles too and keep them in the ammo bunker until I'm convinced you aren't a danger to yourself."

"That won't be necessary, Ralph," Will said calmly. "The crisis is over. I thought I could pull the trigger. But when the chips were down, I didn't have the balls to do it. I was a coward."

"Bullshit, Will. If you had pulled the trigger, you would have been a coward. Suicide is always the coward's way out," Ralph said.

Will was in extremis, but not in the medical sense, as in almost dead. He knew he would only die when the voice in his head allowed him to. Will was in the other kind of extremis—on the brink of going stark raving mad. He wished he could truly lose his mind and with it the image of those two baby girls, everything that had happened, the weight of the guilt he carried.

"I want you to understand something, Ralph. Those sweet and innocent little girls and their kindhearted parents died horribly because of my negligence. I converted their father, played games with them, all out in the open as if there weren't a shitload of Viet Cong informers behind every tree. I didn't follow proper intelligence procedures. I threw caution to the wind. I killed them as surely as if my hand had done the beheading and gutting. I have their blood on my hands. And it will never wash away."

"You're right. You killed them. You fucked up. You're not infallible. But you can't bring them back. Now commit yourself to doing your job the right way. Dedicate yourself to fighting this war in their memory. Don't wallow in self-pity and guilt, stand up tall and annihilate some VC and NVA ass."

"You're right, Ralph. I need to dedicate myself to that family. I have to try to make it right." Will was holding onto his self-control by a slender thread. He wanted Ralph to believe he wasn't suicidal. "I'm OK, Ralph. You don't have to take my guns."

"Don't bullshit me, Will. I gotta know beyond a shadow of a doubt that you're not going to blow your brains out."

"You saw me try and fail. I couldn't pull the trigger. What more proof do you need?"

"OK, Will. What else can I do?" He handed Will the forty-five and the .357. "I'm gonna get some lunch. You coming?"

"No, I'm gonna pass. I don't have much of an appetite," Will said.

Ralph gave him a long appraising look then walked out of the hooch.

Will dropped his pistols on the floor and collapsed onto his cot. He fought to control his thoughts. He tried to practice self-discipline, but he had never been a master of the process. Chaos and anarchy had always ruled his thoughts. He watched and listened as the cinema inside his head screened images of the VC death squad and their evil NVA-uniformed leader burning and screaming in terrible agony. He visualized Lyr Mountain exploding violently and annihilating every last member of the NVA division hunkered within it. Imagining it, his body convulsed and shuddered as the thing inside him struggled to break loose.

Will continued to lie on his cot in a tortured, toxic state. If only he could fall asleep and forget for a while. He needed a sedative. He needed to be knocked out. Maybe a giant syringe of heroin would work, better yet a massive overdose. Could he talk the medic into shooting him up with enough morphine to put him out of his misery for at least a little while? Probably not. Booze would do it. But there was just the supply of beer, and he knew he couldn't drown his sadness in a sea of Budweiser. So he continued to lie on his cot in an impotent funk.

In time Ralph returned to the hooch.

"Good, you're still alive. Thanks for not blowing your brains out. Will, we need to have a talk. Weird shit's been happening around here ever since you fell out of that plane at Buon Sar Pa. The Yards are all freaked out. They think you are one of their gods. What the hell happened out in that settlement?"

Will wished Ralph would just go away and leave him alone. He avoided looking at him. He didn't answer the question.

"Come on, partner. Talk to me. Don't hold out," Ralph prodded.

It took him a few moments to focus on what Ralph was asking. It was hard to think straight. He pulled himself together slowly.

"I have no idea what the hell happened out there, Ralph," he said haltingly. "I heard the same horrendous noise. It was almost deafening. I had to cup my hands over my ears to keep from going deaf and insane. The noise seemed to be coming from behind or above me. It was unnatural. I have never experienced anything like it in my life. You say the Yards are freaked out. Well, I'm just as freaked out as they are."

"What about the VC death squad catching on fire? What set them on fire?"

"I don't know. It seemed that the noise just ignited them. But how did it burn them and not Jonny, Y Grok, and me? It doesn't make sense. The only explanation is the supernatural. The Almighty got so upset by what they did to that family that he set them on fire like burning bushes."

"That's crazy talk. There has to be an explanation," Ralph said.

"Does there?"

"Yeah, there does."

Will was drifting, barely able to focus on what Ralph was saying.

"You're acting really strange, Will, like you're not all there. Are you OK?"

"Yes, OK," Will answered with a strange nod of his head.

"You're weirding me out. Are you sure you're all right?"

"Yeah . . . I'm . . . fine . . . exhausted . . . just . . . need . . . sleep."

"That sounds like a good idea. Get some shut-eye. When you wake you'll be right with the world," said Ralph as he left the hooch.

Later, when the sun had dipped below the horizon, Ralph returned to the hooch. He found Will in the same position as when he had left hours earlier. He appeared to be nearly comatose, but his eyes were wide open. He seemed to be unaware of Ralph.

"Will. Will, it's time for dinner. You missed lunch. Come with me and get something to eat. You gotta be starvin'."

Will didn't answer.

"Come on, Will, you gotta eat sometime. You can't just hide in a hole like this."

"Not . . . hungry," Will croaked.

"OK, suit yourself for now. But tomorrow morning you're going to rise up out of your funk and rejoin the real world. I mean it, Will, even if I have to drag your sorry ass out of here for breakfast."

A few minutes after Ralph left the hooch, Will got up from the cot. He dressed in tiger-stripe camo fatigues and lightweight jungle boots. He stuffed a couple of olive-drab towels into the top of his rucksack and looped a strap over his shoulder. He walked out and into the darkness. There were no stars, no moon, but he could see as clearly as if the sun were shining brightly. The strange night vision had come to him. He walked to the inner gate and shocked the hell out of the Nung guards, who hadn't heard him approach. He signaled to them to open the gate. They refused at first but relented when they saw the menace in his eyes. He continued to the outer perimeter gate and surprised the Rhade guards, who almost jumped out of their skins. He pointed for them to open the massive gate. They refused fiercely until they got a close look at his eyes, then they opened the gate quickly. Will walked out, and two of the Yards tried to accompany him. He shook his head and growled. The Yards retreated. One of them offered his carbine, but Will pushed it away and disappeared into the night.

He was barely aware of what was happening. He was in a dream world. Nothing seemed real. The thing inside him had taken over, and now Will was locked deep inside his body while something else moved for him. It was a strange, weightless feeling. He was moving swiftly down a twisting game trail without control. The jungle canopy was thick, but it spread open magically with his approach. He was gliding uphill without effort, sometimes hovering above the jungle's heavy triple canopy. He could feel something brutal and outrageous building. Whatever drove the strange energy was now driving Will.

He was hovering above the entry gate of the NVA divisional base camp on Lyr Mountain, watching an armed security detail setting watch posts on the installation's perimeter. The soldiers in the detail spoke loudly among themselves, knowing—thinking—the enemy was miles away. There was no wariness, no sense of alert, or awareness of impending annihilation at the hands of an avenging force at their gate. The raging creature that inhabited Will struck swiftly and lethally. Without warning, he torched the security detail and a group of soldiers standing near the opening of their underground barracks. It ignited them with a breath from Will's lips. Will's body swooped through the barracks entrance. Pandemonium ruled as naked NVA soldiers spilled from their crude cots to reach for their weapons. Was it terror that made them move painfully slowly as a beam of energy fired out from Will's mouth and blew them to smithereens? By the time it was over hundreds of them were gone. Will could feel the weight of his body again walking on the dirt of the barracks floor. He passed through three or four underground chambers, dealing mayhem and annihilation to any and all living things. He stepped through shredded corpses and felt the thick, slippery flow of blood spreading beneath his boots.

He couldn't stop what was happening if he tried—rage was in complete control now. Will dropped through an open shaft to a lower level of the underground bunkers. His body shot through a narrow passage that opened into a central space like an office. There were makeshift desks, stools, and files. He passed through a curtained opening and into a maze of small billets. All movement other than Will's continued at a fraction of normal time. Eight or nine NVA officers were emerging from their quarters with pistols in hand. Each was eviscerated by a whisper of rage from Will's lips.

At the end of the passage was a sturdy wooden door. A puff of his breath pulverized it. Will moved into a larger, much more elegant room. There were framed pictures on the whitewashed walls. A uniformed middle-aged man sat behind a desk with a shocked look on his face. He was holding a Russian Makarov pistol in his hand. His uniform bore the red-edged epaulets and stars of a major general in the so-called People's Army of Vietnam. Here was the commander of the Lyr Mountain NVA division. Here was the author of the brutal killing of Y Srun, his wife, and innocent baby daughters. The general aimed his pistol and fired at Will. The bullet tumbled lazily past Will's head.

The savage beast inside Will unleashed his fury. His right hand ripped the head from the murderous general's torso. Blood spurted from his neck and painted the ceiling red. The decapitated head was set on the desk, and the green towels came out from Will's rucksack. The head was wrapped in the towels before being stuffed roughly back into the pack. The upper half of the general's tunic was ripped from his bleeding, spasming torso, the epaulets and insignia crammed into the pack along with a map torn from the wall and documents from the general's desk.

Will could tell the beast was looking for something. What? He pulled a file drawer open and rifled quickly through, stopping on a bound folder and tearing it open. A wad of photographs fell across the desk. He was sickened. A photo showed the general having sex with a tiny child. There were more images of the same shocking child pornography. If Will had any control over his rage, it was gone now. He picked up the lifeless pig of a man and tore him to pieces. He ripped the genitalia from what was left of his torso and ground them into the floor with his boots. His only semi-rational thought was that the fiend got off too easy.

Will raged a path of destruction through the remainder of the underground complex, creating a slaughterhouse of each new barracks he entered. Blood, guts, and bone flew in every direction. He was indiscriminate. He came to a separate section of the catacombs and found a series of large empty barracks with hundreds of cots. This section appeared to be recently vacated. A sudden sense of urgency sprang up in him. He raised his chin toward the ceiling, and a burst of energy spewed from his mouth and blew the top off Lyr Mountain. He rose up weightlessly from the broken patchwork of subterranean chambers and glided to the edge of a gaping breach in the earth. The breach had exposed a massive cache of arms, ammunition, and explosives. Another powerful beam of energy erupted from his throat, and what remained of Nam Lyr went up in a cataclysmic explosion.

Rage hurled him down the hillside toward the Duc Lap A-Team at near light speed. Hill 722 was under siege by a regiment-size unit of more than a thousand soldiers. Will had no need for night vision here. The camp was eerily alight, brighter than day from the white-phosphorus illumination flares suspended over the hill. Intense firefights were raging on three sides of the hill. Barrages of deadly mortars exploded on both sides of the battlefront. An AC-47 Puff the Magic Dragon "spooky" gunship was unleashing its lethal miniguns on the NVA positions with violent precision. But it wasn't enough to drive the attackers back from the camp's perimeter. An NVA sapper team had just blown a gaping breach in the mass of concertina wire near the front gate. NVA troops surged through the hole. Will joined the battle, a burst of energy streaming from his lips and incinerating sixty or more enemy combatants at the breached perimeter. Will turned toward the abandoned tea plantation where hundreds of NVA troops were maneuvering and seeking cover. He bellowed out one final horrific, inhuman howl, and the entire plantation exploded in a flaming cauldron of devastation. Hundreds of voices screamed in anguish as the flames engulfed them. Will fell to the ground in exhaustion and horror over the slaughter he had wrought. Mercifully, unconsciousness came to him at last.

TWENTY-NINE

The next morning at first light a platoon of Yards had started counting NVA bodies at the edge of the Duc Lap battlefield when they stumbled over what appeared to be a white man KIA. The body was covered thickly in dried blood. They flipped it over hard with their boots and heard a groan. The Yards realized it was Will and started shouting at the top of their lungs. Y Grok arrived and recoiled in horror. To make sure Will was alive, Y Grok forced his hand down and placed his fingers on Will's carotid artery. Y Grok immediately called Jonny on his radioman's PRC 25. In minutes half of the A-Team drove up in two jeeps. Both team medics, Berwick and Pasquale, started working on Will at once. None of the blood that covered him was his own, but he looked at first to be near death. But his appearance was deceiving: his vital signs were all within normal ranges. Berwick could find no burned flesh, broken bones, wounds, or signs of blunt-force trauma on his body. Will's eyes were half open, and his pupils were only moderately responsive. He was physically unresponsive and inflexible. He was carefully placed on a stretcher, and the Yards carried him gently back up the hill to the team house.

Captain Jack asked Berwick for a diagnosis. Berwick was mystified. The only thing he could come up with was traumatic psychological disorder.

"Captain, I think he's in a state of shock, battle fatigue. I have never seen this before, but if I had to guess, I would say he is catatonic. He's not all there right now," Berwick said.

"OK, that's it. I'm calling for a medevac," the captain said.

An hour later Will was strapped down on a stretcher and loaded into a UH-1 dust-off. The noisy trip to Tan Son Nhut took less than an hour. Will saw clearly everything around him. He heard every word, every sound, but his system of locomotion was temporarily out of order. The thing inside him was still ascendant, in charge, observing, recording, and processing everything eidetically. The real Will was in a recess, a self-induced dissociative state. Despite all that had happened, he felt almost euphoric.

After landing at Tan Son Nhut, he was transferred into an M-718 army ambulance. The ride was very short, just four or five minutes. He was removed from the back of the ambulance in front of 10 Ton Son Hoa, the US Army's Third Field Hospital, which two years earlier had been the American Community School. A group of nurses flipped him onto a gurney and rolled him to a small private room in the psychiatric ward. Will was amused. I always knew I would end up here, he said to himself, the army's version of an insane asylum.

During the next several days Will was poked and prodded and examined by a string of specialists including two psychiatrists. They found nothing wrong with his body. But the shrinks did arrive at a consensus: Will had severe classic catatonia brought on by the horrors of battle. Only time could heal him.

The most extreme indignity of Will's deliberate fall into catatonia was catheterization. When a husky-voiced nurse who looked more man than woman grabbed his pecker and shoved the tube inside him, he came close to blowing the charade. He wasn't a fan of the intravenous drip the nurses jabbed into him for severe dehydration either. After nearly two weeks of being fed like a baby and sponge-bathed by a succession of nurses, Will began to consider coming out of his self-imposed catatonic state. The other thing was indifferent. The real Will was ready to leap back into the real world. He had been in isolation since his arrival. In all of the quiet hours of lying nearly motionless, he had been fully focused on devising a strategy for dealing with the questions and eventual interrogation that he was sure to be subjected to. The strategy in a word was amnesia. The only plausible strategy for surviving the barrage of inquiry into what the hell happened in Duc Lap would be that Will wouldn't be able to remember a single freaking thing about Duc Lap. He was never there. He never got into the jeep with Brad for the ride to Tan

Son Nhut to catch the flight to Duc Lap the day after Thanksgiving. And that was that.

In recent days he had eavesdropped on whispered conversations among doctors on the advisability of allowing visitors into Will's room. The shrinks were not in agreement on whether visitors would help Will out of his hole or drive him even deeper into it. Eventually the commanding general himself, William Westmoreland, pulled rank and ordered the commanding officer of the Third Field Hospital to allow Colonel Mahoney, B-57's commanding officer, to visit Will.

The colonel's face was full of anguish. The moment that Will saw the man's kindness and concern, he decided to return to the real world.

"Hello, Colonel Mahoney, how are you?" Will asked.

The colonel's jaw dropped almost comically. Then he smiled and all of the stress and pain dissolved from his face.

"My God, Will, I knew you would recover. You gave us one hell of a scare. Welcome back to the land of the living. How do you feel, son?"

"I feel great, sir. But I'm a little disoriented, just trying to figure out why I'm in this hospital bed. How the hell did I get here?"

"What? Wait. Are you saying you don't remember what happened in Duc Lap, Will?"

"Duc Lap? No, sir, I haven't gone yet. The last thing I remember is I was getting ready to go there," Will said.

One of the psychiatrists entered the room abruptly and asked Mahoney to step out in the hallway for a moment. When they returned, the subject of what happened in Duc Lap didn't come up.

"I don't know if you've had a chance to notice, Will," Mahoney said, "but Christmas is almost upon us. And Cookie is pulling out all the stops for a fabulous feast. Doctor Monroe here tells me you may be well enough to come and join us."

Will's salivary glands went into hyperdrive at the thought of a B-57 dinner.

"That would be the best Christmas gift ever," Will said.

The commanding officer smiled and nodded at Will. The smile slowly faded away and turned to a look of strain and frustration. Will knew that the colonel had a thousand questions to ask about the contents of a unique rucksack removed from his shoulders after the battle of Duc Lap. Will would happily spill his guts, tell him the whole heinous story, but the colonel wouldn't believe a word of it. And the shrinks would gather to diagnose the cause of Will's psychotic delusions of violent omnipotent powers. They would declare him a menace to humanity and attempt to keep him in the cuckoo's nest for the rest of his days.

The gustatory gods did not smile down upon Will that Christmas. He wasn't released from the psych ward. He wasn't allowed to return to his unit for the fabulous feast. Instead, now that he had returned to some semblance of consciousness and sanity, he was placed on lockdown under a twenty-four-hour military police security detail. All of a sudden Will had become the highest-priority item in the entire American intelligence community in Vietnam. The CIA swooped in with a vengeance and told US Army Intelligence that it would have no role in the Will Parish debriefing.

Three days after Christmas the medical team charged with Will's care determined he was physically fit and behaving appropriately from a clinical perspective. The shrinks released him from the psychiatric ward and handed him over to a CIA security detail. He was driven from the hospital to a small villa that served as a CIA safe house off Avenue Louis Pasteur. The villa was richly appointed with an eclectic array of beaux arts and art deco furnishings. Will was shown to a bedroom and reintroduced to his duffel bags, last seen in his Duc Lap hooch.

An hour after his arrival, he was escorted to a small, bare room with a folding table and three folding chairs. Two of the chairs were occupied by a couple of guys in their early thirties who were dressed in khakis and short-sleeved white oxford-cloth shirts. Both men were of pale complexion with close-cropped sandy brown hair, but their similarities ended there. One had a menacing, wide body, not fat but thickset and intimidating. The other was slight and slender. Will was invited to sit in the empty chair on the other side of the table from them.

"So, Sergeant Will Parish, I'm Harpo, and this is my sidekick Zeppo," said the slender fellow in an annoyed tone. No handshakes were offered. "Zeppo and I have been asked to work with you to try to clear up some of the mysteries surrounding your role in the battle of Duc Lap. Our goal is to help you recover from your amnesia. Just think of us as your old college frat buddies trying to help you get your memory back."

"OK, just call me Groucho," Will said with delight. "Wow, this is so cool. Old frat buddies. Secret handshake," Will said, extending his hand. Neither guy offered his hand.

"OK, how about secret password then? Semper." Will waited. "I said semper." He waited a moment longer. "Hey, you guys aren't really my frat brothers, are you? Too bad."

"OK, wise guy, let's cut the shit," said the thickset Zeppo in basso profundo.

"Yeah, Parish, let's cut to the chase," Harpo said sharply as he took over and opened up a fat file marked "TOP SECRET EYES ONLY." "At about nineteen-hundred hours on December 7 of this year you, Buck Sergeant Will Parish, posing as a chief warrant officer two, departed perimeter security at A-Team Detachment 239 at Duc Lap, also known as Hill 722. For the record, you were technically absent without leave. When the Nung and Montagnard gate security details reported your departure to the commander of the A-Team, three eight-man search teams were dispatched into the surrounding jungle to try to find you. They found no sign of you. But one of the search teams encountered an enormous NVA force preparing to attack the A-Team. A fierce firefight ensued. The search team miraculously made it back to the A-Team without suffering casualties. The NVA unit, estimated to be regimentally sized, then proceeded to lay siege to Hill 722.

"Are you following me here, Sergeant Parish? You seem to be bored or distracted," Harpo said.

"I don't know about bored or distracted, but I do know that I'm not following you at all, Mr. Harpo. I'm not following the part about me being at Duc Lap. I've never been there. I was supposed to go the day after Thanksgiving, but I never went. Something happened to me, and I never made it to Duc Lap," Will said.

"Bullshit. You were there, and you know you were there. Why the fuck are you lying about it?" Zeppo said, rising out of his chair.

"Temper, temper, Mr. Zeppo," Will said.

Zeppo's eyes turned murderous, and he started around the table to go after Will. Harpo grabbed his shoulder and told him to cool it. Zeppo got back in his chair. Harpo flipped a page in his file.

"All right, back to Duc Lap. The NVA are pouring it on to Hill 722, hitting it with everything they've got, mortars, rockets, field artillery, heavy machine guns. A spooky gunship arrives within an hour and saves A-Team 239's ass for a while. The cloud ceiling lowers, and spooky can't see what it's shooting at and has to vamoose. The NVA attack the hill with renewed fury and breach the perimeter. Just as they break through, a series of mysterious fireballs erupt and incinerate a thousand or so NVA troops. Fast forward to about zero nine hundred the following morning. A Yard detail doing a body count stumbles over what appears to be another dead body that is mysteriously not incinerated. The body is covered in a thick coat of dried blood. But the guy ain't dead. Turns out that guy is you, none other than the missing Sergeant Will Parish. And still one more great mystery, none of the blood caked all over you turns out to be yours."

The dominant thought in Will's mind was how much he wanted to reach across the table and tear out Harpo's larynx to stop his grating sing-song voice. But he didn't.

"I'm starting to get the feeling that this is a hostile interrogation," Will said. "You guys remind me of a couple of asshole FBI agents who arrested me in the Boston Harbor during my agent operational exercise at intel school. They played the role of Polish security and tried to intimidate me into making a confession that I was an American spy. They couldn't break me. So what are we doing here? I'm hearing a bunch of gobbledygook about Duc Lap, a place I have no memory of. I guess it's possible that I was there and everything you are saying is true. I just don't remember a fucking thing about it."

Zeppo got up from his chair and left the room. He returned twenty seconds later carrying something behind his back. With dramatic flair, he produced Will's rucksack and yanked out the NVA general's decapitated head. He thrust it at Will's face. Will saw it coming and leaned back.

"Recognize this guy?" Zeppo grunted out.

"Is that thing real or is it a Hollywood prop?" Will asked.

"I've got a better question," Harpo said. "What was that head doing in your rucksack? How did it get there?"

"Really, that's real? How grotesque. There goes the appetite," Will said, making a face.

"You know it's real, asshole, and you know whose it is. The documents and partial uniform ID'd the guy," Harpo said through gritted teeth.

"OK, I give. Whose head is it?"

Zeppo put the head back in the rucksack.

"Thanks for the show and tell, Zeppo. But I'm still waiting for the tell," Will said.

"You know damn well who he was," Harpo said. "Before his beheading, he was Major General Trinh Van Sam, commander of the NVA's Twenty-Fourth Division at Lyr Mountain in Cambodia. Here's another bit of trivia for you, Parish. The Twenty-Fourth Division no longer exists. It got annihilated by a mysterious explosion on Lyr Mountain the same night you went missing. Very strange coincidence, eh?"

"Very strange. In fact, I would have to say stranger than strange—weird, bizarre, eerie, downright kinky. I'm hearing the theme music from the *Twilight Zone* inside my head as we speak," Will said, feigning a thoughtful look.

"You need to understand something, Parish. We don't believe your amnesia act. We believe that you remember every last detail of what happened out there. We are going to keep after you like a battering ram until you give up your charade. You've got a choice," Harpo said sharply. "We can do this the easy way or we can do it the hard way. Now, what's it going to be?"

"Harpo, I believe you have been watching way too many B-rated gangster movies. At least you and Zeppo could have played good cop, bad cop instead of two asshole cops," Will said.

Zeppo came out of his chair as the door flew open. An elegant older man came into the room.

"All right boys, I'll take it from here," he said.

Harpo and Zeppo made a hasty retreat with their heads down, tails between their legs.

"Hello, Will. I'm the good cop. Name's Reggie DuPont. I'm the CIA station chief here in Saigon," he said extending his hand to shake Will's.

He did the interlocking-pinky handshake and said, "Concordia."

Will's mouth fell open. "You're really a Phi Kap?"

"Princeton, Beta chapter, class of forty," DuPont said.

"UCLA, Alpha Psi chapter, class of sixty-five," Will replied.

"I know. I've read your file."

Will took an instant liking to DuPont.

"Hey, are you any relation to, you know, those DuPonts?"

"Well, yes, matter of fact, I am."

"Cool," Will said.

"Cool? How so?"

"I can't really say, it just strikes me as cool for some reason."

"Fair enough. Well, I don't believe that you and team Harpo-Zeppo hit it off all that well. They seemed to struggle with establishing rapport with you, Will."

"Oh, is that what they were trying to do, reach rapport with me? I think you may need to send them back to charm school for a few years."

"So noted. Well, young man, we have no way of knowing whether you have amnesia. I'm fairly certain that if I went through what you went through, I would have an incurable case of amnesia. But one can never be sure. We could have tried hypnosis, but you don't strike me as the hypnotizing kind. The polygraph was a possibility, but it's not very reliable in a situation like yours. We considered the less civilized tools—sleep deprivation and Pentothal—but I suspect neither would pry anything out of you that you're not willing to divulge. You strike me as a person with formidable willpower. Your name fits you well. So, I have instructed my driver to load your duffel bags into my sedan. Are you ready to return to B-57 in Cholon, Will?"

"That I am, sir."

When they arrived at their destination, DuPont offered a final thought.

"If it means anything to you, be prepared for a medical discharge from the service in the short term. In the army's eyes you are damaged goods. My intuition tells me our paths are likely to cross again one day. For now, good luck to you, Will Parish."

Will thanked him, shook hands, and waved goodbye.

He was anticipating a warm welcome from his teammates at B-57, but there was no welcoming committee. His homecoming turned out to be a depressing affair. Literally everyone he knew well, with one exception, was gone. Colonel Mahoney got his promotion to bird colonel and flew the coop. Captain Michaels was in the field on special assignment. Sergeant Major Jim Todd was gone, rotated back stateside. Brad had just left for R and R in Bangkok. Wagner and Lewis had been promoted and reassigned back to Nha Trang. He felt sad about not getting a chance to say goodbye to people he really cared about. He felt even sadder that he had no way of finding out where his best friend Rob Landau went. The only familiar face was that of Lieutenant Kavanaugh, who didn't seem all that thrilled to see Will. He greeted Will with a firm handshake, unsmiling.

That night Will went to the penthouse dining room with lowered expectations. He met the new commander, a major whose name he didn't catch. No one seemed interested in sitting with him, so he ate alone at a table for four. The food was excellent, a perfect Caesar salad and delicious Hungarian goulash. No wine was offered for pairing. Crème brûlée was served for dessert. Everything was fine, but it just wasn't the same. There was no sense of joy or celebration or the elegant style that Patrick Mahoney lent to the affair. The magic was gone. Will returned to his room and sulked.

After breakfast the next morning, he was summoned to the office of the unit's commander, who told Will with a tinge of sadness that he was to receive an honorable discharge for medical reasons by authority of the commanding officer of the Fifth Special Forces. Will was barely able to control his joy.

He returned to his room and lay down on his bed, threading his fingers together and clasping the back of his neck as his head sank into his pillows. A glorious notion dawned on him. He was about to become a free man. No more military chains would bind him. He was getting out of prison two years earlier than expected. This was a beautiful thing.

A few days later he boarded a Boeing 707 at Tan Son Nhut airbase. As the aircraft lifted off, he bid a silent farewell to Indochina. Then a portent of the future appeared to him. He saw how it all ended so badly for America and the people of South Vietnam. The vision saddened him, but only briefly. The powerful jet soared into the wild blue and with it Will's spirits. He saw clearly now the infinite, incredible brightness of his future.

ACKNOWLEDGMENTS

I got lucky when my niece Erin's husband, Edmund, recommended his cousin to give editorial assistance to prepare *Do Unto Evil* for publication. That cousin is Lindsey Alexander, and she and fellow editor Salvatore Borriello wielded their editorial scalpels to bring my 160,000-word opus down to a more reasonable 85,000 words. They have an editorial company called the Reading List in Chapel Hill, NC.

I learned about good fiction writing from Lindsey and Sal. The two most valuable lessons I learned from them, now indelibly printed in my gray matter, are "you must be able to murder your darlings" and "never place obstructions in the arc of the plot." The good news is that most of my darlings are still alive in a state of suspended animation, waiting for a possible resuscitation in the future.

To Lindsey and Sal, many thanks for your excellent editing.

CPSIA information can be obtained
at www.ICGtesting.com
Printed in the USA
LVHW082142111119
637069LV00010B/89/P